Repossessin' Texas

By

Don Henry Ford, Jr.

REPOSSESSIN' TEXAS

Copyright © 2007 by Don Henry Ford, Jr. Published in the United States of America. All rights reserved. While some of the characters in this book were patterned after real people, this is a book of fiction. No part of this book may be reproduced in any form or by electronic or mechanical means including information storage and retrieval systems without permission in writing from the publisher, except by a reviewer, who may quote brief passages in a review.

Published by Speir Publishing,
1101 Bailey Avenue,
San Antonio Texas 78210

Cover illustration by Stacy Erin Speir.
Cover design by Paul Michael Speir.

Library of Congress Control Number: 2007940476
ISBN-13: 978-0-9801725-0-8
ISBN-10: 0-9801725-0-0

FIRST EDITION

Ford, Don Henry
Repossessin' Texas/Don Henry Ford, Jr. – 1st ed.

Dedicated to the outlaws of the world. And especially to the greatest among their ranks, Jesus Christ.

CHAPTER I

Tim Grant stared through blurred eyes, carefully aligning the hood ornament of the tractor with the small furrow as he drove. A cold wind numbed his body; each bump added to the ache forming in his back and shoulders.

The tractor was old, a John Deere 4020; a tool bar with listers was attached to the three-point hitch. Each pass through the field left four rows behind the tractor. The absence of a cab exposed Tim to the elements. On this particular day, that meant cold and dust—thick, gritty, blinding dust that found its way into every pore of his body. None of this stopped Tim; he was determined to finish the job so pre-plant irrigation could begin.

Two long hinged arms, each with a small disc attached, hung from either side of the tool bar. Hydraulic cylinders raised and lowered these arms at Tim's command. The extended marker disc prepared a furrow he'd follow on the next pass. At the end of the field, Tim depressed the clutch, and stopped the tractor. A thrust on a lever engaged the hydraulic cylinder arm, raising it and folding it into a vertical position. Another lever raised the tool bar and listers out of clinging earth. Tim turned the steering wheel to the right, depressed the right brake, and released the clutch. The tractor pivoted. When perpendicular to the rows, Tim released the brake, straightened the steering wheel, and then depressed the brake again and turned back to the right. The combined effort left the tractor headed in the opposite direction, hood-ornament directly in line with the small furrow the marker disc had left.

One more pass, down and back, Tim whispered through chattering teeth, as if to encourage himself to hang on a little longer. He worked his numb, gloved hands a few times; he couldn't feel them. He wiped at the steady stream of snot coursing out of his nostrils, leaving a thin, watery layer smeared across his wind-chapped face. Tim's eyes watered from gusts of icy wind, and the tiny particles of dust it picked up as it moved over the freshly tilled earth.

Tim pushed the hydraulic lever and lowered the marker disc on the left side. He released the clutch and lowered the tool bar simultaneously. The tractor lurched forward, pulling to one side. Tim fought to line up the hood ornament with the furrow. A quick glance back revealed that the listers were set at the proper depth; a look to the side revealed that the marker disc was doing its job. Another look forward indicated the tractor was still veering ever so slightly to the left. Tim eased the steering wheel to the right but got no response. A nudge on the right brake brought the tractor back in line.

A pickup pulled up to the edge of the field followed by a billowing cloud of dust. Doug Grant stepped out and opened the gate, eying his son's work and liking what he saw; perfectly formed rows, eighty acres of them, stretched from one end of the field to the other. A sense of pride filled Doug as he watched his son.

Tim arrived at the end of the field and swung the tractor around for the last pass. He spied his father in the distance, but forced himself to concentrate so the last set of rows would be as straight as the first. Tim knew his dad would be proud, even though he wouldn't say so.

Tim reached the end of the field, raised the tool bar, brought both marker discs into the upright position, and idled back the engine. Doug Grant pulled alongside, rolled down the window on the driver's side of the pickup and shouted to be heard above the engine noise.

"Take the tractor home. Your mother has supper ready. I have to go by Ira Jones's place for a few minutes. I'll see you at the house."

Doug Grant closed the window of the pickup and shivered. The few seconds it was open allowed most of the heat in the cab to escape. Doug checked to make sure the heater was on full blast.

Tim maneuvered the tractor through the gate. The falling weight of his body buckled his knees when he got off to close the gate and caused him to grimace as sharp, needle-like pains emanated from his feet. Tim walked stooped over like a crippled old man, picked up the wire gate and closed it. He trudged back to the tractor and pulled himself into the seat.

Tim put the tractor into road gear and started toward his home. A blast of icy air greeted him even though the tractor moved only fifteen miles an hour. He could barely pry his fingers from the steering wheel by the time he arrived. His sister, Susan Grant, met him at the front door. Susan helped him out of multiple layers of thick protective clothing.

"Stop pushing so hard. You're frozen. That field will be there tomorrow. Mom has had supper ready for two hours."

"If I don't do my job, there won't be any supper."

"Where's daddy?" Susan asked.

"Said he was goin' to Ira's."

"I hope Ira's not home," she said. "He got into trouble today."

"Oh yeah? What happened?"

"He asked me not to say anything ... but I don't think he'll mind if I tell *you*. He had a fight with Jaime Garcia, the sheriff's son."

"You're kidding."

"No, I'm not. It's worse. When the cops arrested him, they found a joint in his pocket. I bailed him out of jail. He has a black eye. God, I hope dad doesn't find out."

"Me either," Tim said.

Doug Grant pulled up to the front door of the house. Tim and Susan exchanged a glance. Doug walked up the steps and came into the door.

"Ira wasn't home. Wonder where he went? He asked me to help with a problem on a tractor. You haven't heard from him, have you Susan?"

"No. He probably had to go to town for something. Ira is kind of forgetful sometimes."

"I've noticed that. Come on, let's eat," Doug said. Doug wrapped a strong arm around each of his children and pulled them close. Church music greeted them as they entered the kitchen. Martha Grant stared coldly at the rest of the Grant family. Graying hair was pulled back into a bun, and a conservative skirt hung within inches of the floor. Old fashioned, black, turn of the century lace-up shoes adorned her feet; no make up graced her hard, unsmiling face.

Like many of the people who attended the local Pentecostal church in the nearby town of McCamey, Texas, Martha's well-trained eyes perceived the devil in everything and everyone around, including members of her own family. She whispered constant prayers in *tongues* to ward off the evil one. A *sha la la, ah kron die* loomed near the surface of her lips as Doug Grant entered the kitchen.

In Martha's world, everyone was out to make her sin, everyone, that is, except for the preacher. He—she adored, and any utterance that proceeded from his mouth was as good as the gospel. Martha prayed constantly that her husband would someday see the light and become more like the Reverend Davies. The prayers didn't seem to be working.

The Grant family sat down to the evening meal, an excellent rump roast, complete with all the trimmings. In the eyes of Doug Grant, good cooking was Martha Grant's one last redeeming quality. Tim and Susan bowed their heads, while Martha said grace. Doug served his plate, seemingly oblivious to the prayer. Martha's prayer droned on and on. Tim peeked at his father, who by this time was slurping at some of the beef broth in his bowl. Finally, the prayer ended.

Tim said, "Amen."

"Damn fine prayer, Martha," Doug said. "Food's good too."

Martha almost imperceptibly shook her head.

"Tim did a hell of a job on that field, and it was almost as cold as that Pentecostal preacher's heart out there."

Martha dropped her spoon and began whispering silent prayers. Doug continued. "I hear cotton is a dollar a pound now. If the goddamned government will just keep its nose out of things this year, we might make some money, that is, unless the goddamned bankers figure a way to fuck us out of it."

At this, Martha broke into a steady stream of babbling, machine gun style. Then she jumped up and ran to her bedroom for more really serious prayer. Doug Grant changed the radio to a country music station.

"Fucking church music hurts my ears. If there is a God, I don't see how he can stand that phony shit."

Doug, Tim and Susan resumed eating. Awkward silence prevailed over the meal. Doug finally broke it. "Kids, I'm really sorry me and your mom ain't hittin' it off. Since she got on this goddamned religious kick of hers, I can hardly stand to be around her. This shit has got completely out of hand. She prays so much there ain't no time left for livin'. I still have feelings for your mom, but.... The woman I knew is gone. I don't know whether we'll make it. I hope you understand."

Tim said, "Don't worry, dad. We're not kids any more."

Susan stared at the food on her plate, saying nothing. Doug reached over and brushed her cheek. She raised her eyes and met her father's gaze.

"What's so bad about her going to church? I love you daddy, but I love mom too. I hate what's happening. I try to understand, but it's hard."

"I have needs, needs your mother isn't taking care of. The only thing that seems to concern her any more is that goddamned church and that goddamned preacher. She's flipped plumb out."

"Because she prays?" Susan asked.

"No, not because she prays. Nothin' wrong with praying, though I don't seem to get around to doing it all that often. Let me tell you something though. That phony bunch of shit she and the rest of those bastards at her church do ain't got nothin' to do with God. I'd just as soon die and go to hell as to have to put up with that kind of people. And something else. A wife that doesn't see to the needs of her own husband ain't no wife at all, regardless of what any goddamned preacher says."

The rest of the meal was eaten in silence. That night, Tim and Susan lay down in their respective beds. Doug found a spot on the living room couch. He closed his eyes and tried to sleep, but sleep would not come. Doug Grant needed sex.

Doug slipped to the door of his bedroom. Martha looked hatefully at him from the bed, rolled over to face the wall, and broke out speaking in tongues. The last place on earth Doug Grant was going to find some pussy was his own bed.

Doug walked back to the living room, laid on the couch without even bothering to remove his dirty clothes and stared at the ceiling, feeling very much alone.

CHAPTER II

The alarm erupted beside Ira Jones's bed; a hand reached out from under the jumbled mass of covers and groped for the source of the irritating noise. The clock fell to the floor and continued to ring. Ira covered his head, trying to drown out the incessant screeching. Ira's hand came out again, searching the contour of the floor. When Ira located the clock, he couldn't figure out how to shut the thing off. Finally he found relief; he hit a button and the clock stopped ringing. Five minutes later, it went off again. Ira picked up the clock and hurled it across the room. It struck the wall and died with one final gasp. Ira rolled over and went back to sleep.

Then the phone rang. Ira covered his head with the pillow until it stopped. Several hours later, sunshine poured through the window, forcing Ira into a semi-consciousness state. The taste of last night's party lingered in his mouth. Ira spied a partial joint in the ashtray beside the bed and put fire to it. A couple of hits helped. The phone rang again. Ira answered it from the bed.

"Hello. Jones farm, Ira speaking," he said.

"Hello Ira. Are you still in bed?" Ira's dad, James Jones, asked.

"No, I've been up awhile."

"Did you get those steers moved out of the barley yesterday?"

Ira looked out the window of the trailer. He saw a large herd of cattle, contentedly grazing away.

"Yeah, I did. A couple broke through the fence and got back in this morning. Me and Jose are going to get them out in a few minutes."

"Listen, Ira. We have a meeting scheduled for the day after tomorrow with Mr. Jenkins, at eight o'clock. I want you to load as many steers as you can into the gooseneck trailer and drop them off at the sale barn tomorrow. You can spend the night here in Lubbock and then we'll go see him together."

"I wonder what he wants?" Ira asked.

"We need more operating capital. The interest on our loan is due this month. Things are looking bad, now that oil prices have crashed. I suspect he will want more collateral to extend our note, since I can't make the interest payment."

"But dad. He already has three times as much collateral as we owe."

"I'm aware of that, but I'm broke son. We need money to keep operating or everything is going to come to a standstill, and I mean everything."

"The co-op asked about our bill," Ira said.

"They'll get their money. How are things down there?"

"Outside of the fact that I have no money to pay bills and I can't get the supplies I need to produce crops I need to repay the bank… Fine."

"I'll see you tomorrow."

"Bye, dad."

Ira hung up the phone. The joint was out. Ira relit it. He pulled on his cleanest pair of dirty jeans and drove to Jose's house.

Jose's body was beginning to show signs of aging. As a teenager, he migrated to the United States from his home country of Mexico, married, and settled in West Texas, where he stayed, rarely venturing farther north than Odessa, or further south than the Mexican border. He couldn't read, and spoke little English, but was a reliable, skilled farm hand, except for the days he got drunk, which he did at least every two weeks, right after pay day. The problem was these drunks tended to last until all of Jose's money was exhausted. Ira had learned to live with this. Another problem: Jose was afraid of horses. So deep seated was this fear that he'd sooner quit his job than mount one. Ira had also learned to live with this.

While Jose loaded a few sacks of breeder's cubes and several bales of hay into a pickup, Ira saddled a big sorrel quarter horse. Jose drove the pickup to the spot where they needed the cattle to go and began honking the horn. He got out and spread a few breeder's cubes for bait while Ira began pressing the cattle with the horse. The steers weren't overly interested in the breeder's cubes, considering the green barley field was pretty good eatin' itself. However, the big horse breathing down their backs soon became hard to ignore and they left, somewhat begrudgingly.

Ira and Jose stopped long enough to raise a strand of wire and connect it to insulators on posts already in place in the field. Ira then connected the fence to a battery powered fence charger so they would not return. Then they set to the task of capturing a few of the uncooperative bovines, which proved quite a chore indeed.

Cattle, especially young steers, tend to do things their way, which is rarely what their owners want. The last place Ira's steers wanted to be is the pen where they had been burned with red hot branding irons, had their balls cut off, their ears mutilated, needles poked into their bodies, and sprayed with a variety of irritating chemicals just months before. But that's where Ira needed them.

The horse Ira rode was a good one, but he and the horse were sadly outnumbered. Ira did his best to keep the cattle formed into a group and moving in one direction, but every time he turned his attention to one side of the herd, the other side began to drift in the opposite direction, the end result being Ira and the big horse managed to lose most if not all of the cattle somewhere before the gate leading to the corral. Time and again Ira tried to pen the cattle; time and again he failed. One steer in particular seemed to know when to make his break and once he escaped, the rest followed. Ira pushed the horse until he was lathered with sweat. Jose did little more than stifle laughs each time the herd broke and ran.

After the fourth consecutive failed attempt to pen the cattle, Ira rode up with a desperate look in his eyes. His face was flushed with blood and sweat dripped from his nose.

"Get out your rifle!" Ira yelled.

"Why, Señor?" Jose asked.

"When that God-damned brindle steer makes his break again, I want you to drop him in his tracks. We're gonna eat that motherfucker!"

No more laughing at the patron, Jose thought to himself. Jose got out his Marlin lever action 30-30, moved to the side where the cattle tended to escape, chambered a shell, and waited. This time, when the steer turned to run off, as if to make fun of the idiot on the horse, a bullet dropped him in his tracks. The report of the rifle panicked the remaining steers at the precise moment necessary and the whole herd gladly ran into the corral.

Ira followed them as far as the gate, jumped off the horse and shut it, before they had time to turn around and escape.

The two men spread hay out for the steers, both alfalfa and coastal Bermuda, and made sure that the water trough was working properly. Ira filled feed troughs with a salt, mineral, and molasses supplement, which made the cattle thirsty. The cattle were to be sold by the pound, so the more feed and water they consumed, the more they would weigh.

Afterwards, they took a tractor with a front-end loader, picked up the dead steer, hauled it to an old barn, and began the process of butchering. With the crude equipment at their disposal, this turned out to be a difficult and time-consuming project. The jubilation Ira felt when the animal fell faded to the reality that there will be one less animal to sell, and they needed all the money they could get to stay afloat.

Jose, on the other hand, was overjoyed. The steer weighed seven hundred pounds and yielded 400 pounds of beef or better. Jose knew he would be the beneficiary of that meat. That meant many long barbecues for the upcoming months, which also meant, since he could provide the meat, plenty of free beer his buddies would have to bring for their share of the proceedings.

Ira noticed that Jose collected nearly all the entrails, except the large intestine and the lungs. Poor Mexican immigrants tend not to be wasteful.

The next morning, Ira gave Jose instructions on the running of the farm, loaded the cattle into a gooseneck trailer, and started for Lubbock. Ira smoked joints, drank beer, and listened to outlaw country music on the road to Lubbock, forcing the big .454 into a steady strain all the way with the throttle pegged nearly to the floor. Rather than stop by his dad's house as he had been instructed, he unloaded the steers at the auction and headed for his favorite titty bar and the arms of his favorite titty bar dancer.

An infamous biker gang—the Desperados—owned the burlesque parlor; evidence of this fact surrounded the place; no less than fifty Harley-Davidsons stood in the parking lot in neat rows. Ira looked for someplace to hide the trailer, just in case one of his parents happened to drive by.

* * * * *

Angela Romano's mind roamed as she waited for her turn to dance—her past playing like a movie in front of her eyes.

Angela was a big girl—a Russian mom provided the genes for that and the ice blue eyes. Her skin however, was darker than most blondes—evidence of the Italian man that had sired her before going his own way, leaving Angela and her mother to fend for themselves.

Angela's childhood dream had been to participate in the Olympics as a gymnast. She had honed and chiseled her body into the exacting specifications required by the sport, until one of the many stepfathers that came and went through her home decided that body looked good for something else as well. After her mother blamed her for this indiscretion, she hit the road, at the ripe old age of fifteen.

A few weeks of hitchhiking around the country, eating out of trashcans and living like a stray dog, taught her the value of the well-formed body with which she had been blessed. The first time she sold herself, she earned forty dollars and a free night in a motel with a warm shower. The next day, the trucker asked her to marry him. After that, it became easier.

Not too long afterward, a *momma* from a motorcycle gang spotted Angela in a truck stop. They talked for several minutes. The momma walked off and returned with a man Angela found attractive. Black leather covered a hard, muscular build; long jet-black hair hung far down his back in a braid, and piercing brown eyes searched Angela's face. The momma belonged to RJ; from that moment forward, so did Angela. Later, she would learn that RJ was the National Sergeant of Arms for the Desperados.

RJ's band of whores adopted Angela, bought her clothes, taught her to dance, and introduced her to crystal methamphetamine, the drug of choice of many bikers. The girls also introduced her to almost every form of sex practiced on planet earth.

In spite of his rugged, handsome exterior, RJ proved difficult to please sexually. Years of massive doses of speed had left him impotent. Added to that was the fact that he had many good looking young whores from which to choose. Angela had one thing going for her that set her apart from the rest. Years of gymnastic training and good genetics had given her nicely shaped, muscular legs and one of the tightest asses to be found in Texas, with muscular control most men only dream of experiencing; between those legs was a bonified snappin' pussy. Even RJ recognized the value of her rare gift.

RJ however, liked money far more than sex, so he dedicated his time to turning Angela's rare gift into dollar bills. He crossed the first hurdle by acquiring a fake ID, which made Angela old enough to work in his Lubbock tit bar. Soon, Angela was making five hundred dollars a night. By the time she turned eighteen for real, she became his number one whore.

About that time, Ira Jones came along. Angela liked the redheaded cowboy from the start, which was quite unusual; she had learned to think of most of her Johns as little more than meat to be devoured. Ira seemed interested not only in her ass, but also in her as a person. The first three times he took her out, in spite of the fact that he paid for her time, he declined the sex. Ira took her on the first old-fashioned date she experienced in her young life. Angela found it easy to talk to the young man; sharing things with him she had never before shared with anyone.

While men loved having sex with Angela, she rarely enjoyed the act. By the time Ira finally did get around to bedding her, this changed. He treated her gently and patiently, and for the first time ever she experienced pleasure while making love to a man. They spent the entire night in each other's arms. Angela awoke thoroughly confused.

Ira bought her several more times after that; each time the result was the same. Angela began to live for the days he showed up and began to resent making him pay for sex.

Ira tried to talk her into quitting her job and marrying him. She refused, yet begged him to return each time he left. Ira failed to understand. You just don't quit being a whore for the Desperados.

Then, Ira stopped coming around; no word was said; he just disappeared. Angela was heartbroken. Her job performance declined. RJ began to treat her cruelly. She, in turn, became cold, and their relationship deteriorated into a war—a war Angela lost.

Ira Jones stood five foot seven—an inch taller than Angela and weighed one hundred and eighty pounds to her one-fifty. Neither had much body fat; both were young and strong. Ira was not however, strong enough to support the projectile Angela became when she saw him enter the bar. Angela threw herself on the young cowboy. Bouncers came running, prepared to do harm, until they noticed it was she who had tackled him, and what they were doing on the floor wasn't fighting. The bikers looked on with disgust as Angela aggressively kissed Ira.

"I thought I had lost you, " Angela said.

Ira picked up his hat and led her to a table.

"Why didn't you come back?" she asked.

"I got another girl friend, down in Bakersfield. I couldn't afford to keep seeing you. I had to steal money from the farm every time we went out. We're going broke."

Angela looked down for a moment, and then raised her eyes. "Is she pretty?"

"Yes."

"Prettier than me?"

"I wouldn't say that. She's good looking."

"Do you still love me Ira? You used to say you loved me."

Ira looked into her eyes. Her presence aroused him. That had been the very reason he had avoided her. Ira wanted her—badly—too much for his own good, it seemed.

"Yes, I do Angela. I can't help myself."

Angela looked back at the young cowboy. Tears welled in her eyes. She kissed him again, and ran her fingers through his curly red locks. She then whispered words she had never before told any man.

"I love you too."

Ira stared, almost in a state of shock. "What did you say?"

"You heard me."

"I want to be sure my ears didn't deceive me."

"I love you, Ira Jones."

"Holy fucking shit. Now what am I going to do?"

"Take me away from here. I want to be yours."

Ira was at a loss for words. He loved Susan Grant, or so he thought—yet when he looked at Angela, he wanted her too. Somehow just being around Angela made him feel like a king.

"Ira, I have money put away, enough to keep RJ happy tonight. Please, take me out of here. I need to be with you."

"You mean—for nothing?"

"Yes."

"That's a deal too good to pass up."

Angela smiled, and then walked over to another of RJ's whores, to let her know she would be leaving early. Ira felt the blood quicken in his veins as he watched her bounce across the room like a graceful young doe.

They drove to a motel in her car, after leaving Ira's truck and trailer at a truck stop. At the motel, they wasted little time, quickly discarding clothes and falling into each other's arms. Ira struggled to get into Angela; each move was answered with shudders, pants, and begging. By the time he got all the way in, it was over.

The second, third, and fourth times lasted a little longer.

The next day Angela went back to RJ, but not until she had secured a promise from Ira—a promise that he would return.

Ira drove to his father's house. On the way, his mind roamed, reliving the experiences of the previous night. Once again, Ira found himself confused, wanting two women at the same time; one a whore that spread her body all over town; the other who would give it to no one—Ira Jones included.

CHAPTER III

James Jones looked at his watch and ran a hand over his freshly shaved face one last time. The faint odor of cologne permeated the air around him. Grey streaked hair was neatly combed and held in place by VO-5 and his black leather shoes shined with a fresh coat of polish. A financial report Ira had prepared stared up at him from his desk. James disliked what he saw.

James Jones worked hard, devoting himself to his family, a family born and raised on a ranch. Many years of backbreaking work on his father's ranch had taught him the value of an education and left him determined to live another life than what he had seen his father endure—suffering year after year to support a family on agricultural income. James held a degree as a petroleum engineer, but his work had led him over the years into varied facets of the business world. James married young, while still in college, and immediately began having children. Six consecutive sons were born to the union, and then they stopped having children. Wanting a girl, the Jones's tried one last time, and along came Ira—the seventh son.

Much to his surprise, nearly all of James's children grew up interested in agriculture—the very thing James worked so hard to distance himself from. Wishing to support their interests, James reluctantly got back into farming and ranching. The older boys eventually either owned or managed farms, feedlots, and other agricultural related businesses; all stayed in the Texas panhandle.

Ira was considerably younger than his siblings, but shared their interest in agriculture. Unlike his brothers, he exhibited a terrible streak of rebellion. At the age of sixteen, Ira quit school and left home, to the dismay of his parents. Ira wanted to be a cowboy. He traveled the country, taking one poor paying job after another on ranches throughout the western United States, usually earning barely enough money to keep himself clothed and fed. On his nineteenth birthday, Ira showed up on his father's doorstep, completely broke, having abandoned his pickup at a roadside park when he ran out of gas and money to fill the tank.

James Jones bought a small, irrigated farm near Bakersfield, Texas, primarily to give Ira something to do. Unbeknownst to James, Ira had developed an addiction to marijuana while traveling around the country.

James hadn't expected the farm to make money immediately. Equipment needed to be purchased, wells reconditioned, and the cost of buying land on borrowed money at very high interest rates had to be considered. James counted on oil income to bear the burden of the place until it became productive. James hoped to hand the land over to his son, once it became profitable. Things hadn't worked out like he planned.

On rare occasions, James made a swing by Ira's place; when he did, it usually seemed well kept. However, when harvest time came, and all the money was collected, expenses were always far higher than expected and yields far lower.

At first Ira had attacked his work with enthusiasm, and had been optimistic about his chances. Two years of backbreaking labor and consistent losses left Ira bitter. Ira began to neglect his job.

James bore the load; hoping time would alleviate the problem. Then, the bottom fell out of the oil market. OPEC opened the spigots and left them open until oil was less valuable than water. Ira's place had to pay its way now, or all would be lost.

James looked at his watch again, shoved the financial statement into a briefcase, and walked out of the house and straight into the grinning face of his son. Ira stood in the door dressed in dirty jeans and a western shirt that looked as though it had been slept in. Ira's body emitted a wave of various odors—a mixture of sweat, stale beer, mildew, perfume, cow shit, and recent sex. His overly long, curly red hair billowed out from under the brim of a dirty, sweat-stained cowboy hat, and his face sported several days worth of wispy beard stubble.

"Hi, dad," Ira said.

"Where have you been? I was about to leave without you."

"I didn't get away from the farm until pretty late yesterday. By the time I got the cattle unloaded, it was too late to disturb you, so I just went ahead and rented a room for the night."

"Well, let's go then."

Both men walked to James Jones's car, a new Mercedes Benz, and climbed in.

"Ira, you should have cleaned up for this meeting. This isn't a dog fight we're going to," James said, noticing the cow shit from Ira's boots soiling the carpet of his new car.

"I know. I didn't get around to washing clothes this week. Sorry, dad."

James noticed that Ira's eyes were bloodshot and glassy. "Did you go out drinking last night?" he asked.

"I had a couple of beers, but not many."

James looked at his son. "I'm going to level with you son. First, the report you sent is terrible. The figures do not balance—it is incomplete, unorganized, unprofessional, and far less than what you are capable of producing. I expect better. I will not show this crap to Mr. Jenkins."

"Sorry, dad."

"Sorry isn't going to get it forever, Ira. I suspect you have been drinking too much. Sometimes I wonder if you are on dope or something. Just so you know—that cannot and will not be tolerated on *my farm*. We are going under if you are not as sharp as you can be. I need the best you have to offer and you can't give me that while fucked up on drugs and alcohol. That goes for you and for any hand working on that place. Have I made myself clear?"

"Yes, sir."

"All right. About the meeting… Mr. Jenkins knows we're hurting—maybe not how bad—but he knows we are in trouble. As I see it, our only chance for survival is to get more operating capital. You are aware we already owe four hundred thousand to Jenkins's bank. I am going to ask for a hundred more."

"Do you think he'll give it to us?"

"I hope so. The bills won't be paid if he doesn't. I simply don't have the money to pay them."

"That bad, huh?"

"Yeah. The oil business has gone to hell. I invested in a bank that went under and the FDIC will only cover a portion of what I lost—a small portion. We are headed for a recession, if not a depression. I need you to show some enthusiasm here, even if you don't believe it. We will probably get the money; the question is, what he will want in return. I may have to sign over damn near everything I still own. I'm counting on you, Ira."

"I've been doing my best, Dad."

"Bullshit. I realize you put in a lot of hours. I am aware that farming is a tough business, but you are *not* doing the kind of job you are capable of. I don't expect you to do all the work yourself, but you need to know everything happening on that farm, down to the minute detail. In order to do that, you must keep accurate records, not some pile of unorganized, scribbled shit like you sent me."

"OK," Ira says.

"What kind of barley crop do you expect to make?"

"At least forty bushels to the acre—maybe more."

"Tell Jenkins sixty. How is the hay looking?"

"Good. I started the irrigation. We should be able to get an early cutting. There are some aphids, but not enough to bother spraying for, especially if we get a spring rain."

"How about the equipment? Have things held up well?"

"We need another swather and a baler. The ones we have stay broken half the time. It's so far to get parts that I seem to spend half my time on the road. I know they're expensive, but a bale-loading machine would come in handy also. Last year, we lost a lot of hay, just because we didn't get it picked up when we should have. I have hell finding anyone wanting to haul hay."

"Anything else?"

"No."

The two Joneses pulled into the parking lot of the bank. "Are you ready?" James asked.

"Ready as I'll ever be."

Ira felt like he was shaking hands with the devil when he grasped the limp, sweaty palm of Floyd Jenkins. Subconsciously, he fought the urge to wipe his hand on his jeans after the experience. Jenkins smiled at Ira with his face, but his eyes conveyed something else—something far from friendly. Jenkins quizzed Ira about the working of the farm, asking him what he needed, what he expected to produce, and where he thought he might be able to make spending cuts, occasionally writing a note on a tablet after Ira's reply. Afterward, Mr. Jenkins turned to James Jones and the serious business began. Ira was left feeling like his part in the meeting had been nothing but a simple formality.

"I am going to need more collateral," Jenkins stated, looking down at James Jones's financial statement. "Farming in this day and time is a risky business. What can you give me?"

The haggling began. Ira sat quietly through this part of the meeting; his disgust for the banker grew as the conversation progressed. When it was over, the Joneses received the money and Mr. Jenkins got his collateral—far too much of it for James Jones's liking.

More formalities were exchanged and the Joneses got up to leave. Once again, Ira endured Mr. Jenkins's shit eating grin and dead fish eyes, but the sweaty palmed handshake got the best of him. Ira wiped his hand on his jeans as though he had come into contact with a contagious disease. It did not go unnoticed.

As they walked out of the bank, James asked his son, "Well, what do you think?"

"Do you want me to be honest?"

"Of course."

"I don't trust that man and I damned sure don't like the son-of-a-bitch."

"Me neither. He's a piece of shit. He does what he has to, to cover his ass. He;s convinced we will fail, and when we do, he will move in for the kill. Sometimes you have to deal with assholes to make it in this world."

"That's a tough one, dad."

"I know. I just signed off a lot of property to keep us in business. I can't give all the money to you, but I will do what I can. I'm counting on you to do your part. That means no drugs, no booze, hard work, and paying attention to detail. I want you to prove Mr. Jenkins wrong."

"I'll try, dad."

"That may not be enough. Sometimes you have to *make* things work. There will always be an excuse for failure. Trust in God and believe in the abilities he gave you. The two go hand in hand. Without faith, nothing of significance can be accomplished. Ira, you are a special person. You are blessed with many natural talents. What you do with them is up to you."

* * * * *

After the meeting, Ira went to the livestock auction and watched the steers sell. They weighed heavy and brought a decent price. It would appear that he had done well. Ira knew better. Far fewer animals remained on the farm than there should have been; some had died due to an unnaturally cold winter; others had been lost to thieves. Anything left unattended in the Bakersfield valley of Texas was subject to come up missing.

Ira started his truck and started for home after cashing the check for the steers. He stopped by the liquor store several miles south of town. Lubbock County was dry and did not allow convenience stores to sell alcohol. Ira noticed the pre-rolled joint in the ashtray. *That shit can't hurt anybody*, he thought to himself. He lit the joint. While driving, he went over the meeting with the banker and the words of his father.

About halfway home, he stopped for gas and another six-pack of beer. He left the station pointed for home, stopped about a quarter of a mile later, crossed the median of the highway, floored the truck, and headed back toward Lubbock and the tit bar where Angela worked. On the way, he considered his predicament.

* * * * *

Susan Grant was a strikingly beautiful blond, with her father's blue eyes and a small but perfectly proportioned body. On top of the good looks, she was intelligent; a trait often found lacking in women of her beauty. In Ira's eyes she had only one glaring fault. Susan was still a virgin.

Ira had received a taste or two of the female anatomy at an early age and developed a liking for what he found there. When Ira tried to introduce Susan to the pleasures of the flesh, he encountered stiff resistance. Susan would only go so far.

At first that meant extended sessions of kissing and maybe a feel of her breast through various layers of clothing, and only then for a brief period. As the relationship progressed, Ira finally coaxed off Susan's shirt, revealing small, firm, nicely shaped breasts. Ira did everything he could think of with these newfound treasures, before proceeding to the next logical step. About the time he was ready to explode in his pants, he reached for the button to Susan's jeans. She stopped him dead in his tracks.

"Oh, come on Susan," he begged. "I'm about to die for you."

"Not yet, Ira. I want you too, but not until we get married."

Susan took advantage of the break in the action to pull her shirt back on.

A couple of days later, Ira lured Susan into a hay barn. This time, he quickly got back to the point where they had left off in their previous session, and then crawled between her legs, pinning her to her back. Both were still clothed from the waist down. Ira ground himself into Susan's crotch; she responded by meeting his thrusts with her own, quietly moaning all the while. Ira lavished her upper body with kisses. When he was sure she was ready, he reached for the fly of her jeans. Once again, Susan's claw-like hands thwarted his efforts.

A few more days passed. The two went to see a drive in movie together. This time Ira was sure that he had won the extended battle when he got Susan out of her jeans, exposing her beautifully proportioned body. Ira kissed and massaged her, adoring all he found, feeling the moist warmth through the one small piece of cloth separating him from the treasure. She would not remove her panties. When he tried, she became angry.

"Susan, this is killing me! You don't understand how a man is built, or you wouldn't do this. I need a release. If you don't give it to me, I'm going to have to find it somewhere else."

"You better not."

"We're going to get married. What is the difference if it is now or later?"

Susan did not reply, so Ira proceeded again.

She stopped him cold.

"No, Ira," she said breathlessly, her face flushed with blood. "Not until we are married."

Susan grabbed her jeans and pulled them back on.

Ira grabbed her hand and directed it to his swollen penis, which was almost purple by now. One stroke was all it took. Ejaculate spewed into her hand.

"Gross, Ira. Why did you do that?" she asked.

Since that day, Ira had come nowhere near getting her clothes off again. Back to dry humping. She said, "I can't let you do that again. I am afraid I won't be able to stop you. I can't wait until we're married Ira. It is going to be so good."

"I can't wait either," Ira had replied, meaning something entirely different.

* * * * *

Ira slipped into the bar unnoticed, and took a seat in an obscure, dark corner, and watched Angela work a man from across the room. All around him, prime pieces of female anatomy walked in the tiniest of tiny thongs and other forms of seductive attire. Girls danced on stages and tables; men cheered them on. Ira watched Angela

Angela was larger than Susan and coarser. Both were blondes, although Angela's now came from a bottle. Susan went to church. Angela was a whore. Susan would make Ira socially acceptable. Angela wouldn't. Susan had good manners. Angela did not. Angela smoked and did drugs. Susan didn't. *Surely Susan is the better person of the two*, Ira thought. He looked at Angela, and he wanted her. *Is it just the sex?*

Finally, as though Angela sensed him from across the room, she looked in his direction, stopped in the middle of her table dance and walked over.

"How long have you been here?" she asked.

"Oh, I don't know. Maybe thirty minutes."

"Why didn't you let me know?"

"I was spying on you."

"That's not fair." Angela gave Ira a kiss and sat beside him. Once again, Angela's presence brought his blood to a boil.

"I though you were going home," she stated.

"I was. I turned around and came back. I'm really confused. I thought I had gotten over you; now I'm in as deep as ever, maybe deeper. Something you said has been bugging me."

"What's that?"

"You said you love me, yet you carry on with other men. You also said you didn't mind if I had another woman. How can that be?"

"RJ has more than one woman. I'm used to it."

"I don't like what you do for a living, Angela."

"Then why do you come around? I'm a dancer. I like being a dancer. For you, I might stop selling myself, but not unless you can give me the things I want and need. I've been poor, Ira. I don't do well without money."

Ira smiled sadly and shook his head, but said nothing.

"What's wrong?" she asked.

"I don't know. You're crazy I guess, and I must be too. Come here."

Ira kissed Angela. "I want you tonight."

"I need to make some money first or RJ will be mad."

"Fuck RJ."

"Until you take me away from here, I have to pay him. If I leave here with you, I can't come back empty handed."

"That mother fucker doesn't own you."

"Yes, he does," Angela replied.

"Where is this guy? I need to have a talk with the bastard."

"I don't want that. Just take me away."

"I will Angela, but I need a little time to think this over. I have money. Come on, let's get out of here."

"Are you sure? You don't have to do that. I can earn enough before closing time to take care of RJ and then we'll leave. That guy I was sitting with is loaded."

Ira looked across the room at the man Angela had been entertaining. He looked lonely.

"I'm sure you could, Angela. Let's get the hell out of this dump."

Ira took Angela out to eat at a restaurant. Over the meal they talked.

"You told me RJ has connections all over the state of Texas. If I take you away, what is to keep him from coming after you?"

"There is a way," she replied.

"How is that?"

"You can buy me."

"Buy you?"

"Yes. Desperados sell their old ladies all the time."

"You're shitting me."

"No, I'm not."

"Slavery went out years ago."

"That's what you thought."

"You're serious, aren't you?"

"Yes."

"Damn … Out of curiosity, how much would you be worth?"

"I don't know. We're not getting along. Probably ten or twenty grand. I could pay you back in less than six months if you let me dance. Other than that, I would have no choice other than leaving the state. The Desperados own Texas."

"They don't own shit. Let them bring their ass down to my part of the country and see what happens."

"Yes, they do, Ira. They own at least half of the topless bars in this state. Do you have any idea how much money one of these places makes? They also control the meth market. Try selling some here, or in Dallas, or Houston, or Corpus, and see how long it is before you get a knock on your door. They pay off the police. They own prosecutors, and even a few local judges. They *kill* people who get in their way. Just last week, a girl died here. The police called it a suicide, but it wasn't. RJ had it done. I am sure of it."

"Like I said before, let him cross that Pecos River and see what happens to his ass."

"He is smarter than that. He'll just put the word out and dangle the money. Sooner or later someone will catch up to you."

"The thought of buying and selling people is hard for me to take... Ten grand, huh?"

"Probably. I can't say for sure."

"I don't see how he can do that. I could never sell you to another man. I can hardly stand sharing you now. Even the thought of you dancing in tit bars is hard for me to handle. Have you ever considered doing anything else?"

"Of course, but sometimes you find yourself where you are and the easiest thing to do is to keep on doing what you do. I've had very few opportunities in my life."

"I need to go home, Angela. I have serious thinking to do. I'll see you later."

"You come back. Ira. Whenever you get ready to take me out of here, I'm ready to go."

* * * * *

On the way home, Ira considered possibilities. *Two women at the same time? Nah. But, then again...*

I might be able to get away with it for a while.

How am I going to tell Susan? This is going to hurt her.

I can't tell her. It will hurt her too much.

I can't live a lie either.

Why does life have to be so damned complicated? he asked the air around him.

He got no answer.

CHAPTER IV

While Ira and his father were busy securing operating capital in Lubbock from the bank, Doug Grant was busy securing his own operating capital, using another method —a method he called *the noble art of Repossessin'*.

Doug Grant was a relative newcomer to the state of Texas, having migrated from Kansas when his habit of repossession' had nearly gotten him put in prison. Doug was farm raised. As a teenager, he developed quite a reputation as a tough customer in a fight. His father took pride in that fact and pitted him in free for all fights against others for money. In these fights any tactic was permitted, so long as it didn't involve a weapon. Eventually he whipped most of the grown men in his neck of the woods inclined to think they could fight as well. Doug wasn't particularly large; he stood about five feet ten inches tall and weighed a hundred and ninety pounds. What made him bad to the bone was his temperament. He was ruthless and ferocious in a fight, having been known to bite off an opponent's ear or nose, when the opportunity presented itself.

Doug was strong for his size, due partially to genetics, but also to many hours of manual labor on the farm. His one weakness tended to be his wind.

Doug smoked heavily, having started at the age of twelve. The day came when a big, redheaded Missouri farmer was able to withstand Doug's horrible initial assault. This man also had a mean streak. Doug tired after cutting the guy's face up unmercifully with his fists. The big man kept coming. Eventually, he got a finger into each of Doug's eyes, almost gouging them out of his head. Doug's dad had to hit the huge farmer with a tire iron to get him off of his son, even though he had conceded. The incident put Doug into the hospital for two weeks and ended his career as a fighter.

Repossesin' was another skill Doug learned at a young age. Repossesin' was what most people refer to as stealing, though Doug didn't consider them the same. The distinction came in that Doug never repossessed indiscriminately. He thought of himself as a modern day Robin Hood. Of course, Doug tended to forget about the distribution among the poor part of that story. The way Doug saw things; the system was out to rob honest laborers of their just rewards, especially independent ones like farmers. Anyone who aided this system out to enslave the world quickly found himself or herself on Doug's shit list.

Government workers and bankers held their rightful places at the top of the list—insurance companies weren't far behind. If you valued your property, you'd have been well advised never to let Doug Grant know it was insured. Lawyers were there only to protect those in power. Farm equipment companies or any number of companies supplying products to farmers also had a place on the list, since they probably charged unfair prices for their products or services they provided. Anyone who bought agricultural products at unfair prices was guilty as well. Most people tend to eat once in a while and like to buy their food as cheap as they can get it. If you paid taxes or showed your support for the government in any way, you became guilty. Police were the system's bullies; Doug harbored a special hatred for them, and anyone of them who crossed his path was in jeopardy of losing his life. Preachers were nothing more than con men by Doug's standards. When Doug got through compiling his list, very few people were safe from his noble art of repossessin', but to be fair to Doug, he tried to limit his repo jobs to the most deserving.

One sure way to get your ass shot off was to try to stop Doug Grant from rightfully repossessin' what was actually his to begin with. Doug Grant went nowhere without a gun. Many years of fighting had taught him the value of such a tool. The way he looked at it, there was no sense in getting all sweaty and dirty, and risking getting hurt, when a few ounces of properly applied trigger pressure did such a nice job on a man. Somewhere down the line, Doug had decided that the only way anyone was ever going to take his gun was the day they pried it from his cold, dead fingers.

* * * * *

Doug pulled up to a John Deere dealership not many miles from Lubbock. A large Rottweiler dog ran up to the chain link fence guarding a yard full of new tractors. Doug smiled, withdrew a rifle from his gun rack and called the dog.
"Here, puppy dog. Come and get it."
The dog barked and growled viciously. Doug walked up to the fence and shot him right between the eyes. Both of the dog's eyes popped from their sockets and his legs scrambled for a few seconds, propelling him aimlessly, scattering blood from the small dark hole in his forehead.
"Now that's a nice puppy," Doug commented, as the dog settled into his final resting position.
Next, he went back to the truck, extracted a large set of bolt cutters, and cut the chain off of the gate leading into the yard, where he proceeded to help himself to two new tractors.
Doug was a mechanical genius; he could steal anything on wheels or tracks in five minutes or less, armed only with a large screwdriver. On this particular day however, fate almost caught up with him, or rather, with the owner of the dealership Doug had selected. Just as Doug was snapping the last chain boomer in place, a car pulled up to the front of the building.
Luckily, Doug had the foresight to close the chain-link gate after entering the yard. Upon hearing the car's arrival, Doug positioned himself behind a tractor's tire, withdrew his gun, and waited. The man walked into the building. Doug waited for him to exit. The man came out of the building, got

back into his car, and left, without a single glance in the direction of the yard, unknowingly saving his own life.

Must have forgotten something, Doug thought to himself. He replaced the gun and went back to work.

* * * * *

While driving down the highway, Doug Grant thought about the many virtues of farm equipment, when selecting material for repossesin'. First, the stuff all tends to look alike. There aren't many identifying marks. Each company has its standard color, and every piece of equipment they make bears that color. Even the rightful owner of a piece of machinery would not know his piece of equipment from any other, once Doug got it several miles from where it had been. There were no license plates to worry with. People rarely safeguarded farm equipment well. Most important in Doug's mind was the fact that farm equipment is valuable. New John Deere 4440's, like the two riding on the back of his trailer were worth between forty and fifty thousand dollars.

An Oklahoma farmer was overjoyed to get them for twenty thousand apiece, cash money, no questions asked.

CHAPTER V

Tim Grant pulled up to check his irrigation ditch. What he saw made him shout in anger. The dirt ditch had broken again and the precious water the field so badly needed was running through a hole in the side of the ditch into another drainage ditch near the road, supplying moisture to an already healthy patch of weeds.

The field was a new one, without a cement ditch from which to irrigate so Tim had been forced to make one from dirt using a blade on the back of a tractor set at a forty five degree angle. Several passes had been required to make the ditch; the end result was a V-shaped groove in the ground with dirt berms on either side.

To water the field, Tim cut a small trench across the ditch and buried one side of a long poly tarp in the bottom. A two by eight board was suspended above the trench and the top corners of either side rolled around it. Pieces of sucker rods were suspended from the board to the bottom of the ditch, underneath the tarp, for added support; the result was a dam, which would stop water introduced into the ditch. When the pump was started, water filled the ditch to a point above ground level. Siphon tubes were then inserted to extract the water from the ditch and into the individual rows.

Irrigating out of a newly constructed dirt ditch is a tricky operation. Tim had to balance the output of the well with the amount of siphon tubes he started; not enough tubes, and the water would overflow the ditch, eroding the sides and breaking it; too many tubes, and the water level would fall until some of the tubes sucked air, lost their siphon, and then the level would rise, leaving dry rows, or worse—too many would lose their siphon at the same time and the water level would rise too high and once again, break the ditch. Other factors further complicated the procedure: sometimes an engine sped up or slowed down inexplainably, or maybe the well's output would change after several hours of pumping. Either of these scenarios meant trouble.

The wells, under ideal conditions ran twenty-four hours a day, seven days a week, and required constant monitoring and supervision. Every twelve hours a new dam had to be set and the water moved further down the ditch.

The first few days of the irrigation season had been frustrating for Tim. Periodically, the engine, a Minneapolis Moline, which ran on natural gas, started missing, causing it to slow down. Consequently, the water output and the level of water in the ditch decreased, and a few tubes lost their siphon. The engine then resumed running well. Because several tubes no longer were extracting water from the ditch, the remaining tubes still drawing water could not keep up with the supply, and the ditch overflowed and blew out. Each time this happened, Tim was forced to shut down the well, repair the ditch by hand with a shovel, and restart everything, requiring at least an hour of intense concentrated labor, if not, more. He also lost whatever time the water had errantly run somewhere besides where he needed it to be.

Tim drove back to the well. The engine was running smoothly, pumping a ten-inch pipe full of water at one thousand gallons a minute into the ditch. The oil pressure was good—same with the water temperature—no smoke was evident in the exhaust.

What in the hell is going on here? he wondered.

Just then, Ira Jones drove up.

"Blown out again?" Ira asked.

"Hell, yes. This motherfucker's eatin' my lunch. Sometimes, I feel like takin' a sledgehammer and beatin' it all to hell. I've taken this engine apart and put it back together three times already, and can't find anything wrong. At this rate I'll never get this field watered."

"It wasn't the engine this time," Ira said.

"Oh no? What was it then?"

"Tumbleweeds. The windstorm last night got you. Same thing happened in my field. Fuckin' wind picks up trash and it collects in the ditch, stopping up the tubes. They get to where they ain't drawing any water—next thing you know, your fuckin' ditch blows. Follow me. I'll show you."

Ira floor-boarded his pickup, making a hundred and eighty turn at full throttle—the spinning wheels sprayed dirt and gravel like a contrail—and headed toward the break in the ditch. By the time he reached the dam, he was doing fifty miles an hour on a road designed for ten. He locked the wheels of the truck and slid to a stop just a few feet from the dam, hopped out, and began pulling on a pair of black rubber irrigation boots. Tim's truck slid to a stop, just a few feet behind Ira's.

Ira extracted a pitchfork and began to fork crud out of the ditch. A huge wad of twigs, tumbleweeds and other pieces of organic matter and trash had formed near the dam. He picked up a siphon tube and showed Tim how it had been clogged by the debris.

"I clean all of that crap out every time I move the fuckin' dam," Tim complained.

"I know," Ira replied. "Last night, I spent half the fuckin' night forkin' weeds. It was a cold son-of-a-bitch too. Do you think we can get the ditch plugged without shutting down the well?"

"I've tried a couple of times. It's impossible by myself. I shovel like hell and the water rises, washing me out again before I can get the tubes started."

"Get your shovel and we'll try." Ira suggested. "Maybe between the two of us we can get it done. It would sure save you some time."

Both men armed themselves with a shovel, took a few deep breaths, and began to scoop loads of heavy, sticky mud out of the ground and into the break in the ditch. At first the rushing water immediately washed each clump away. Eventually, a few held. At this point, the two began to pick up their pace. The race was on. They shoveled in rhythm; one dug deep while the other dumped his load, and then visa-versa, as fast as they could manage. Each man loaded as much mud as he could get on the shovel at one time; shovel handles creaked to the point of breaking under the strain. The water level began to rise, putting pressure on the newly made patch, and the men were forced to thicken the wall so it would not explode under the weight of the water. Finally, the water rose to a level a few inches above ground level.

"Start some tubes. Quick!" Ira shouted. "I'll keep on shoveling."

Tim ran around the dam, through the dry part of the ditch, and began starting the siphon tubes. To accomplish this feat, he picked them up with his left hand, leaving one end of the curved tube in the water. Using the palm of his right hand, he alternately opened and closed the end of the tube while pulling it up and down with this left hand, forming a crude pump of sorts. When the tube was full, he sat it down and it began to siphon water. Tim worked quickly, priming each tube in seconds and then moving on to the next. Nevertheless, the water level gained on them and began to leak over the weak spot. Ira continued to shovel at a maniacal pace.

"Hurry, Tim! The ditch is getting too full!"

"I'm going as fast as I can."

By this time, Ira had filled the hole until it was as high as the rest of the ditch. Water was leaking over the sides in new spots. Tim got all the tubes started and the water began to recede a fraction of an inch at a time.

"I think we got it," Ira said, continuing to shovel to make sure the weak spot held. Then the ditch began to break in a new area.

"Damn it. Look, Ira!" Tim yelled, trying to jump the ditch full of water to get to the new break. His foot fell short and he slipped on the muddy bank and fell into the ditch. He got up spewing curses while Ira laughed. Tim recovered and the two of them patched the new leak. The water level crept down and stabilized, so they slowed their pace, reinforcing weak spots and building the entire side up a couple of inches to prevent further blowouts should the water level rise later.

After all was under control, both men leaned against their shovel handles and watched the shimmering rivulets of water run through the rows. Squaw tit peak loomed over the field in the distant background, like an ancient monument to times gone by. Most people wouldn't take a second glance at such a sight; the young farmers found beauty in it.

Ira removed a joint from his pocket and lit it.

"Want a hit?" he asked, after taking a drag.

"Sure. Where did this come from?"

"Some guy Jose knows in Fort Stockton. He picks it up for me by the quarter pound. I get it cheaper that way."

"Didn't Jose go to prison one time?" Tim asked.

"Yeah. Not too many people know about that. He just got off on federal parole. He got busted driving a load out for someone seven or eight years ago and did a couple of years in La Tuna."

"Does he smoke?"

"Hardly ever. For him it was strictly a way to make money. Can hardly blame him. Things are tough for a man who can't speak English in this country."

"You know what, Ira? I'm starting to think my old man is right. We've been working our asses off for quite a while now and I haven't seen the first dollar of a profit."

"Me neither," Ira said. "I'm beginning to feel like a leech. Every time I turn around, I have to ask my old man for money."

"I know the feeling. Maybe we're crazy to keep trying. Every time we produce a good crop, so does everyone else, and then the shit ain't worth nothin'. Prices get good and we ain't got nothin' to sell. Every damn thing we buy keeps getting' higher and higher. I love growing things. I understand the plants and the animals, but the business end of farming eats me alive."

"I'm going to grow a patch of marijuana this year," Ira said. "I grew a few plants last year for my own use. It came out pretty good. At least *that* shit is worth some money."

"You may find this hard to believe, but me and dad have discussed the same thing."

"You're shitting me. I thought your old man hated marijuana."

"He ain't got nothin' against marijuana. He just doesn't want *me* smokin' it, or for that matter, anyone else in our family."

"I'll be damned. I woulda never figured that in a hundred years. Somehow, I just can't picture Doug Grant sellin' marijuana."

"My old man is a lot cooler than you think."

"Why, I guess so. If I were to tell my old man that I wanted to grow marijuana on his place, he'd disinherit me for life."

"How much are you planning to grow?" Tim asked.

"I figure I'll start out with about a thousand plants and thin them down to the best three or four hundred females. I'm going to grow *sin semilla*."

"Do you know how to tell the difference between the males and the females?"

"Yeah."

"What about seed?"

"I've got lots of it."

"You'll have to give me some. Maybe you can show me and dad how to grow *sin semilla*."

"Shit, I don't know. I'm a little leery about talking to him about that."

"Ira, I'm telling you he's cool. We've already got one growing in the barn, testing it out. Besides, you're almost family. The only thing we need to do is come up with a story about how you found the seeds. Don't let him know you smoke the stuff and you got nothin' to fear."

"I figured he already knew. A time or two he has come up on me right after I finished a joint."

"Be careful. If he finds out you smoke that shit, you and Susan are through. He don't want us using marijuana, or hanging around anyone who does."

"What do you reckon he'd do if he found us out?"

"He'd probably kick the shit out of us. That might well be the last joint we smoked."

"I don't believe I'd want to tangle with your old man. I may be young, fast, and strong, but he's mean. I see it in his eyes sometimes."

"He can be. He ain't all bad though. I don't think he ever gave me a whippin' I didn't deserve. He loves me and Susan more than a lot of fathers do their children."

"I better go, Tim. Tell Susan I'll see her tonight."

"How are you two getting' along? You haven't come around much lately. Is something wrong?"

"I've been feeling a little guilty lately. The last time I went to Lubbock, I went by a tit bar and picked up a whore."

"Damn, Ira. You better not let Susan find out. She's liable to shoot you."

"I know it. I feel bad about it, but I haven't had any pussy in ages. I've tried switchin' hands, using KY jelly, and just about everything else I could think of. When I was twelve, I thought jackin' off was the greatest discovery I'd ever come across. Somewhere down the line, it kinda lost its thrill."

"I know what you mean. The real thing is hard to beat. Lisa takes good care of me though. I figured you and Susan were getting it on a long time ago."

"Nope, but it damned sure ain't my fault. Sometimes I get the feeling she enjoys teasing me, just to watch me suffer. She'll let me get close, damn close, and then cut me off and watch me flounder. I can't take that forever. Maybe you could drop a hint for me."

"I don't know man. Me and Susan don't discuss those kinds of things. I'll see what I can do, but it won't be easy, with mom whisperin' in her ear every ten minutes."

"Thanks, Tim. See you."

"Later, Ira."

Tim watched the ditch for a few more minutes and then looked at the joint Ira had handed him before leaving. A seed was stuck in one end. He pulled it out and held it in the palm of his hand, eyeing it closely.

"Maybe—just maybe," he said, and plunged it into the moist soil near the ditch.

CHAPTER VI

Doug Grant, Walter Dean, and Bubba Cooper sat in their customary seats at the farm co-op near Bakersfield. Each held a thick cup of coffee in one hand and a cigarette in the other. Just about every morning, Walter and Bubba were there; Doug often joined them. The meeting was part of the morning ritual each went through, a ritual usually carried on throughout the rest of the day. At one time this activity would have been called a *spit and whittle* session, but the term no longer applied, as each had forsaken chewing tobacco for the more instantaneous gratification cigarettes provided, and rarely whittled. The gossip however, was the same as always. Of course, none of the three would have ever admitted to gossiping; that is something only women do.

At one time, the Bakersfield valley of Texas was alive with farmers; on any given day or night; tractors could be seen, working away in the fields. Natural gas was free for the taking, and fueled stationary engines atop wells over underground streams—supplying abundant water. The rich soil above was fertile. Times do change though.

In their hey-day, the two old timers had done well and had been known as the best farmers in the area. Walter Dean had the state record for per acre cotton production and Cooper's wasn't far behind. In those days cotton was picked by hand and between the two men, upwards of five hundred Mexicans were employed during harvest season. Now, they spent most of their time reminiscing about those days, occasionally cussing the government, or bankers, for bringing it to an end.

Just about anyone in the world was fair play in their discussions. Whoever or whatever happened to be in the newspaper usually got kicked around. Both old men figured that if the world would just stop and listen to them for a while, all its problems would be solved. Shame on your ass though, if you happened to be born black, brown, yellow, or for that matter, north of the Red River. In their utopia, those people would cease to exist, along with all Texas hippies and some of the city slickers. The whole world would be wearing Stetson hats and listening to country music.

Doug Grant was an exception to the rule, having been born originally in Kansas. They figured he, at least, had sense enough to leave Yankee land and move to Texas—besides all that, Doug also got around to cussing Yankees once in a while hisself.

Walter Dean propped his sweat-stained hat back on his head, and leaned back in his favorite chair. "Is that Jones boy still sweet on your daughter, Doug?"

"I believe so. He's a good kid though. Damned hard worker. Only thing that worries me about him is his unrealistic view on life."

"How's that?" Bubba Cooper asked, leaning forward and adjusting the volume on his hearing aid to hear better.

Doug spoke louder, so the two old men could hear. "That boy actually thinks he can make money farming. Can you believe that shit?" Doug shook his head and smiled at the two men.

"I'll guarantee you he ain't making a dime now," Cooper said. "I owned that place and farmed it for years. He's making decent crops, but nothing like what we used to, and he is spending twice the money we did. We went broke. The only way I figure he has a chance is to grow some of that marijuana them hippie kids smoke now."

"You don't think he uses that, do you?" Doug asked the old man.

"Hell if I know. I wouldn't know what it was if I was lookin' at it. They tell me a lot of the youngsters do nowadays.

I bet he knows a lot of rich city kids that do. I wouldn't blame him a bit if he grew some and sold it to those sorry bastards."

"I would," Walter Dean said. "I have grandchildren living in those cities. Besides, it is against the law."

"So is cheatin' on your income tax," Cooper said. "You ever do that?"

"Well—yeah—but that's different. Everybody does that, or goes broke."

"What about the sour gas you steal to run your irrigation wells?"

"Yeah, but..."

"The way these youngsters see it, there ain't much difference between those things and what they do."

"But, that shit hurts people," Dean said, taking a big drag off of his cigarette and coughing violently.

Doug Grant finally joined in on the argument. "There ain't nobody twistin' their arms to buy the goddamned stuff. Don't get me wrong now. I have never smoked any. I don't want my kids fuckin' with it either, but I'd sell it to them rich bankers, and politicians, and their sorry ass kids in a minute if I had any to sell, and I don't blame anybody else that does either. Them brats will grow up just like their parents. They're seeds. If a seed comes off of a weed, and you plant it, the next generation is going to be a weed too."

Neither Dean, nor Cooper commented, sitting back and absorbing what Doug had said for a moment.

Doug continued his tirade.

"Yes sir, so long as my kids leave the shit alone, I don't care if the rest of the world chokes to death on it. Some would be doing us all a favor if they did. Seems like ever other person is a government employee, a banker, or some other kind of leech, like that goddamned preacher my wife likes so much. Sometimes I think I'd be better off sellin' my place and movin' to Mexico. I hear those women know how to treat their men. Far as I am concerned, these spoiled white bitches up here can go straight to hell. They're useless as tits on a boar hog. If they didn't have asses on them, there'd be a bounty on their heads. Outside of lettin' you fuck 'em ever once in a while, what good are they? Spend all your goddamned money, bitch at you when you come home from a hard day's work—hell my woman ain't even any good for fuckin' any more, since that goddamned lyin' asses preacher got his hooks into her—the sorry son-of-a-bitch."

"I ain't got much use for a preacher, either," Dean said, finally finding something he could agree with. "Most of them wouldn't hit a lick at a snake if it was fixin' to jump up and bite them."

"How's things looking at your place?" Bubba Cooper asked, trying to change the subject, which had become uncomfortable.

"We've got water goin' on that cotton field. Prices look good. They'll figure a way to fuck that up before we got any to sell though. That boy of mine had the same disease that's eatin' Ira Jones up."

"What's that?" Cooper asked

"He actually thinks he is goin' to make money growin' cotton. He's been workin' his fool ass off. Can you imagine that? Makin' money growin' cotton?" Doug asked, shaking his head.

"We used to," Cooper replied, with a faraway look in his eyes. "Everything is too expensive now. In the fifties, I bought a brand spankin' new tractor, complete with equipment, for twenty-five hundred dollars. That tractor Ira Jones has cost him fifty thousand, without any equipment. Barley is still the same price. There just ain't no damn way, short of goin' in and registerin' with the government for a handout. I just never quite could get used to doin' that."

"Tell me about it," Doug Grant stated. "If I didn't have outside interests, we'd have folded a long time ago. The only reason I farm at all is to teach Tim. Farmin' has been a way of life for my family for generations. I just couldn't stand to see it die with me."

"I know how you feel," Dean said. "If it wasn't for those oil wells they found on my place, I couldn't eat. I haven't made a dollar on my farm for ten years runnin' now. I don't know what I'd do with myself if I didn't have my place though."

"Hell ain't it—to be in love with such a bad habit," Doug commented.

Both old men grinned sadly and nodded their heads. Doug got up and left. The two old timers immediately switched the topic of their conversation to him.

"I wonder how he pays his bill." Cooper said. "He don't have a bank account. I've checked all over the country, and I can't find a thing in his name."

Dean replied, "I don't give a shit how he comes up with the money, so long as he keeps doin' it. If it weren't for those two kids farming and the money they spend in this store, we'd be out of business."

Both old timers wouldn't give a dime of credit to either of the two young farmers left in the Bakersfield valley had not there have been outside wealth to pay the bills. They knew where Ira Jones' money came from. They did a lot of speculating over where Doug Grant got his money. They figured there was more to the story than they knew. They hadn't yet decided whether that was a good or a bad thing.

CHAPTER VII

Martha Grant sat in the front row, eyes locked on Reverend Delton Davies as he preached, with a look on her face not unlike that of a young schoolgirl at a Beatles concert during the sixties, hanging on to every word and movement.

Delton Davies was handsome, and he knew it. He strolled from one end of the stage to the other as he preached. He lowered his voice to a whisper. When the congregation leaned forward to hear, he spun around and shouted loudly, damn near jolting some of the eager listeners out of their seats. Martha sighed in admiration. Then the singing began. This was Martha's favorite part. Delton Davies had a wonderful voice. At least once during each service, he sang a solo; every time he did, Martha Grant broke into tears.

After the song, he went into a whole series of hallelujahs. "Hallelujah! Hallelujah! Hallelujah! Hallelujah! Hallelujah!" he shouted, and then broke into a barrage of unknown words, sounding something like *Sha la la shish cum bah.*

Reverend Davies waved his arms from side to side and the crowd joined in. A man in the audience rattled off a whole series of unknown words. At this point, Reverend Davies had already made two collections, one for tithes, and another for the cost of a new church he hoped to build.

"I've been given the interpretation of Mr. Graham's holy words. Yes. Yes. Yes. There is a financial need among us. Yes, indeed. Praise God. It will be met. Hallelujah! Praise God! I'm being instructed to take up another collection today. There's something else. Glory to God. All who give unselfishly to this cause will be repaid ten-fold, yea, some even a hundred fold. Praise the Lord! What a wonderful God we have! Praise his wonderful name! Glory hallelujah!"

The plate went around again, and the congregation dug deep. A hundred-fold return on your money is hard to beat. Another song was sung, and the service ended.

Reverend Davies went to the door of the church and shook each man's hand as they exited. At night he used a spring type wrist exerciser to strengthen his grip. Most of the women got a hug and a compliment on how nice they looked. When Martha came by, he whispered into her ear.

"Martha, I need to see you after the service. God gave me a special vision concerning you."

"Me?" she asked, delighted that God would do something especially for her. After everyone had left, she went back into the church.

Delton Davies took her by both hands and stared directly into her eyes. She felt her breath quicken.

"Martha, this may be hard for you to accept, but I must tell you, for God himself has instructed me." He paused for effect.

"What is it?" Reverend Davies."

"The devil is working hard to destroy you, Martha. This has been revealed to me. You are a very special person in God's plan, and the devil is out to stop you. I have been sent to prevent that from happening."

"Praise God," Martha replied. "I knew he had been after me. Tell me what I should do."

"Martha, God has told me that the man you are now living with is not your true husband. You have been living in sin. I would never intervene in another's marriage for God said, *Let no man break apart what God has joined together*, but God revealed to me that he did not ordain your marriage."

"Oh my," she exclaimed, almost fainting. Reverend Davies caught her. Tears began to form in her eyes. "I've tried so hard, prayed so many prayers."

"But Doug Grant is not a man of God. No, he is a son of the devil himself, and he is out to destroy you."

"I knew it. Oh my God. How could I have been so blind?"

Delton Davies hugged Martha. She sobbed like a baby in his arms.

"Its OK, Martha."

"What of my children?"

"There is a war going on over them. Keep the faith and you will be victorious."

She looked up at him and he kissed her on the forehead. Martha began to feel a stirring in her loins, a feeling she had successfully fended off for over a year now.

"God has selected another man for you."

Delton Davies kissed Martha flush on the lips this time, and then reached around her back and pulled her close.

"I am that man, Martha."

"You…and me?"

"Yes. I saw it in a dream."

Delton Davies kissed Martha again. She began to tremble with excitement. Many times she had fantasized about being with Delton Davies, and then felt guilty afterwards. Now, she felt a huge sense of relief. *Delton Davies was her ordained husband. That explained it all—why she was so strongly attracted to him—why she could no longer stand Doug Grant.*

"Praise God," she whispered. When Delton Davies kissed her again, she kissed him back. Reverend Davies ran his hands up and down her back and cupped her buttocks, squeezing and pulling, pulling and squeezing. When the time was right, he led her to a back room and the action continued. Soon both were on the floor, fucking like a pair of minks.

Afterward, Reverend Davies had a few more words of wisdom for Martha.

"We must not tell anyone about this yet, Martha. Not all the people's understanding of the word is advanced as ours. They might misinterpret. Soon, God will prepare them, and then the truth will be revealed. From this day forward, you are my wife. It is a wonderful thing, isn't it Martha—being in love and knowing God has ordained it? He has made me a happy man."

"And me a happy woman. God, it has been so long—waiting. I knew something was wrong but it took God speaking through you to show me the light. Thank you so much Reverend Davies."

"Don't thank me, Martha—Thank God."

Martha left church with a glow and a bounce in her step she hadn't had since she was a teen-aged girl.

Reverend Davies smiled as he watched her go.

CHAPTER VIII

Ira Jones watched the windrow of alfalfa feed into the pickup reel of the baling machine from the cab of his tractor. Dust was starting to fly from the baler, indicating it would soon be time to stop for the day. Ira looked at his wristwatch. It read 11am. He stopped the tractor and got out to check the last bale made.

"Too dry," he said. Ira looked at the counter on the baling machine. It read five hundred and seventy seven. Ira shook his head in disappointment. He had started baling at midnight, stopped at 4 am, and resumed at nine, after moving the irrigation water on another part of the field. Ira looked over the field and the long strips of neatly rowed bales, fifteen hundred of them, ready to be picked up, yet, the boys from the neighboring town of McCamey supposed to be hauling the hay hadn't shown again. More hay was ready to bale and Jose was cutting more still. Ira scratched and yawned, rubbing bloodshot eyes, red partially because of the marijuana he had consumed, but also because of the hay dust and pollen he unwillingly bathed in while working.

Alfalfa faming in arid West Texas was tough work. Most farmers tried to get at least six cuttings a year, the Jones's patch was two hundred and fifty acres, so that meant a whole lot of watering, cutting, baling, and hauling. Because of the hot, dry climate, baling was often done at night when the humidity went up, moisturizing the precious leaves so they wouldn't be pulverized by the baler. On an average day, Ira put in fourteen to sixteen hours.

Ira drove the tractor back to the barn, got into his pickup, and continued on to a field of barley he was in the process of irrigating. It too, like Tim's cotton field, had a dirt ditch. Ira set a new dam, and then released the one he had been using. Water invaded the new territory in the ditch. While the level rose, Ira scooped up the siphon tubes and laid them out in the next rows to be watered. When the water level reached sufficient height, he began to start the tubes.

Doug Grant pulled up to the field.

"That is one beautiful patch of barley you have there, Ira. Looks even better than ours. Damn stuff must be over four foot high already. You're right on time with that water too."

"Yeah, I think so. I'm hoping to make a good crop."

"You should, unless bad weather gets you. This country will really put out the grain. Shame that prices are so bad."

"Sure is. Five bucks a hundred, last I heard. That's pathetic." Ira looked out at the field. "You know, I really love this kind of work. Plants and animals really respond to good treatment. I feel proud when I can look out and see living things growing because I've done my job."

"I know the feeling, Ira. Sometimes it still hits me. Course, year after year of goin' broke at it has kinda taken the edge off of those feelings. Being proud of your work doesn't put money in your pocket or food on the table."

"How have you managed to stay in business so long Mr. Grant? I've only been farming for three years and I have lost so much money I'm driving my dad into bankruptcy."

"I have my ways. Maybe when you get desperate enough, I'll talk to you about them."

"How desperate do I have to be?"

"You ain't there yet. How did your meeting with the banker go?"

"We got funded."

"Are you going to be needing any equipment?"

"Yeah. My baling machine broke down about twenty times last night. I should have made another thousand bales, but I spent more time under it than I did baling."

"What brand are you interested in?"

"John Deere, or maybe a New Holland."

"John Deere is one of my favorites. I can get a new baler and a hydroswing swather for the price of a new baler."

"Is that right?"

"Yes sir. Of course, I'm talking cash money."

"How can you afford to do that and still make any money on the deal?"

"I have good connections for farm equipment, particularly John Deere stuff. Iowa and Missouri are full of broke farmers right now. How about a bale wagon? Looks like you're havin' trouble getting your hay picked up."

"I do need one, but I can't afford it. They're worth about fifty grand for a self-propelled model aren't they?"

"Normally, yes, but for you, I just happen to know where a really special deal is. What would you say if I were to tell you I could bring you one for twenty thousand?"

"New, you say?"

"Not quite, but almost. Not even broke in well."

"Bring it on."

"You do realize that I do all business on a cash only basis. None of that damn write-your-own money for me. That won't be a problem, will it?"

"No sir, I don't think so."

"By the way, Tim told me to let you know that four wetbacks showed up this morning. Bastards walked four straight nights to get here, all the way from Mexico. Can you imagine that? Shit—these locals won't walk two miles to look for a job, and then complain when we give a job to someone who wants it so bad he is willing to risk gettin' arrested, robbed, or even killed to get here—not to mention gettin' bit by rattlers or doin' without food for a couple of days and walkin' 'til his damn shoes wear right off of his feet. People in this country have forgotten the price our ancestors paid for their freedom. We Americans are so goddamned soft now, it makes me sick —a bunch of fat lazy bastards."

"I can use the wets. Those kids from town didn't show again and I have lots of hay on the ground."

"You speak their lingo, don't you?"

"About half assed."

"I can hardly understand a word of that shit. Sure wish I did sometimes. Those fellas ain't afraid of work. From what I hear, their women know how to treat a man too. I've been contemplatin' going down there to see if I can't find myself a señorita. Maybe you could help me communicate. You want to go?"

"I wouldn't mind, but I don't know when or how I'll be able to find the time."

"I spent many a year working like you and Tim. When you get my age, you learn to *make* a little time to enjoy yourself."

"I don't see how I can."

"Maybe someday, I'll show you, Ira. Take my word for it. Slavin' you ass off to make some goddamned banker rich ain't where it's at. You ever notice how they live?"

"Not really."

"Well, let me tell you. While you're out here working one hundred hours a week or better, hot when it's hot, cold when it's cold, wet when it rains, and tired all the time, they're drivin' around in the fanciest new cars, livin' in mansions, with servants around to do all the work, eatin' in the finest restaurants, and fuckin' the finest whores on the planet. They work from nine to two, and take off for every goddamned holiday known to man. While they're *at* work, they do nothin' except develop schemes to fuck the workin' man out of his money, and pat pretty secretaries on the ass. Take a look at your hands."

Ira opened his palm. The skin on his hand was so thick and dry it was cracked and bleeding.

"How many bankers do you think have a hand that looks like that? It don't make any sense to work that hard, and then let some slime sucking bastard get rich off of you. I personally would like to see a hunting season on bankers, insurance men, and lawyers. I doubt you'd be able to get much lean meat off of their bodies, but you might render quite a bit of lard. And their heads would look good over my fireplace."

"Oh come on, Doug. You don't really want to kill those people, do you?"

Doug Grant's eyes narrowed and his jaw clinched. His fingers tightened on the steering wheel of the truck.

"You goddamned *better* believe it. I'd kill ever damn one of em, if I could figure out how. I'd be doin' us all a big favor, too. I'll see you in a couple of days with that equipment. Work on gettin' the cash together."

"Sure will, Doug. Thanks for the word on the wets. Tell Tim, I'll be right over to pick them up."

After Doug left, Ira thought back to their conversation. He looked again at his calloused, bleeding hands, and pictured Mr. Jenkins propped up in his comfortable air-conditioned office. Part of what Doug Grant said made sense; another part scared the hell out of Ira—the part about killing.

CHAPTER IX

Ira pulled up to the Grant's house. Tim met him at the door. Together they walked to a run-down tool shed. When the door opened, four sets of eyes stared out with blank, scared looks.

"*Yo tengo trabajo para ustedes si quieren trabajar,*" Ira stated.

One of the group stood, speaking for all.

"*Claro que si.*"

Ira continued on in Spanish. "How are you called?"

"I am called Leonardo. And you."

"I am called Ira."

"Hira?"

"Yeah, Ira."

"How much do you pay?"

"I can offer twenty dollars a day, plus a place to stay and groceries."

Leonardo looked back at his compatriots. All grinned and nodded their approval.

"You do know we are still somewhat close to the border and that the border patrol comes around. You will be at risk of getting picked up."

"Yes sir, that is a risk we are willing to take for awhile, at least until we can find a way to get further into the country. We have no money and have not eaten for two days. One of the guys with us did not make it. We left him in the mountains."

Ira noticed that the men looked exhausted and dirty. They had no possessions other than the clothes they wore.

"Did you pay a coyote?"

"No, sir," Leonardo replied. "I have come before and knew the way. We were caught trying to come with a coyote a week ago and had no money to pay another, so we crossed and walked here on our own."

"What do you mean you left a guy behind? Do you want to look for him?"

"No, he is dead."

"Dead? How?"

"I don't know. He was sick and became very tired. He told us to go on without him, but we did not. He laid down to rest, and when we tried to wake him, he was dead."

"Was he a friend?"

"No, I did not know him. He was with us when we got caught the first time. He had no identification. I heard him say he was from San Luis, but that is all I know."

"What did you do with his body?"

"The ground was very hard, and we had no tools, so we just stacked rocks on him."

The men loaded into Ira's pick-up, Leonardo in front, the remaining three in the back.

"What kind of work do you have for us?" the young Mexican asked.

"Right now, I have some hay that needs to be hauled from the field. Do any of you know how to drive a tractor?"

"I do. None of the rest can."

"Good. You can drive while they load. You will need to stack the hay in that barn," Ira said pointing toward a tall building covered with corrugated tin. "Do you want to eat first?"

"No. Let us begin working. If you wish, you can bring some food."

Ira showed Leonardo how to operate the tractor, and hooked it up to a flatbed trailer for him. He dug out a handful of assorted used gloves and distributed them among the men. They loaded onto the wagon, drove to the field, and tore into the hay with enthusiasm, happy to have found work.

Ira spent the afternoon getting a small house in shape for the men, while they worked. He took them a box of crackers, canned sardines and links of dry sausage, and acquired a list of groceries they would like. The list was simple: flour, shortening, baking powder, sugar, salt, dried beans, peppers, onions, tomatoes, and eggs. Ira also threw in some additional items while at the store: hamburger, chorizo, a box of crackers, pre-made corn tortillas, a box of cookies, instant coffee, and a sack of candy.

That evening, the men grinned in appreciation as they inspected the contents of the bag.

The shack had no running water, but did have a nearby spigot and a water hose. The men heated water over a fire, took bucket baths, and rested on cots, all very much happy to be where they were.

* * * * *

The following day, a Friday—Jose's payday—Jose decided to take it upon himself to throw a party for the employees of the Jones's farm and their friends. A few of Jose's friends came out from Fort Stockton, dressed to the nines, and ready to have a good time. Several of them fancied themselves musicians and had instruments in tow. One—a man referred to as the tarantula, due to his talent at flying over the strings of a twelve-string guitar with his fingers, proved to be quite good.

Ira provided beer for the occasion, supplemented by an ample supply the men from Fort Stockton brought. They were well on their way to being drunk when they arrived. Jose and his wife provided the food.

Jose started a fire using mesquite hearts. In the desert of Southwest Texas, a plant or an animal must adapt to survive the harsh growing conditions. Mesquites are one variety of plant that has done well. In other areas, where rain is more plentiful, mesquites are capable of growing into rather large trees, with trunks in excess of three feet in diameter. Around Bakersfield, the annual rainfall averages about ten inches, and it is not uncommon to receive all of that rain on several days of the year. The rest of the time, it is dry. Mesquites grow a large knot of wood under the surface of the ground, and send up thin, thorn covered branches with small delicate leaves, capable of folding up during extremely hot days, and opening to receive sun when not so hot. These branches rarely get over four feet tall. The thorns are vicious, and any creature attempting to eat one of these plants, or not watching where he goes will soon take notice of them. The thorns are so sharp, and rigid, that they will easily puncture a tire passing over them, and many are they in West Texas who have felt the pain of a mesquite thorn as it pierced the sole of a tennis shoe. Due to mesquites, and other similarly armed desert plants, wearing boots is a necessity around Bakersfield, not a luxury.

Trees being few and far between, local residents discovered the dead hearts of mesquites buried under the soil can be extracted and burned satisfactorily for cooking—in fact the food cooked over such wood, is left with a unique, pleasant flavor now highly sought after by some of the world's finer restaurants.

Jose waited until the hearts had burned down, leaving a very hot bed of shimmering coals, and then grilled strips of beef cut in various odd shapes over the coals. The meat had been marinated in a mixture of lemon juice, various spices, and Jose's secret ingredient—beer—for several hours prior to being placed on the grill.

Jose's wife had prepared enchiladas early in the day for lunch, the real way—thick handmade corn tortillas stacked flat like pancakes—in between each layer was a thick chili sauce made from reconstituted dried red peppers like those often seen hanging on the walls of Mexican restaurants in West Texas and New Mexico. A fried egg—cooked sunny side up—adorned the top of each stack of enchiladas.

That evening she made fresh *guacamole*, or avocado salad, homemade flour tortillas, and each man roasted fresh green chilies over the coals, peeling the skins when done.

Since Ira's encounter with Angela, he had avoided Susan, using the long hours he was required to work as an excuse. That night, he picked her up to share in the fiesta. The wetbacks joined the party as well, but sat by themselves, grinning shyly and saying little. Everyone ate to his or her heart's contentment, and then the music and drinking began. Actually the drinking began long before the meal; it just moved into a higher gear after the feast. Ira could tell when Jose began to get drunk; he started speaking English.

The four wetbacks sat, huddled together, reluctant to do much more than observe until the music began. The tarantula soon captivated all with his songs, some which were well known by his long lost Mexican cousins. Ira noticed the men joined in when a song they recognized was played, and occasionally one would let out a Mexican *Ay Yay Yay* during a happier tune. A time or two, during sadder tunes, he saw tears in their eyes, as their minds roamed across the Mexican desert, to where they knew their families waited, suffering in poverty, many kilometers away.

Ira watched the proceedings from the tailgate of his pickup, seated next to Susan with his arm wrapped around her. Susan understood no Spanish, but seemed to enjoy watching and listening to the music. A time or two, the tarantula drunkly dedicated a song to her, making her blush.

Ira came up with an excuse to leave the party early; it had been several weeks now since his sexual encounter with Angela and the pressure was building again. He drove to a secluded spot in the fields and stopped.

"Come here. I want to show you something," he said, opening the door on her side of the truck.

Ira turned on a flashlight and the two of them walked about a quarter of a mile through the dark night air to the one piece of native ground left on the Jones's farm. They stopped at a small clearing in the middle of a thick stand of thorn covered brush and cacti. Enclosed in a chicken wire cage of sorts were thousands of small green plants.

"Are those marijuana plants?" Susan asked.

Ira produced a joint and lit it. "Yep."

Susan bent down to inspect them closer. "They are pretty. Aren't they too close together, though?"

"Yeah. This is just a starter bed. I've already started transplanting them to that big ditch right behind my trailer house. All I have to do is crank that engine ever once in a while and let it fill the ditch with water. I'm going to let Kochia weeds grow up in the ditch so they'll be hard to see."

"What if someone finds them?"

"Then it'll be my ass. I don't think they will though. Marijuana looks a whole lot like Kochia weed. I have to take the chance. I damn sure can't make any money farming legal crops like I've been doing."

The two sat down on a small mound of dirt next to the plants and smoked the joint.

"They are pretty plants," Susan said. "It is hard to believe something so innocent looking could cause so much trouble. How much money do you think you can make off of these?"

"If I can grow three hundred pounds of *sin semilla*, it ought to bring around one hundred and fifty grand—wholesale —if not, a little more. I still have to figure out how to get it harvested and packaged. There is more work involved than you might think. Sure beats the hell out of raising cotton though. Last year, I grossed thirty-seven thousand dollars on my cotton crop, and spent forty thousand growing and harvesting it—not including my own labor. That don't count the interest I owe the bank either.

"Why do you keep farming then? Your dad would help you get a start doing something else, wouldn't he?"

"Sure he would. Ever since I was a kid, I wanted to raise cows and grow crops. My granddad was a farmer and a stockman. I can still remember when he took me out behind his house and made me work in his garden. I didn't come up to his waist then. He buried a peanut in the ground, one of the ones we were eating at the time, and watered the ground. I laughed at him when he told me it would turn into a plant. I thought he was trying to trick me or something. You should have been there to see my face when that plant started growing out of the ground. To me, it was kind of like witnessin' some kind of a miracle. And then, when that same plant ripened and we dug up some more peanuts, well... I was hooked for life.

"Later, he had me rototill a patch of ground in his garden. We made up rows together, using a hoe. He poked little holes into the earth with his cane, and I dropped in the seeds. I was one proud boy when it came time for the family to eat *my* vegetables. I couldn't stand tomatoes before I grew my own. I have loved them ever since. I've seen nothing more beautiful on the planet than a new-born foal sucking on it's momma unless it's a fresh born baby calf doin' the same."

"But, if there's no money in it..."

"Not everything can be measured in dollars and cents. I keep hopin'... I mean ... there's got to be a way. People have to eat. Sooner or later, prices will go up, when enough farmers go broke. The ones who survive will be in the driver's seat then. That's how I got it figured, anyway."

"Tim thinks just like you. You're both idiots. Ask my dad how long it has been like this for farmers. He says because farmers are ignorant and don't band together, they have no political pull. So long as there is plenty to eat no one gives a damn whether they starve or not."

"He is probably right, to a point. I don't think it will be that way forever."

"But what about now, Ira? We have to live now."

"That is what these are all about," Ira said, pointing at the young plants.

"But they are illegal. You could go to jail."

"If they weren't illegal, they wouldn't be worth anything. The very fact that they are illegal, and not allowed by the government is why people pay so much for the shit."

"I guess that's better than what daddy does."

"What does he do? I've wondered about that for a long time."

"I'm not sure, but I have an idea. Time after time, when we're broke he disappears for a few days. When he comes back, he always has money. He won't say where it comes from."

"What do you think?"

"I think he steals. I think he has for years. It's getting worse though. I'm worried about him. He takes his guns out and shoots box after box of bullets. Daddy is very bitter."

"I don't doubt it. I'd be pissed off too if I set the Kansas state record for bushels of corn to the acre and went broke doing it."

"I still don't understand why you all don't quit and do something else," Susan said.

Ira reached over and kissed Susan. When he reached into her shirt and tried to cup her breast, she pulled away, and looked suspiciously at him.

"Ira, Tim tried to talk me into letting you... you know. He said you were getting weak, and that you went into one of those places where women dance naked. Did you?"

"Yes. I'm sorry Susan, but I did."

"Is there another woman?"

Ira had made it a practice never to lie to Susan. When he looked into her eyes, he figured now was as good a time as any to begin. He said no.

"Are you that weak, Ira? Why can't you wait? I have to wait too."

"Nobody *has* to wait, Susan. You choose to because of some bullshit your mother has fed you."

"It is not bullshit!"

"I reserve the right to my own opinion on that subject. If what she and the rest of that church do were anything like heaven, I'd just as soon go straight to hell. At least I'll have a little fun along the way."

"Don't say that, Ira!"

"I'm not saying I don't believe in God. Because I do. What I am saying is that the church you and your mom go to is full of phonies and she's one of them. Wake up Susan."

"You are so... so... cruel. You don't understand. Take me home, right now. We're through!"

"Susan..."

"I mean it. Take me home, or I'm walking. I don't care if I ever see you again."

Ira drove Susan home. Not a word was said on the short drive. As soon as they arrived at her house, she opened the door of the pickup, got out, slammed the door as hard as she could, and ran into the house.

Fucking Bitch! You're just like your God damned mother, Ira thought to himself.

Ira drove by Jose's house. The party was still in full swing. Ira wanted no part of it. He waved and continued driving. Ira went home, poured a big glass of whiskey over ice and took a gulp. He looked at his watch and made quick calculations. At eighty miles an hour, he could make it to Lubbock and the bar where Angela worked before closing time. He pulled on his clothes. On the way by the party, he stopped and called Jose over.

"I'm going to Lubbock, Jose. I'll be back Sunday. If anyone calls, tell them I'm around, but not available to answer the phone. Got that?"

"Sure, Señor," Jose answered, slurring his speech as he spoke. Ira could smell the alcohol on his breath. Jose swayed slightly and stood grinning.

"If you sell any hay, record what you sell for me. You can pay the *Mojados* with hay money."

"No problema, boss. You have goood time."

"Bye, Jose."

"Bye boss. Don't worry bout notheen. Jose will take good care of evertheen."

Ira drove a hundred miles an hour all the way to Odessa, stopping there long enough to fill his gas tank, grab a cup of coffee, a box of no-doze tablets, and a two liter bottle of coke. Miraculously, he made the trip without a single traffic ticket. He arrived at the bar with time to spare, but to his dismay, Angela had already left with another paying customer.

Ira drove slowly through the streets of Lubbock, lonely and horny. He finally stopped at a convenience store, purchased a skin magazine, rented a motel room, and masturbated on the bed.

On the way to the bathroom to cleanse himself, he saw his reflection in the mirror. "Weak mother fucker," he stated, spitting at the image of himself. Saliva drizzled down the glass.

Ira went back to the bed and shut off the light. The massive doses of caffeine running through his veins would not let him sleep. An hour later, he turned on the light, picked up the magazine and jacked off again. This time, he had foresight enough to get a roll of toilette paper first, and he skipped the trip by the mirror.

CHAPTER X

The next day, Ira woke up in the motel alone and bored. He decided he wasn't ready to go home without first seeing Angela. He called Jose on the telephone. Jose was still drunk when he answered.

"I won't be back until tomorrow," Ira said. "Is everything OK?"

"Yes, sir." Actually, Jose had no idea. He hadn't been out of the house to check.

"How are the hands doing?"

"They are fine too." He hadn't seen them either.

"You are the boss while I am gone Jose. Keep those men busy."

"*Si Señor. No problema.*"

"Bye."

"Same to you Señor. You get a señorita and have gooood time."

Ira knew it would be late that night before Angela went to work again. He didn't know where she lived, or even her phone number; RJ didn't allow such things. Rather than lay around all day feeling sorry for himself, Ira rented the room for another night and made the short drive to Plainview, the home of Ernie Coontz, Ira's best childhood friend.

Ernie called Ira the *Wild Man,* but the term more appropriately fit him. Ernie stayed on the edge, driving fast and living hard. *Sex, drugs, and rock and roll* was his motto. By the time Ira arrived at Ernie's house, Ernie was well on his way to what he termed a *high-speed wobble. A high speed wobble* was what Ernie did after taking massive doses of amphetamines of one type or another, a handful of downers, once again of various and assorted types, all of which he washed down with generous amounts of vodka or beer. The amphetamine gave him the *high speed*; the downers and the alcohol contributed the *wobble*.

Ernie was a blast to be around; when he wasn't passed out, he was the life of the party, and at his house, the party rarely ended. He sold dope to support himself, having given up farming years before. Any kind of pharmaceutical substance with a reputation for getting someone high was liable to be found at Ernie's house.

Ernie was a handsome young man: blond haired, and blue eyed, with looks not unlike those of a young Robert Redford or Brad Pitt. That fact, and plenty of free dope, kept an endless supply of young girls coming by his place, looking for a good time. Pills were left on the table in a candy jar, the refrigerator was full of beer and meat stolen from the local meat packing plant and traded at discount prices for dope. The powder was parceled out more sparingly, still, Ernie tended to be generous to those who were generous in return, and even a few who weren't. Over the years he had picked up his share of leeches, which contributed nothing but themselves.

Ernie answered the door with a can of Budweiser in hand, dressed in cutoffs and cowboy boots. He had on no shirt, but a battered cowboy hat adorned his head.

"Wild man! Good to see you," Ernie exclaimed, giving Ira a powerful hug.

A short, plump girl with a cute smile walked up. Ernie introduced her as Denise.

Ernie peered closely at Ira's face. "You need some pussy, don't you?"

"No."

"Don't lie to me. I can see it in your eyes. That is why you came, isn't it?"

Ira said no.

"I know you better than that, son."

Ernie wrapped an arm around Denise. "Denise here is a wonderful girl. Best thing about her is, she don't mind sharing, ain't that right sweetheart?"

Denise blushed and smiled at Ira.

"You do want some pussy, don't you Ira?"

"Come on Ernie. Let it be."

"How about some head, then. Denise gives good head."

Denise blushed again.

"I'm sure you're wonderful," Ira told her, "but I ain't used to having sex with someone until I get to know her first. I ain't like Ernie here."

"I like Ernie," she said.

"I do too. We're just different."

"Bull shit!" Ernie exclaimed. "Show him you stuff, Denise."

Denise began to remove her shirt, revealing firm-looking breasts, jutting straight out. She looked a few pounds overweight, but was still pleasing to the eye.

"Show him your ass, Denise."

"You don't have to do that." Ira said.

Denis unbuttoned her jeans, pulled them down a ways and flashed Ira. She wasn't wearing any panties.

"OK Ernie, you're right. She's a fine looking woman, and I do find her attractive. That doesn't mean I have to screw her though, does it?"

"No, but you'll hurt her feelings if you don't. Listen, Denise. This guy is just playing like he's shy. He's the biggest stud ever to come out of Plainview, Texas. I don't let him touch most of my women; it ruins them for life. No one can satisfy them after Ira Jones has had them."

"Enough of your bull-shit Ernie. Put your clothes back on Denise. I *am* getting uncomfortable looking at you. You are a very pretty girl. Maybe I'll take a rain check."

"I'll be looking forward to it."

"What in the hell is wrong with you, Ira?" Ernie asked in a whisper. "It is not like you to pass up a shot at some pussy. I wasn't kidding about her. She is mean in bed. She can suck a baseball through a garden hose."

"I bet she can, but I have a date tonight—in Lubbock. I can't be spending myself too early."

"I should have known. Is this a regular, or what?"

"Yes."

"You aren't falling in love again, are you?"

"Kind of."

"Oh shit. Denise. Take this man to the bedroom and give him the works. You might be able to save this poor fool's life."

Ernie grabbed Ira by one arm and Denise grabbed the other. They led him to a bedroom, opened the door, and shoved him in. Ernie slammed it shut behind.

Denise began removing her clothes. When naked, she started on Ira's.

"Wait Denise. You don't have to do this."

"I know. I want to."

"Please, Denise. Stop."

"What's wrong? Don't you like me?"

"Oh yes." The bulge of Ira's hard on was obvious, even through his jeans. He didn't want to have sex with the girl though. She looked very young—too young, and he wanted to save himself for Angela.

"I didn't want to say anything, Denise. Please don't tell anybody, but I have a case of the clap."

Denise stepped back, eyes open wide.

"Lets just kill some time in here and act like we did our thing to keep Ernie happy. How does that sound?"

"That'll work for me. I sure don't want to catch gonorrhea."

Ira and Denise sat on the bed talking for a while. Occasionally Denise provided sound effects for those in the other room. About a half an hour later they returned to the party. Ira came out with his hair messed up and his shirttail hanging out. The people in the room all clapped. Denise came up from behind and wrapped her arms around him.

"Oh no," Ernie exclaimed. "I've lost another one. It'll be years before she gets back to normal."

Ira and Denise exchanged a knowing glance.

Ira spent the rest of the day at Ernie's house. Ernie spent most of it trying to convince Ira to bring a load of marijuana from Southwest Texas. Plainview was completely out of marijuana, and a lot of money stood to be made by the first person to show up with a load.

That evening, Ira drove back to Lubbock. He thought about Denise, wondering if he had done the right thing by passing up what for him was a rare chance at having sex with a real live girl not charging for her services. He decided what he needed from Angela was probably more than just sex. The spirits driving Ira, be they bad or good, drove him straight into the tit bar where Angela worked.

CHAPTER XI

Susan Grant woke up after a restless, nightmare-filled night, after going to bed angry. She decided to go to Ira's house to make amends. She found him gone. Susan spotted Jose, who told her he had gone to Lubbock. Susan knew what that meant.

"When will he be back?" she asked.

"Tomorrow."

"Did he say where he is staying?"

Jose shrugged his shoulders to say no.

"Thank you, Jose."

Susan drove home. On the way she broke into tears. *If it's sex he wants, then it will be sex he gets,* she finally decided.

Susan wrote a note telling her mother that she would be back the following day and left—headed for Lubbock.

CHAPTER XII

"What the hell happened to you?" Ira asked, when he saw Angela enter the club. The thick layer of makeup and sunglasses did little to hide the fact that her face was bruised and beaten.

"Thank God you came," she exclaimed, when she saw him. "I was hoping and praying you would come."

"What happened, Angela?"

"I need to get out of here, Ira. RJ beat me up really bad. I'm bruised all over. I think he broke a couple of ribs."

"Why?"

"Because of you."

"Me? What did I do?"

"I made the mistake of telling one of the other girls that I was sweet on you. She told him. I should have known better."

"Why that sorry son-of-a-bitch. Where is he? I think it's time I met this mother fucker."

"No, Ira. Just get me away from here."

"I don't have the money to buy you."

"I thought you owned a farm."

"My *dad* does. I just work there. I can't spend his money on something like that. Shit, I'm already a couple of grand in the hole to him."

Ira spotted several hefty looking bikers, checking him out from the bar. He returned their looks with an icy stare.

"Who are those guys?" he asked Angela.

"They are some of the brothers—you know, *Desperados*. Don't look at them, Ira."

"Why not?"

"I'm going to be in trouble as it is. I was told not to see you any more. Don't make things worse than they already are."

"I'd say it is time to leave the bastard—right now. Fuck what they think. Come on Angela. Let's go."

Ira stood up as if to leave; Angela remained seated.

"I can't go right now. I don't have my clothes. Besides, if they see you take me, they'll stop us. They aren't going to let me leave with you."

"I'll get you more clothes. Listen, you do exactly as I say. I'm going to walk up to the bar. You ease over toward the door. As soon as the shit hits the fan, run straight out that door to my black Chevy pickup. Here are the keys. Get in and start the engine. I'll be right behind you."

"We'll never get away with this, Ira."

Ira looked back at her. A determined fire burned in his eyes.

"What about my clothes. I can't go out dressed like this."

"Yes you can. I told you I'd get you clothes."

Ira removed a heavy handled folding hunting knife from his pocket, took a good grip in it, and started walking toward the two bikers, eyes focused on them, like a predator eyes its prey—nothing else in the room was visible to him at that moment.

Angela got up and warily started in the direction of the door. Her mind raced. *Do I really want to do this? What about the speed?* Angela panicked. Ira looked tiny compared to the two bikers. *What is he going to do? He is fucking crazy!*

Ira walked up to the two men, moving a dancer out of the way as he approached. Ira began the conversation with a right hook, thrown from the floor. The punch landed squarely on the jaw of one of the men, crunching bone and knocking him out of the chair. He hit the floor unconscious. Before the second man knew he was in a fight, he too was on the floor, the victim of a perfect three-punch combination. When he tried to get up, a boot heel to the teeth changed his mind, knocking out half of them. Ira began kicking and stomping the first man to the head and body; each blow broke bones and dislodged cartilage.

Angela stood paralyzed, hardly believing her eyes. *How can such a small man deliver such violent blows?* she wondered. Each time Ira struck the fat men, it sounded like a gun going off in the bar. A bouncer came running from the back of the bar to stop Ira—a huge black man hired exclusively for his fighting skills.

"Ira!" Angela screamed, just in time to warn him.

Ira spun around, but now the knife was open. He slashed at the black man's extended arm. The blade cut a huge gash, all the way to the bone. A knot of bulging muscle and a gush of blood erupted from the wound. The black man backed up in horror, trying to push the flesh back into its proper place.

Another biker came running up. "Get him Leroy," he yelled at the black man.

"You don't pay me enough to fuck with that crazy bastard! You want him—you get him!"

Ira turned his attention to the biker, flashed the bloody blade, and moved in his direction. The biker turned and ran. Ira then grabbed Angela and shoved her toward the door. When the bouncer watching the door did not yield, one look changed his mind. He stepped aside and let them pass. Ira hustled Angela to the truck. On the way, she twisted her ankle and lost a shoe—one of the high-heeled varieties favored by strippers. She tried to stop and pick it up but Ira kept her moving. He opened the door to the pickup and shoved her in.

"Those shoes cost a hundred dollars," she declared.

"We'll get you more. We need out of here before reinforcements show up. They're probably calling cops right now."

Ira started the engine and drove off.

"Ira, you're fucking crazy. They're going to hunt you down. They're going to hunt *me* down. Look what you've gotten me into. I won't be able to show my face in a bar in this state."

"Exactly," he said.

Ira sped through town and headed south.

* * * * *

Susan pulled into the parking lot. She had looked through the yellow pages for burlesque houses and discovered there were not many in Lubbock. An ambulance was parked near the front door of the club. A bloody man with a long beard was being loaded. He appeared to be missing half of his teeth.

The bartender looked at her with apparent interest, liking what he saw.

"Looking for a job?" he asked.

"No. I'm looking for someone." Susan searched the room for Ira. "What happened here?"

"Some little red-headed cowboy went fucking *off* in here. I've never seen anything like it in my life. Motherfucker looked like Paul Bunyan in a forest of saplings, the way he was cutting motherfuckers down."

"Red-headed, you say?"

"Yeah. Dude about this tall," the man said, holding out his hand. "Seemed like he grew a foot once he started throwing down though."

"Where is he?"

"Hell if I know. He grabbed Angela and headed for the door. I sure as hell wasn't interested in following him. You know the guy?"

"Maybe." Susan looked down dejectedly.

"Are you sure you don't want a job here. A girl looking like you can make a lot of money here."

"Not today, thank you," she replied.

Susan drove aimlessly around Lubbock, going from motel to motel, hoping to spot Ira's pickup. She didn't find it. Finally she headed for home. She had no way of knowing it, but she wasn't far behind him. About an hour down the road to Odessa, she passed a John Deere dealership, where, also unbeknownst to her, Doug Grant was, at that very moment, busy repossessin' a baler and a swather.

* * * * *

Ira stopped at Odessa, and rented a room for the night. He and Angela bathed and lay down for the night. Ira tried to get next to Angela, but she repelled his advances.

"What's wrong with you?" he asked.

"You know I'm hooked on meth, don't you?"

"Yeah, I think you mentioned that."

"Then, where are you going to get me some?"

"Don't you think now might be a good time to quit?"

"Who says I want to quit? I like the stuff."

"The only place I know of where I can get any speed is in Plainview, just north of Lubbock. Something tells me it might not be a good idea for us to show up there right now. Besides, you *need* to quit."

"I know it, but it will be harder than you think. You're going to have a real bitch on your hands for a few days."

Ira rolled a joint. "Smoke this," he said handing it to her. They smoked the joint together.

"I love you," Ira said.

"What are we going to do, Ira? I should have thought this out. Maybe I should go back."

"Go back? You want to go back to the bastard that beat the shit out of you, and may now kill you?"

"No, but what can I do? I can't go home with you. What will Susan think? I don't have any clothes or a place to stay. I can't work. I am not the type who would be happy locked away on some desolate ranch all day while you are out working, even if Susan wasn't in the picture."

"We broke up the other day," Ira said.

"You did? Why?"

"I guess she thinks I'm not good enough for her. I'm wild. Susan is a church girl. You said it yourself one time. You're more my type."

"So, what now, Ira? You have me. What are you going to do with me?"

"Well, for starters…" Ira began removing Angela's clothes.

Angela moaned softly as Ira entered her. "I *am* glad you took me," she whispered moments later.

They spent the rest of that Sunday in bed. Ira went out one time to get food and coffee. That night, they ordered pizza. After watching movies, they slept, snuggled closely together.

*****

A hundred miles away, Susan Grant lay awake, lost in hatred. For a time, she had cried. Now, her sorrow ripened into anger. She was mad, not only at Ira; she was mad at herself.

CHAPTER XIII

Ira woke up early Monday morning, went to a department store and bought clothes for Angela. When he got back to the motel room, he tried to wake her, finding it almost impossible.

"What time is it?" she asked.

"Ten o'clock."

"It's too early. Let me sleep."

"Come on, Angela, we need to get out of here."

"I feel terrible," she complained. "Take me to your friend's house and get me some crystal."

"That's a three hour drive from here, and we'd have to go through Lubbock. Here, smoke this," he said, offering her a joint.

"I don't want any of that shit. I don't even like marijuana."

Ira offered Angela a cup of coffee. She glared at him. She eventually did accept the coffee, and lit a cigarette.

"Now what?" she asked.

"I have some business to take care of. A man is supposed to bring several pieces of equipment by the farm today, and I need to go to the bank and get his money for him."

"How much?"

"Ten thousand dollars."

"You can walk into a bank and write a check for ten thousand dollars?"

"Yes, but only if it's for something we need at the farm."

"What are you going to do with me?"

"Let's go. We'll decide on the way."

"You're not ashamed of me?" she asked.

"Of course not. Get dressed."

Angela got up and tried on the clothes Ira had bought.

"I'm not wearing these. They don't fit."

"I'll let you pick out what you want later. You have to have something to wear out of here. You can't go walking around dressed like that," Ira said, pointing to the skimpy clothing Angela had worn out of the bar.

Angela wore little make-up, so it didn't take long for her to get ready. They left Odessa in the direction of McCamey, where he did his banking.

"Have you ever been to Mexico?" Ira asked.

"No."

"Do you want to go?"

"I don't know. What's down there? I don't particularly care to see a bunch of starving people. That is not my idea of a vacation."

"They have nice places in Mexico. Have you ever heard of Acapulco?"

"Yeah. That's in Mexico?"

"Yes."

"Then I'll go."

Ira stopped by the bank in McCamey and withdrew twelve thousand dollars from the farm account, ten thousand for the baler, and two thousand for the trip. Ira had no money of his own. Ira was formulating a plan in his head at that very moment—a plan to have a vacation and make money at the same time. Ernie wanted marijuana. Acapulco was supposed to have marijuana—gold marijuana—worth lots of money. The trip would allow him to spend time with Angela—a honeymoon of sorts. While there, he would score some dope and pay for the trip. *Who knows, maybe I'll find a good enough connection to save the farm,* he thought to himself.

Ira made a swing by the farm and left the ten thousand dollars with Jose and gave him hastily delivered instructions concerning the running of the farm during his absence. He didn't want to see Doug or Susan Grant with Angela in tow, so he didn't stay long. Rather than take the most direct route to Mexico, which would have been via Del Rio, or Presidio, Ira headed west on I-10, toward El Paso, so Angela would have the chance to do some shopping before their departure. Angela snuggled up to him, sleeping while he drove. Ira felt proud to have such a beautiful woman at his side.

At El Paso, the two went shopping. Before they were done, Ira had spent five hundred dollars. Everything Angela purchased fit into one small canvas suitcase. It seemed to Ira, the smaller an article of clothing happened to be, the more it cost. Most of the things Angela picked out were tiny. She bought a black bikini, some very short shorts, and several halter-tops. Angela seductively modeled each item. Everything she wanted, he bought.

Ira took out an insurance policy on his pickup. While at the insurance desk, he learned he would need proof of American citizenship to get Mexican visas. Neither had any ID, other than driver's licenses, but Ira discovered that he might be able to get by with a sworn, notarized affidavit, so he paid a justice of the peace to fill out one for each of them.

Angela put on the pair of short shorts and a halter-top before they crossed the bridge.

"Don't you think you should put on something a little less revealing?" Ira suggested.

"Why? What's wrong with this?"

"Nothing here in the U.S. or at the beach in Acapulco. We're about to go through the interior of Mexico. People don't dress that way down there, not in public, anyway."

"Tough. I do."

Ira crossed the international bridge and pulled up to a fat Mexican Customs official. The man peered into the cab of the truck from the driver's side. His gaze soon homed in on the long, shapely legs occupying the passenger seat, and stayed there. Ira could hardly get the man to listen to what he said.

"I need visas to go to Acapulco," Ira said, in passable Spanish.

The man stared, dumbfounded. Ira repeated himself. Finally, the man pointed toward a parking lot. By this time, he was motioning to his buddies. Ira and Angela got out and walked into the Custom's office, hand in hand. Every man for two hundred yards around stopped what they were doing, frozen in place, watching Angela as she strolled toward the building, ass cheeks swaying from side to side as she walked, barely contained by the tiny shorts. One car driving by screeched to a stop in the middle of the road.

Angela's blond hair hung down her back in long, loose curls. Her face was pretty, not beautiful, but pretty. It was not her face that attracted all of the attention. Her body could have been sculpted right out of most men's imagination. Nowhere on it was a pound out of place. Her breasts weren't overly large, but stood straight out without the aid of a bra; pointed nipples were visible through the thin fabric of the halter-top. Her stomach was flat, her legs smooth and tan. Angela had been taught to walk seductively; now it was something she did unconsciously. She appeared not to notice the wave of confusion that emanated from her as she approached the building.

Once in the door, all activity inside the office came to a standstill. The men stared; women pointed and whispered among themselves. One woman, seeing the awe-struck look on her husband's face, quickly grabbed him by the arm and hustled him out the door, casting hateful glances at Angela and muttering under her breath as they passed by.

Ira and Angela approached the counter.

"I would like two visas," Ira told the official. "We want to go to Acapulco."

The man looked at Angela and gulped deeply. Finally, her tore his eyes off of her and asked in English, "What can I do for you?"

Ira smiled and repeated himself. The man looked at the papers Ira handed him.

"These won't do. You need proof of American citizenship."

Ira pointed at the affidavits. "That is what those are."

"Anyone can make something like this," the man stated.

"Those came from a judge's office."

Ira showed the man the letterhead and the official seal.

"It will not do." The man handed the papers back to Ira.

Undaunted, Ira extracted two twenty dollar bills; put them under the affidavits, and handed them back to the man.

"How about these then?"

"Why, yes sir, these will work just fine," the man said, pocketing the money in a fashion no one would notice. "Where did you say you wanted to go?"

"Acapulco."

The man began to write on a form. "For how long?"

"A week."

"I will make the visa for a month."

The man asked for various bits of information while he filled out the visas: date and place of birth, reason for the trip, marital status, etc.

"I notice you have different last names. Are you not married?"

"Not yet," Ira said, squeezing Angela's hand.

Angela began to notice all the people staring at her. "Why do they stare so much? They act like they have never seen a white woman before."

"I warned you about dressing like that. It causes problems down here."

"Well, that's not my problem. It's theirs. This is the way I dress. If they don't like it, they can kiss my ass."

"I am sure that is *exactly* what they would *like* to do, among other things."

Ira asked the official for a map of Mexico. There were none. Instead, the man drew the route on a piece of paper. First they had to go to Chihuahua, then to Torreon, then straight through the central Mexican plateau, all the way to Mexico City. From there, it was further south to Acapulco. He lost Ira long before Mexico City.

Ira had an ounce of marijuana hidden in the seats of the pickup. After getting the visa, another customs agent quickly searched the cab and then turned to Ira. "Should I search again, or do you have a little something for the coffee?"

Ira didn't immediately understand.

The man made a signal with his fingers.

Ira handed the man a ten-dollar bill.

"I like cream and sugar with my coffee," the man said.

Ira handed him another ten.

"Enjoy your stay in Mexico," the man said. "With such a beautiful woman, you should have a nice time."

"I hope so," Ira said, winking at the man.

Rather than stay in Juarez, Ira drove on to Chihuahua City before stopping. On the way, he was introduced to driving Mexican style. He was not impressed. The road was narrow, and rarely had a shoulder. Long stretches were not mowed and the tall grass severely impaired his vision. Livestock wandered loose all over the highway, appearing out of these grass hedges in a way that gave a driver little time to react. They passed the carcasses of several dead animals that had been hit, left to rot on the side of the road. If that weren't bad enough, the people driving made up for it.

Some of the cars crept along, weaving all over the highway; others drove as fast as their car would go; both types were oblivious to the fact that others were trying to use the same road. A time or two, Ira found himself behind one of the slow drivers. Each time it looked as though the way was clear for Ira to pass, the man turned on his left blinker, forcing Ira to remain behind the creeping vehicle. Thick, black exhaust fumes rolled out of the car. The third time the man pulled this stunt without turning, Ira passed him anyway, shooting him the bird as he went by. A few miles down the road, another car did the same thing. Finally, Ira realized they were trying to signal that the way was clear with the left blinker when this man stuck his arm out the window and waved him around.

"What in the hell do you reckon they do when they want to turn left?" he asked Angela, shaking his head.

Angela shrugged her shoulders.

The multicolored lights of Chihuahua greeted the young couple as they entered the city. Although it was past midnight, street vendors still sold their products from little roadside stands or mobile carts. Ira found an old downtown hotel and rented a room. The man at the desk looked suspiciously at Angela as Ira filled out the registration forms, but did not have the courage to ask if the two were married. In many Mexican motels, it is not permitted for a man and a woman who are not married to share a room.

Both Ira and Angela arrived exhausted from the drive and quickly fell to sleep. The room had two single beds; they both slept in the one. They did not make love, but clung tightly to each other throughout the long, dark hours, when spirits of loneliness are at their best.

CHAPTER XIV

Doug Grant pulled the semi up to Ira Jones's house; on the trailer behind rode a brand new baler and a swather. Doug noticed Ira's pickup was gone, but went to the door and knocked anyway.

A moment later, Jose drove up in his ranch truck.

"These is very nice," Jose said, looking at the hay equipment. "Hira tell me give you these money." José held out the ten thousand dollars.

Doug took the money and counted it. "Good enough. Where do you want it?"

Jose pointed in the direction of a barn, got in his pickup and drove that direction. Between the two, they unloaded the trailer with nothing but hand signals.

"Did Ira say when he'd be back? I've located a bale loader he wanted."

"He come back these week."

"Where did he go?"

Jose shrugged his shoulders.

"Do you think he still wants the loader?"

"He boss. He want it, you get it, no problema."

"OK, Jose. Thanks for the help."

Doug Grant drove home. He found Susan staring out of the window.

"Have you seen Ira?" he asked. "He's not home."

Susan started crying.

"What's wrong honey?" Doug asked, wrapping his arm around his daughter.

"He ran off with some bar girl."

"Wait a minute. Back up a little bit."

"We had an argument. He said bad things about mom. I got mad and broke up with him. I guess he got lonely and went to Lubbock. I knew he used to date a girl there, one of those topless dancers. I looked for him, but I was too late. He beat up some guys and stole her from the bar. I haven't seen him since. It's my fault."

"Why do you say that?"

"Because what he said is true. Mom is a phony."

"Well, I'd have to agree with that. That doesn't mean it's your fault he ran away with some whore."

"But daddy, I still love him." Once again, she burst into tears.

Doug stroked her hair and tried to comfort her. "Listen, Susan. Don't you worry about a thing. No bar girl will hold Ira Jones too long. He's got more sense than that."

"But, I bet he's… You know…"

"Screwing her? Probably. It won't amount to nothin'. In this day and time, a young man is better off having had a few experiences like that before he gets married."

"How can you say that Daddy?"

"I know. There are differences between men and women. Women, I have never been able to figure out. I know what makes a man tick. Most young men think with the head of their dick for a while. Let a young man with half a brain run into a rotten assed whore a few times, and he'll learn to appreciate a good woman, one that is there for him, and only him. The man who never experiences that before getting married—the guy who marries the first girl he has sex with… Well, he'll always wonder what he missed out on. I was that kind of man. Your mom was the first for me. I did my running around after I got married. I'm partially to blame for your mom being crazy as she is."

"So you don't think he'll fall in love with her?"

"Oh yeah. He will, for a day or two anyway. You don't ever know for sure. Not all whores are bad folks. If I was a bettin' man though, I'd bet after he gets a real good dose of her, he'll be back, and he'll be better off for the experience. Even if he doesn't, it isn't the end of the world. I know you don't want to hear this now, but he isn't the only fish in the sea. You're beautiful, intelligent, and loyal—what more could a man want?"

"Ira wants sex."

"Don't we all?"

"But I wouldn't let him…"

"If you want him, that was a mistake. You'll never hold on to a young, hot-blooded man like that without it. He's got to have it."

"Thanks for talking to me, daddy."

"Any time, sweet heart."

CHAPTER XV

Ira and Angela got an early start, 9 o'clock in the morning being early for Angela. Ira woke up with a piss hard on and decided to take advantage of it. Angela wasn't in the mood and repelled his advances. Angela tended to be grouchy when she awoke. That natural inclination was compounded by withdrawal symptoms of a heavy meth user doing without.

"Leave me alone," she said, trying to push Ira away.

"Come on babe. I want you."

Angela finally rolled over, flexed her muscles, and stared icily while Ira while tried to enter her. After almost a minute of fruitless effort, he gave up and went to the shower. It wasn't happening without her cooperation.

Ira turned on the hot water and waited for the water to warm up…and waited…and waited. *Must be the other side,* he thought to himself. He opened the other valve. More cold water greeted him. He left it running for a while, but it stayed cold. *No fuckin' hot water.* Ira jumped into the icy water for a few seconds. It took his breath away. A few seconds later, he jumped out, shivering from the cold. *That didn't take long*, he thought.

"Get up, Angela. We need to hit the road."

Groggily, she got out of bed, totally naked. The sight of her body aroused Ira again. He tried to kiss her. She stood there, unresponsive. He might as well have been kissing a corpse.

"What's wrong with you this morning?" he asked her.

"I told you I'd be a bitch without my dope. You should have gotten me some. Where's the soap? I need a shower."

"I couldn't find any."

"No soap? What kind of motel is this? By the way, I need special shampoo for my hair. I use Jhermax."

"I doubt you'll be able to find that down here. We can probably get something similar."

"I use Jhermax."

Angela went into the bathroom and turned on the shower. Ira said nothing. "Which one is the hot?" she asked.

"I couldn't find any on either side."

"What? No soap, no hot water. What the fuck is wrong with this place?"

Angela strolled across the room and stepped out into the hall, naked, and yelled, "I want my money back. What kind of a motel are you running here? No soap, no hot water, single beds..."

Ira grabbed her by the arm and hauled her back into the room. "What are you trying to do, get us thrown in jail?"

"I'm mad. I need a shower. A motel comes with soap and hot water. Go get our money back."

"Take it easy Angela. It's no big deal."

"The hell it isn't."

"Look, Angela, sometimes motels in Mexico aren't quite as nice as what you're used to."

"What in hell are we doing here then? Take me home."

"Give the place a chance. I guarantee you it will be different in Acapulco."

"I'm not going anywhere without a shower."

"No, you're not," Ira said, the hotheaded Irish blood rising to his head. Ira grabbed Angela and hustled her to the shower. The cold water was still running. He shoved her in.

"No," she shouted. "Let me out of here."

He refused. Ira had a hair trigger temper; he rarely held grudges, but when he went off, it was instantaneous and furious.

"Let me out."

"You stop yelling and I'll let you out. You keep up this shit, and I might decide to knock your fucking ass out." Ira stood, with fists balled.

"Let me out," she said, quieter this time.

Ira stepped aside. She walked out, grabbed a towel and dried off.

"I thought RJ was bad. You were about to hit me," she stated.

"I don't tolerate being pushed around by anyone." Ira cooled off. Now he felt bad.

"I'm sorry, Angela."

Ira walked over and tried to give her a hug. She received the hug passively, saying nothing in reply.

"Come on. Let's get out of here. I promise I will find a better motel next time."

"I need some cigarettes and a Pepsi."

"Don't you want any breakfast?"

"Cigarettes and Pepsi *are* my breakfast."

"Oh. OK."

Ira and Angela walked down the stairs to the front desk. While there, Ira exchanged dollars into Mexican pesos."

"Where is the coke machine?" Angela asked.

The clerk looked curiously at her.

"They don't have coke machines," Ira told her.

"Tell him his motel sucks."

Luckily, the hotel clerk understood no English. He grinned and nodded, flattered that such a beautiful, blond haired American woman would speak to him.

Ira hustled her out the door.

"You don't have to be so rude to these people."

"I just told the truth."

Ira and Angela walked to a small store near the motel. Ira bought a few pastries for himself, and ordered two Pepsis.

"No Pepsi," the clerk stated. "Coke?"

"Yes," Ira answered.

"No, I want Pepsi," Angela said.

"They don't have any. Two cokes please."

"I drink Pepsi."
"Didn't you hear me? They don't have any Pepsi."
"I don't like Coke."
"What the hell is the difference?"
"There's a lot of difference."
"Bull shit."

The clerk handed the cokes to Ira. They were lukewarm. Ira handed one to Angela.

"This thing is hot," she exclaimed.
"Do you have any ice?" Ira asked.
"*Si, Señor.*" The clerk got out an ice pick and chipped a piece off of a block in the coke box."
"Do you have any plastic cups?"
"Sure." The clerk handed two cups to Ira.
"I am not drinking Coke. And I'm damned sure not drinking anything that man has handled with his nasty hands," she said, referring to the ice.
"I'll stop somewhere else and get you a Pepsi. Just take the Coke to the pickup. I'll drink it later. What kind of cigarettes do you smoke?"
"Merits."

A sinking feeling hit Ira in the stomach. Angela turned and walked back to the pickup.

Ira looked at the cigarette rack. There were no Merit cigarettes. In fact, the only brands he even recognized were Marlboros and non-filter Camels.

"Give me a pack of Marlboros."

Ira carried the things he had purchased back to the pickup. "They didn't have Merits. I got Marlboros."
"Marlboro? You're kidding, right?"
"No, I'm not."
"I don't smoke Marlboro cigarettes."
"Listen, Angela. This is Mexico. I doubt you're going to find Merit cigarettes anywhere in this goddamned country. Try those. If you don't like them, you can try another brand, until you find one you like."

Ira shook his head and drove off, in search of Pepsi. He stopped at one place after another, but found none.

"Now, I suppose you're going to tell me they don't have Pepsi either?"

"They have it. I've seen it down here. I just can't find any right now."

"I don't like cold Coke, much less *hot Coke*. I want a cold Pepsi."

Ira felt his temper rising again. He drove to another place —still no Pepsi—but they did have cold Cokes. He bought one and finally got Angela to try it. Before she had time to taste it she said, "Yuck!"

When she lit a Mexican Marlboro, the shit really hit the fan. "What the fuck is that? It sure isn't a Marlboro. That tastes like dried cow shit."

"That is a nasty habit anyway. You ought to quit."

"You…telling me to quit? And you sit there smoking one fucking joint after another? Fuck you, Ira. You smoke your weed; I'll smoke mine."

Ira thought about that for a minute. "You got me there."

Ira started out of town.

"Stop," Angela shouted.

"What?"

"I want that dress." Angela pointed toward a display window in a store.

"Oh, Angela. You're driving me crazy." Ira stopped, and they walked to the store together. Angela was still wearing her short shorts. The walk to the store brought traffic to a standstill. Men gawked; a few even whistled from a bus stopped in the middle of the road.

Angela tried on the dress. It didn't fit, but another like it did, so Ira bought it for her. Much to Ira's dismay, she chose to put it in a box, and wore her short shorts out into the street again.

Soon after they got onto the highway, Angela fell asleep. Ira looked over at her. She looked like an angel lying there. He reached over and brushed her soft cheek. She smiled in her sleep.

Must have woke up on the wrong side of the bed, Ira thought to himself.

Ira hauled ass through the Mexican Desert. He decided to drive straight through, fearing that he wouldn't be able to find anything that would satisfy Angela in the interior of Mexico. He stopped on the side of the road and bought a few soft tacos from a street vendor; he was careful not to wake her, knowing if she saw the guy that made them, she would never eat them. As it was, she liked the tacos. Ira finally spotted a Pepsi sign in a small town, and bought six large bottles, and some chipped ice. He put the drinks in a plastic bag and the ice on top of them. When Angela woke up again, he pointed at the drinks.

"There are a few Pepsis."

Angela opened one, took a drink, and looked at the bottle. "That isn't Pepsi. I don't know what it is, but it sure as hell ain't a Pepsi. I want an American Pepsi."

"Shit," Ira exclaimed. "Has anybody ever told you you are hard to please sometimes?"

She corrected him. "No, I'm hard to please *all* the time."

Ira lit another joint and kept driving. Angela drank the Pepsi; grimacing each time she took a sip. "I need to use the bathroom," she declared, once they got out into the middle of nowhere.

"Why didn't you tell me that before we left that last little town?"

"I didn't need to then."

"You'll just have to wait, unless you want to squat on the side of the road."

"I'll wait."

At the next town, Ira stopped at a filling station, and refueled the pickup. "Where is the women's restroom?" he asked the attendant. The man showed him and he conveyed the directions to Angela. The man's eyes were locked on her as she walked to the bathroom, as were those of every male for a hundred yards in any direction. In a moment, she returned.

"If you think I'm going to put my ass on that toilette seat, you're crazy. They don't even have any toilette paper. It looks like a pig pen in there."

"Shit," Ira said in disgust. "I'll take you somewhere else."

Ira stopped at a restaurant to let her use the bathroom. She came back again. "Don't these people use toilette paper? They don't have any either."

By this time, Ira was ready to cry. He dug a roll out from under the seat and handed it to her.

"Take me somewhere else. This place doesn't look very clean."

"Look. Put some paper on the seat."

"No. I want to go somewhere else."

"Get in."

Angela got into the pickup. Ira drove off, straight out of town, without stopping.

"What about the bathroom?" she asked. "I still need to go."

"I don't care if you shit all over yourself. You had two chances."

"I don't need to take a shit. I just need to pee."

Ira slammed on the brakes and skidded to a stop. The move almost put Angela through the windshield.

"Get you ass out and piss," he ordered.

"Here?"

"Yes."

"I can wait."

Ira shook his head and resumed driving. At the next town, he stopped at another gas station. Angela went to the bathroom. She came back. "That place is disgusting. I saw a roach on the floor. There is no way I'm going to use that bathroom."

"I am not stopping again until I need gas. That may be several hours down the road."

Angela looked coldly at Ira. He wasn't budging. She stormed to the bathroom. When she came back, she said, "If I catch something, it's all your fault."

"That sounds strange, coming from a woman who has had half the dicks in Texas stuffed up her ass," Ira replied.

A look of pain crossed Angela's face.

Ira immediately felt bad, but words released cannot be withdrawn.

The rest of the day was much like the first half; nothing satisfied Angela. As night fell, a bus passed Ira, who was already doing eighty miles an hour. He further depressed the accelerator and fell in behind the speeding bus. It was all the pickup could do to stay with the flying load of passengers. They averaged ninety miles an hour, sometimes reaching speeds in excess of a hundred. By 4 am, they reached Mexico City. Miraculously, Ira made it through the city without getting lost and continued south to Cuernavaca. Angela slept the whole way.

All that night, Ira drank coffee, cokes, and smoked joints. Pot acted like a stimulant on Ira; rather than making him sleepy, it helped him stay awake, especially when taken in conjunction with caffeine.

Angela woke up about eleven the next morning.

"Where are we?" she asked, groggily.

"About an hour away from Acapulco."

"Really?"

"Yes."

"Good." She stretched and looked out the window. They were now driving through mountainous territory; the surrounding hills were lush green with vegetation and small waterfalls cascaded down.

"It's pretty here," she commented.

Ira couldn't believe his ears. This was the first good thing she had said about Mexico.

"I think you'll like Acapulco. It is a well-known international resort. Rich people from all over the world come here to play."

"Sounds like my kind of place."

Ira lit a joint. "Want a hit?"

"Maybe just one." Angela took a hit and handed the joint back to Ira.

He took another hit. The pickup rounded a bend and Ira's heart almost stopped. A road block loomed, not a hundred yards away, manned by at least twenty soldiers, all armed with automatic weapons. Ira threw the joint out the window.

"Roll down your window," he ordered Angela.

She did, just in time to hit a Mexican soldier in the face with a thick cloud of marijuana smoke.

CHAPTER XVI

Ira wasn't exactly sure what the soldier said, but he did catch one word—marijuana. That, he understood. He had no trouble understanding something else—a soldier pointed a fully automatic Thompson sub-machine gun right at Ira's face. Another yelled, ordering him to get out of the pickup. On the passenger side, a third soldier opened the door and ordered Angela to step out of the vehicle.

"What do they want?" Angela asked; terror etched in her face.

"Just get out. Keep your hands where they can see them. Don't reach for anything," Ira told her.

"*Que Quieren?*" Ira asked. The man with the Thompson replied in Spanish, "I smell marijuana. Move to the side while we search the vehicle." He then motioned to a subordinate. "Search him."

The private quickly patted Ira down. Ira looked at Angela. She stood, dressed in her short shorts and the tiny halter-top; the private pointed his weapon at her, and looked her over. Ira looked around. Soldiers gathered from all directions; most stared at Angela. A vision of the entire group having their way with her entered his mind.

One of the soldiers searching the pickup shouted, and then ran up to the man with the Thompson, referring to him as sergeant. In his hand rested two marijuana seeds.

"Is this marijuana?" the sergeant asked, looking at Ira.

"I don't know," Ira said.

The sergeant still had the Thompson trained squarely at Ira's chest, operating it with one hand, while a sling over his shoulder held it in place. He motioned toward a tent with the barrel and told Ira to move in that direction. Angela moved close to Ira, and the two walked together. The soldiers stared at Angela's ass as she walked.

They both watched as the soldiers tore the truck apart. There was no further indication they had found anything after ten minutes of searching. Ira knew there was still at least an ounce, stuffed deep into the foam padding of the driver's side seat, through a small hole in the upholstery.

"Is there any more marijuana in the truck?" the sergeant asked.

"No," Ira replied.

The sergeant ordered one of the privates to move the truck to the side of the road so other vehicles, forming a long line now, could pass. As these vehicles came by, curious faces peered out of windows.

"What are they going to do to us?" Angela whispered.

"I don't know. You better hope they don't find that bag of weed."

"What will happen if they do?" she asked.

"We might go to jail—that is, if we're lucky."

"What do you mean, 'if we're lucky?'"

"There *are* fates worse than jail. Put it this way. You may deeply, and I mean deeply, regret not having listened to me about dressing like that."

"They wouldn't rape me, would they?"

"Not over fifty or sixty times, that is unless more soldiers show up."

Angela looked in the direction of one of the privates. He smiled hugely—gold-lined teeth glinting brightly in the morning sun.

"What are you going to do, Ira? You wouldn't let them do that to me, would you?" Angela asked, moved closer to him.

"Well what do you fucking propose I do to stop that from happening Angela? I am sorry for putting you in this position. I should have known better. Right now, the best thing you can do is to act like you have nothing to fear—nothing to hide. Can you do that?"

"I will try."

Ira walked toward the sergeant. The man raised his weapon. "What is the deal here?" Ira asked. "You have searched for fifteen minutes now and haven't found anything. Why don't you let us go?"

"You had marijuana in your truck. It is illegal to have marijuana in our country. You can go to jail for that."

"For two seeds? Those might have been there since I bought the truck."

"You lie."

"Let us go. We are not criminals."

"You were smoking marijuana when you arrived."

"If I was, are you going to stand there and tell me you never smoked a joint?"

"That has nothing to do with it. You violated our law."

"I want to talk to your superior." Ira sensed he was getting nowhere with this man.

"He will be here soon."

Ira walked back to where Angela stood.

"What was all of that about?" she asked.

"We're in trouble. That son-of-a-bitch is not going to let us go. His boss is on the way. I hope he's easier to talk to than this guy. If not... Hell, let's not think about that now. We need to figure a way out of this mess. Angela, if you believe in God, now would be a good time to do some serious praying. I am going to get us turned loose or buried, one way or the other."

"What are you going to do, Ira?"

"I'm not exactly sure. Let's see what his boss is like. If he's no better than this fellow... You better hope these guys have some KY jelly around here."

"Ira!"

"Keep smiling."

Ira grinned at the sergeant. About then, a thin, young looking man walked up to the sergeant. The sergeant saluted and handed him the two seeds. Ira heard the word *teniente*. The man had an air of arrogance about him. He left no doubt who was in charge, quickly dispatching the sergeant with one curt word.

"So you had marijuana in your truck," the lieutenant stated, in educated sounding Spanish, spoken slow and distinctly, so Ira would understand.

"No, sir. They found two seeds on the floor."

"And you had no more?"

Ira looked closely into the young officer's eyes, trying to read him. He decided to take a chance. "No sir. But I was smoking a joint when we pulled up to the roadblock."

"Then, you do use marijuana."

"Yes, sir."

"What about the girl? Does she also smoke marijuana?" Angela bravely smiled at the man.

"No sir."

"Is she your wife?"

"Not yet. We are engaged."

"I think you are a *cabron*.

"I prefer to be thought of as a black sheep. I am not fond of goats," Ira replied.

"Are you a smuggler? Are you here to buy marijuana?"

"I am going to tell you the truth."

"I would hope so."

"I am no smuggler. The reason I came down here was to have a good time with her, you know… But, I *am* interested in becoming a smuggler. I hoped to look around a little and see what I could find down here. Acapulco is known for its marijuana. I have smoked marijuana from Northern Mexico and know others who traffic in it, but I have never before been here."

"You are aware that trafficking marijuana is illegal and carries severe penalties?"

"Of course. You know how it is though. Sometimes a man must take chances, or he is no man at all."

"Prisons are full of people who think like that."

"And so are palaces of the rich. I would bet some of your bosses have learned to look the other way."

"I don't think so."

"Come on man. Where do you think all the marijuana comes from? Right here. The quantities coming into the United States cannot be produced without coming to the attention of the authorities, yet, year after year, it keeps pouring in. That sir is a fact."

"Are you suggesting there is corruption in our government?"

"Some may call it that. Others might call it being smart. How much money do you make a month?"

"That is none of your business."

"Maybe not. Just for your information then one pound of high quality Mexican marijuana now sells for a thousand dollars in my country. I would bet your next check you don't earn that much."

"You might be surprised," the lieutenant replied, grinning now. "You are a *cabron*! It says you are from Texas on your visa. What do you do there?"

"I am a farmer."

"A farmer?"

"Yes."

"You don't seem the type. Why, if you are a farmer, do you want to traffic in marijuana?"

"It has become almost impossible to make money farming in my country. I'm going broke."

"So, you are attempting to save your farm?"

"Yes, sir."

"Did you bring money to purchase marijuana?"

"Very little. I hoped to look around first, and then come back later if I found any."

"I am curious about something else." The officer looked at Angela, starting at the legs, and working his way up, traversing every inch of her body with his gaze. "The girl—is she your *novia,* or is she a prostitute?"

"She is both."

"Both?"

"She is a prostitute, and I love her. I hope she'll retire and marry me."

"A prostitute…retire, looking like that? Blond haired beauties such as this are very rare in my country. She must be nice. Mr. Jones. I assume prison does not fit well in your plans."

"No sir, it does not."

"I too will be honest with you, since you have done the same with me. Being poor the rest of my life does not fit well into my plans. We have that in common, as well as another thing—an appreciation for beautiful women. I have a few things you desire—the ability to let you go, and marijuana. It seems you have something I desire as well—access to money, and beautiful women. I can take what you have here—all of it," he said, glancing in Angela's direction, and then back at Ira, "or, we can work something out that would be good for the both of us."

"What do you have in mind?" Ira asked, fearful of the reply.

"How much money do you have?"

Ira removed his billfold, opened it, and counted the contents in front of the lieutenant. He had thirteen hundred dollars. Ira also had an extra hundred folded up and hidden in the lining of a second billfold; this he did not show the man.

"How much money would you require to spend, let's say, two days in Acapulco, and return home?"

"Probably three hundred dollars, if I watch my money carefully."

"For one thousand dollars or, twenty minutes with the woman, you can go free, and take a small load of marijuana with you."

"You can have the money. The woman is not for sale."

"And what if I decide to take her anyway?"

"If you do that sir, you better not leave me alive."

"Is that a threat?"

"Yes sir, it is."

"Very well. Maybe one day you can bring me one like her. It has long been a desire of mine to experience a blond haired *gringa*."

"That, I may be able to do," Ira replied.

"Follow me," the lieutenant said to Ira. "You stay," he told Angela, in English.

Ira followed the man into the tent.

"The money sir?"

"OK."

Ira handed the man one thousand dollars and they walked back out. Angela looked relieved to see Ira return. She had a ring of interested soldiers checking her out until the lieutenant arrived, at which time they returned to their duties.

"You both may wait in the tent now," the lieutenant told Ira. He then ordered one of the soldiers to do something, but Ira could not hear what he said. The soldier got into Ira's pickup, started it and drove off.

"What did the guy want?" Angela asked, once they were alone.

"You are not going to believe it when I tell you."

"What?"

"I am buying a load of dope from him. I gave him a thousand dollars."

"How much does that leave you?"

"About three hundred."

"Can we make it back on that?"

"It is enough to get home. It may not be enough to do anything while we are here. I have an idea though."

"What?"

"I'll try to get someone to wire more money to us."

"You can do that here?"

"Yes."

"I would sure feel better if we had more money. We are a long way from home."

"Well, I could have let him fuck you instead. He offered to take that in place of the money."

"Really. You should have taken that Ira."

"I can't do that Angela."

"Listen, Ira. All the time you have known me, I have been a whore. Whether you realize it or not, that means I was fucking other guys. One more wouldn't have killed me—for a thousand dollars no less. I am a whore!"

"I am not some goddamned pimp, though. I care about you."

"Maybe you need to stop caring so much. I'll hurt you in the long run."

The lieutenant reappeared. "Take this as a gift," he said, handing Ira a bag of marijuana. It was the bag he had hidden in the seat. "You may leave. Come back at this same hour, and you will have no problem getting through the roadblock. Here also is a list of nice but inexpensive hotels in Acapulco. Have a nice time. I hope we can do more business in the future—however, I must caution you. Do not tell anyone what happened here today. Also, do not buy from anyone else. If you want marijuana, come to me and no one else. Do you understand?"

"Yes sir, I do."

"Good, then. You may go. Enjoy your stay in our country."

"Where is the merchandise?" Ira asked.

"In the doors. You will not be able to lower your window, so be very careful. Do not smoke while you drive. Should you be caught, you do not know me."

"Yes sir, I understand completely."

Ira and Angela got back into the pickup and continued toward Acapulco.

"How much money did you say you have left?"

"Three hundred bucks."

"You should have sold me. We would have more money."

"Screw you. And shut the fuck up."

"What did I do?"

"I'm not in the mood to talk about it."

The rest of the trip to Acapulco was spent in silence. Ira drove and Angela hugged the passenger side door, as far away as she could get from Ira, and still be in the moving vehicle. Both relived the experience at the roadblock; at one point, Ira's hands began to shake. He tried to hide this from Angela. She too was shaking and fighting back tears.

CHAPTER XVII

All the motels on the list the lieutenant had given Ira were either full or failed to meet Angela's expectations. Ira finally found a villa, far from the main concentration of hotels. The villa was expensive by Mexican standards—fifty dollars a night—but very nice. Each villa had its own kitchen, complete with a refrigerator, a stove, cooking and eating utensils, and a large, comfortable, king-sized canopied bed. The villas overlooked a private, secluded beach, surrounded by gardens teeming with exotic plants.

Both Ira and Angela were dirty and exhausted from the trip and the ordeal at the checkpoint. They showered, ate some excellent charcoal broiled chicken at an outdoor restaurant, and stared across the bay at the city of Acapulco. The sites and sounds of the ocean and the town provided a romantic setting. When they did go to bed, they fell into each other's arms, but Ira could not perform; the incident at the roadblock still haunted and distracted him.

"What's wrong?" Angela asked.

Ira did not reply.

"Do you think I'm dirty?"

"Look, Angela. I don't like what you do, not one bit. I understand your reasons. Now, you must try to understand mine."

* * * * *

Angela woke up in a bad mood, once again.

"My hair hasn't been washed for days. We need to go find some shampoo."

"There's shampoo in the shower," Ira told her.

"I can't put that stuff on my hair. It will ruin my permanent. I use Jhermax."

"OK, we'll look for some."

"I need some sandals too. It is hot down here. I need another pair of shorts and several other things."

"You know we are on a tight budget since our episode with the soldiers."

"You shouldn't have given him your money. I still can't believe you did that."

"I had no choice."

"Sure you did."

"You are never going to let that die, are you?"

"No. You told me I could go shopping when we got here. Here we are and you spent all of our money on marijuana."

"I have an idea. Wait here."

"Where are you going?"

"I am going to talk with the owner of this place."

Ira walked up the path leading to the owner's house through an exotic garden; splashes of bright color and beautiful fragrances greeted him at every bend in the trail. The villas employed two gardeners on a full time basis; one was down on his knees in one of the beds, working in the dark, fertile, humus-rich soil with bare hands. The manager of the villas, a woman of about fifty or so, invited Ira in when he knocked.

"How are you today, my American friend?"

"Much better, after a good night's rest. I was very tired when we arrived yesterday. We drove all the way from Chihuahua without stopping."

"Oh my. That is a long trip. What can I do for you?"

"I had a few unexpected expenses on the way here, and will have to cut our honeymoon short if I can't get more money. Do you have a Western Union office, or its equivalent, where I might be able to get money sent from the United States?"

"Yes, of course we do."

"How long does it take for money to get here from the United States?"

"A day, or maybe two, at the most, I believe. Let me check to make sure."

The woman made a phone call.

"Yes, it is as I said. Two days."

"May I use your phone to make a call? I sure do hate to leave, after spending all that time getting here."

"Of course you may, sir."

Ira dialed Ernie's number in Plainview.

"Did I hear the operator correctly?" Ernie asked. "She said collect—from Acapulco, Mexico?"

"Yep, you did."

"What in the fuck are you doing in Acapulco?"

"It's a long story. I have a girl with me. I came down here to look over a few things you expressed an interest in the other day. I ran into a little trouble, but I ended up finding those things, and need a little money to get home on."

"How much?"

"Probably about five hundred bucks or so."

"How do you want it sent?"

"Western Union."

"They do that down there?"

"Yeah."

"I'll be damned. Sure Ira. I'll send seven, just to make sure."

"Thanks Ernie. I'll make it worth your while, assuming I get out of here in one piece."

"I'm sure you will. You be careful."

"I will."

"Bye."

Ira handed the phone back to the lady. "I guess we get to stay a little longer."

"Good. It is a pleasure having you."

Ira walked back to the villa and told Angela what he had done. They went to breakfast together. Angela complained about the food. They went shopping for shampoo; Jhermax didn't exist in Mexico, and nothing else would do. Ira bought another pair of sandals for Angela, after trying on at least ten pair—minutes later, they hurt her feet. Everything that caught her eye, she wanted. Before the day was over, they had spent a hundred dollars she carried and some of Ira's money as well.

"We better take it easy until that money arrives," Ira warned. "It may be two days before we get any more. I only have a hundred and fifty dollars left. The room will eat fifty of that tonight."

"Just one more thing, Ira. I need that bag to put my things in."

"It will still be here when the check arrives. I am not spending any more money today."

"Cheapskate."

"Bullshit. I am looking out for our asses. When that money order arrives, you can get a few more things, but not until then."

Angela sulked around for several hours, saying she did not want to go out improperly dressed. After considerable effort, Ira finally coaxed her into going for a swim at the villa's private beach. They had it to themselves. Being near Angela in the tiny, black bikini, aroused Ira. Angela teased him. Before it was all over, they slipped into a secluded group of trees and made love to the rhythm of the pounding surf, completely oblivious to the world around them.

CHAPTER XVIII

Susan Grant was furious. Ira had been gone for several days, without calling to let anyone know where he was, or if he was OK. She cut every picture she had of him to pieces. Later, she took the pieces and burned them. She threw away every gift he had ever given her and anything that reminded her of him. None of this made her feel any better. Finally, a thought came to mind. Susan picked up the telephone.

"Hello, is Jason there?" she asked.

Jason Adams had gone to high school with Susan. He was big, strong, handsome, and popular. For years, he had pursued Susan, but she had always ignored his advances. Any and every other girl in the school would have done anything short of killing for a chance at a date with Jason. Besides having been the starting quarterback on the football team, he was a loyal churchgoer, came from a wealthy, influential family, and drove a new BMW.

"Hello, who is this?" Jason asked.

"Susan Grant."

"Oh, Hi, Susan. What's up?"

"Do you still want to go out with me?"

"Yes!"

"Well, I'm ready."

"All right. What happened to that red-headed cowboy?"

"I'd rather not talk about it. We broke up."

"Where do you want to go?"

"Anywhere would be OK. I'm lonely and just want to get out of the house."

"How about a drive in movie?"

"That would be great."

"Far out. I'll be by in a couple of hours."

Susan hung up the phone and smiled. Jason took Susan to an R-rated movie, with a considerable amount of sexual content. Watching the characters engaged in various sexual encounters aroused the two youngsters; before long Jason's hands roamed all over Susan's body. Susan removed her clothes and Jason moved in for the kill.

Accomplishing the feat in the small car was difficult, but they managed.

That night, when Susan bathed, no amount of washing would get rid of the dirty feeling. She cried herself to sleep, regretting what she had done.

CHAPTER XIX

Friday morning, the money order still had not arrived. Ira began to worry. He was almost broke, miles from home, and in a foreign country. To further complicate matters, Angela had resumed constant complaining.

"How long does it usually take a check to get here from the United States?" Ira asked the man at the desk.

"One, or two days at the most. They first go to Mexico City; from there, they are sent here."

"I had a money order sent two days ago. Are you sure it has not arrived?"

"What was the name again?"

"Ira Jones."

"I see nothing here. Check back tomorrow."

"You are open on Saturday?"

"Yes, for half a day."

"Thank God."

Ira walked back to the pickup, where Angela waited.

"The damned thing still has not come in," he informed her.

"You're kidding."

"No, I'm not."

"I'll bet the bastard didn't send it. How well do you know this guy?"

"He sent it."

"You better get someone else to send more, just in case. Why don't you call your father?"

"I'm not going to call my dad from Acapulco. I'll call Ernie to make sure he sent the money."

Ira returned to the villa and explained the situation to the owner of the villa. She proved understanding, and offered to allow him to stay on credit until the check arrived. Ira called Ernie from her office, and Ernie verified that the money had in fact been sent. In addition, Ernie promised to send another three hundred dollars, just in case the first check somehow had been lost.

Ira felt better on the way back to the villa.

"Ernie sent the money. He is sending three hundred more, just in case. Surely, the first check will be here tomorrow," he told Angela.

"I sure hope so. It's torture to be in such a nice place and not be able to enjoy it. Let's go partying."

"We're down to twenty dollars, Angela. Part of that is going into the gas tank—the rest is for food. I'm sorry, but that is the way it's going to be."

Angela refused to come out of the villa the rest of the day, choosing instead to wallow in self-pity. Ira spent most of the afternoon at the beach, swimming alone. That night, she rolled to her side of the bed and ignored him.

Saturday arrived. Ira went to the Western Union office. There was no check in his name. The office was closed Sundays. Before the weekend was over, the pair was broke and out of food. Sunday night, they went to bed in the beautiful, exotic paradise, hungry. From Ira's point of view, things could have been worse; he still had marijuana to smoke. Angela was pissed.

"I should have known better than to run away with you," she said. "At least I had food to eat and nice clothes to wear with RJ. Look what you have gotten me into."

"Believe me, if I could give you back to that bastard right now, I would. This hasn't been fun for me either. Do you think I like this shit any better than you?"

"Well, it's your fault. You are the one that wanted to go to Mexico."

"Why don't you shut up?"

Angela did. She refused to say another word well into the next day. Ira thought it was the most miserable day he had experienced in his young life. That was because he hadn't yet lived the next few.

CHAPTER XX

Jose was worried. Ira hadn't come back, and he hadn't called. Jose could operate any piece of machinery on the farm, and he knew more or less what needed to be done. Running the business end was another matter entirely. Engines had broken down and needed parts to be put back into operation. Jose didn't know where to get the parts; had he known he wouldn't get them. It was not his job. Then Doug Grant showed up with a brand new bale loader, wanting money for it. Jose had sold some hay during Ira's absence, but nowhere near the twenty thousand dollars Doug wanted for the machine. When Jose told Doug Ira was nowhere to be found and had left no money, the crazy gringo became excited and began cussing and swearing.

Jose hadn't understood all of what Doug said, but he did understand that the man was mad, and appeared unstable. Jose feared Doug Grant. Deep inside, he knew Doug was dangerous. Since that day, Jose had taken to carrying a gun. *A man can't be too careful with that crazy blue-eyed devil on the loose.* Jose had seen people lose their lives. If anyone was to die around the Jones farm, Jose intended for it to be anyone *but* him.

CHAPTER XXI

Monday morning found Ira at the Western Union office. The check had not arrived. The clerk told him to try back later that evening. He did; it was still not there. Neither Ira nor Angela had eaten that day. Ira discovered that there was a Mango tree growing near the villas, so he climbed it and gathered fruit. Later, he tried his hand at scaling a coconut palm, skinning the inside of his legs in the process. The coconuts proved difficult to dislodge from the tree, but he did get a few for his efforts. Getting into them without a machete to extract the contents proved a difficult task as well, leaving Ira cussing and sweating.

The next morning, Ira awoke hungry. While Angela slept, Ira walked to the beach. Each morning, local boys collected oysters from the ocean at that particular location. The men swam out with inner tubes with small nets woven into the inner hole.

The men used the tubes for buoyancy and also to hold their catch. All wore flippers and diving masks. Watching them work gave Ira an idea.

"If they can do it, so can I," Ira declared.

Ira was a good swimmer, and had no trouble getting out to where the boys dived for oysters. However, without an inner tube to rest on, he was forced to tread water, and could not fully prepare himself for a deep dive. The first time down, he barely made it to the bottom before returning to the surface, empty handed. The second time, he prepared mentally to stay down longer. Sand swirling around large rocks on the bottom made it difficult to see. He found no oysters. Thinking, *surely*

I'm doing something wrong; Ira swam over to one of the other divers. The boy looked at him curiously.

"How deep is the water?" he asked.

"Ten meters."

"Where do you find the oysters?"

"Right below us."

Ira watched the boy dive. He returned to the surface with two oysters in hand. Ira took as much air into his lungs as he could hold and dived. Once again, he found it difficult to see, but Ira was determined. He searched through the sand alongside a large rock. He grasped at several objects that looked like they might be oysters. Only when it felt like he was about to pass out from lack of oxygen did he return to the surface, barely making it back to the surface. The young man laughed when Ira held up a rock about the size of an oyster. Ira decided to head to shore before he drowned.

About fifteen minutes later, the boys also returned to shore, each with a net full of oysters. Ira watched enviously while they broke the oysters, preparing them to be sold to local restaurants. In the end, Ira traded his wristwatch for one boy's catch and took them back to the villa.

"I got us some breakfast," he told Angela.

"What is it? I can't handle any more mangos right now."

"Raw oysters."

"Really?"

"Yeah."

"I love raw oysters. How did you get them?"

"Oh, I went diving for them."

"And you found that many?"

"Well, not exactly. I bought a few from another diver with my wrist watch." Ira couldn't bear to tell Angela that he had not been able to find a single oyster. Angela began to suck down the creatures while Ira watched. Finally, he decided to try his hand at eating one. It almost gagged him. He decided that one was enough.

The check did not come again that day.

That night, Ira took a small amount of marijuana to the beach until he found a likely looking American couple and sold them a few joints. He took the five dollars for his effort and bought some bread and sausage. They ate in silence that night, occasionally exchanging hateful looks.

Ira lost it on Wednesday. When the Western Union clerk told him his money still had not come, he began to cuss him in front of a large group of people shouting, "*Hijo de puta, me dejiste que un cheque dura dos dias para llegar de Los Estados Unidos. Ya lleva una semana y todavia no está aqui. Pinche mentiroso. Dime otro mentira y verá que voy a hacer a usted, cabron.*" In essence, he threatened the guy.

The clerk got on the phone. "Your check has been found. It will be here tomorrow."

Ira and Angela walked dejectedly down the sidewalk, in the direction of Ira's pickup, which by now was getting low on gas. On the way, they passed a sidewalk bar. For what seemed the thousandth time, a group of Mexican men whistled and hollered at Angela. By this time, Ira had learned to ignore such behavior. One waved at the pair.

"I don't want to go over there," Ira stated. "Come on."

"Let's see what they want," Angela argued. "What else do we have to do today, besides sitting around hungry, with nothing to do?"

"What the hell," Ira finally conceded.

"Do you want a beer?" one of the men asked Ira.

"I have no money to buy beer," Ira replied, "We have had troubles and have been waiting a week for a money order."

"I'll buy. Have a seat."

"What does he want?" Angela asked.

"He has offered to buy us a beer."

"Well, accept his invitation."

Ira looked suspiciously at Angela for a moment and then turned his attention to the semi-drunk Mexican. "I don't care for one, but the lady says she does."

The man ordered a round for everyone; Ira included, and began a conversation directed primarily at Angela. Ira served as the interpreter. It became obvious the man was far more interested in getting to know her than he was the red headed cowboy.

On an empty stomach, the beer hit hard and fast. Ira soon felt weak at the knees.

"Is she your girl friend?" the man asked?

"Not really. She is a dancer. I brought her down here to have a good time. Things are not going well for us right now. The only reason I haven't abandoned her is that I feel obligated to get her home in one piece since I am responsible for getting her down here."

"Then she is not your woman."

"No sir. I tried to make her mine. No one owns that woman, and no one ever will."

"Is she a prostitute?"

Ira did not answer.

Angela watched the man's body language trying to figure out what was being said. She knew she was the topic of the conversation. "What is he asking?"

"He wants to know if you are a whore."

"Tell him I am."

"Are you sure?"

"Yes."

"I don't like this, Angela."

"Tell him."

"Yes, she's a *puta*."

"Since you no longer seem to care for her, would you object if I purchased her services? It has always been my fantasy to have a beautiful, blond woman."

From what Ira had seen, about ninety per cent of Mexican males seemed to share this fantasy.

"I don't want to see her do that, but I cannot speak on her behalf, so I will ask her for you."

"The guy wants to know if you will sell him some pussy. I'd rather you didn't."

"Tell him I will. I'm not going to bed hungry again waiting for you to come up with something."

"There has to be a better way. Shit, let me sell more weed. I can find somebody."

The truth was; Ira was still in love with Angela, in spite of their differences. Nevertheless, he did as she asked. Several hours later, Ira sat, ashamed and disgusted outside a motel room in his pickup, while Angela fucked the Mexican man. Somehow he had never pictured himself as a pimp; sitting there, he realized that was exactly what he had become. When they returned to the bar, the guy's brother decided he too wanted a piece of Angela; she screwed him in Ira's pickup while parked right on a major street of Acapulco in broad daylight. Ira sat on the sidewalk, watching the pickup rock back and forth to their motions. The man apparently blew his load prematurely and was dissatisfied, wanting another shot. Angela said no. When he persisted, Ira stepped in. One look convinced the man. Ira made sure she got her money and they left. Angela went by a store and bought food.

That night, she prepared a meal, but in spite of his hunger, Ira refused to eat. They argued. At one point, Ira found himself close to hitting Angela, but rather than do so, he walked to the beach, sat on a rock, and watched the waves roll in. Several hours later, Angela found him. She had a part of a bottle of tequila in her hand and was drunk. She was crying.

"Ira, I'm sorry."

"Bullshit. You'd do it again."

"Yes. I would. I won't go hungry if I don't have to. I've been poor all my life. I want more—nice things—to be able to go where I want, when I want, without worrying how much it costs. Being a whore allows me to do those things. It is the only way I know."

"You could do something else."

"No, I can't, Ira. I have no education. The only thing I have going for me is my body. That is the only thing men want from me—even you."

"That's not true, Angela."

"Yes, it is."

"Angela, right now you couldn't pay me to fuck you."

Angela tried to wrap her arms around Ira.

"Get away from me," he told her.

Angela sat down on the sand and began to sob.

"Angela. I wanted you to be my wife. I now see that's not what you want. The terrible thing is, I still love you. It tears me up to see you destroy yourself."

"I'm a whore, Ira. I don't want to be your wife. I don't want to be anybody's wife. I want to be your whore. In my own way, I love you too. Sex means nothing to me; it's not much different than eating a meal or taking a shit. My stepfather was fucking me by the time I was thirteen. We could have a good life together. You wouldn't have to work. I could get you more girls. There are a lots of women like me out there."

"I can't be that Angela. Not me."

Angela cried and began to rock back and forth. She looked pitiful. Ira sat beside her and wrapped his arm around her. She laid her head on his shoulder; the wetness of her warms tears moistened Ira's cheek and neck. Ira held her for a long while, watching the waves.

Later, he led her back to the villa. He made no attempt to have sex with her. The two fell asleep holding each other through the night. At one point he woke. *God, I love this woman,* he thought, *but this will never work. I should have known better.*

Ira's mind roamed. When it finally rested, he was sure of one thing. He was ready to go home.

CHAPTER XXII

Doug Grant pulled through the gate leading into the Jones farm. He had been busy. Pieces of farm and construction equipment had been shuffled all over the country; each move left more money in his pocket. Such activity goes unnoticed only so long, and all of Doug's senses indicated it was time for a change in scenery. This time, when he moved, he was going alone. He would leave the farm with Martha, Tim, and Susan. Doug had enough money to buy a place in Mexico.

On the way by the barn, Doug noticed Jose warily checking him out. Doug never quite knew what to think about Jose, because of their inability to communicate. Ira's pickup was still not back. Doug noticed the irrigation well near the house was not running—an ominous sign for anybody trying to grow alfalfa in the arid soil of Southwest Texas.

Ira's disappearance troubled Doug. It was not like him to neglect his duties for so long. Other people in the community had noticed his absence as well; Walter Dean and Bubba Cooper talked about it during their spit and whittle session that morning.

Doug turned the pickup around and drove out of the Jones place without stopping, waving at Jose on the way by. As Doug passed, he noticed the butt of a revolver jutting from the Mexican's waistband.

I'll be damned, Doug thought. *That Mexican may have a little more salt than I gave him credit for.*

Doug continued to his own farm, pulled up to the barn, and parked. Doug noticed the Reverend Delton Davies's car parked in front of the house. Seeking to avoid contact with this highly despised adversary, Doug decided to piddle around the barn for a while, in hopes that the preacher would finish his visit quickly and be gone. However, after an hour, curiosity crept into Doug's mind. He walked to the house.

Doug opened the door, hoping to slip into his bedroom without being heard. When he opened the door to the room, a shocking sight greeted his eyes. Martha Grant stood near her dresser with the buttons of her dress open in the front; Delton Davies's face was buried between her pendulous breasts. His hands were busy exploring territory south of the border at the same time; the hem of Martha's long conservative dress was pulled up somewhere around waist level. Her face was flushed and became even redder when she spotted Doug Grant staring at her. Delton Davies sensed Doug's presence shortly thereafter, and turned around. Martha quickly adjusted her dress, pulling the front closed.

"Well I'll be damned. If it ain't the Reverend Davies? What you doin' there preach?"

Delton stared at Doug with a horror stricken look on his face. His normally powerful voice squeaked when he tried to speak.

"What's wrong preacher, the devil got your tongue? Oh, I know. You're trying to heal my wife's tits. Why didn't you tell me?"

"Get away from me Satan," Delton Davies finally managed to say, in a less than convincing voice—then more authoritatively, he said, "I command you in the name of Jesus to get behind me Satan!"

"You made a big mistake here buddy. While I may look like Satan to you, I'm not. I'm Doug Grant. You may *wish* I was Satan when I get through with your ass. This happens to be my house, and that tit you had in your mouth, belongs to my wife." Doug looked at Martha. "She used to be my wife, anyway."

Doug Grant walked up and bitch slapped Delton Davies. He then turned and knocked Martha to the floor with a backhanded blow.

"Get away from me Satan!" Delton Davies commanded again, this time, sounding like he meant it. Doug bitch slapped him again, and again, and again, until Delton fell to the floor, sobbing.

"Get the hell out of here. Now. Before I change my mind and kill your weasel ass," Doug said.

Delton Davies tried to get up, but Doug Grant slapped him to the floor again.

"Please," the preacher cried, "Don't hurt me any more."

"You are a fucking worm, Davies. Every worm I ever saw crawls when they want to go somewhere. If you want out of my house, you are goin' to crawl. Then again, if you'd like to stay…" Doug Grant pulled a loaded .357 magnum out of his belt and leveled it at the preacher's head.

The Reverend Davies began crawling out of the room. Doug Grant kicked him in the ribs and shoved his ass down to the floor with his boot heel. "On your belly, you son-of-a-bitch. Worms don't have hands and knees… Now crawl, motherfucker."

Delton Davies began crawling, crying like a baby and mumbling prayers.

"Stop it!" Martha Grant screamed. She stood up and ran at her husband. Doug struck her across the bridge of the nose with the butt of his revolver, shattering bone and cartilage, and showering the room with crimson droplets. The blow knocked her down and out. Doug Grant removed his belt and began lashing Delton Davies as he crawled out of the house, down the stairs of the front porch, and all the way to his car.

Tim Grant drove up.

"What are you doing dad?" Tim asked his father.

"This worm likes to suck your mother's tits. Get on your knees, preacher. I am in the mood for a prayer."

Delton Davies assumed the position children are taught while praying. His cheeks were streaked with dirt and tears. Doug Grant leveled the revolver at his head.

"Please," Delton Davies sobbed.

"Pray for me preacher. I seem to be in the need right about now."

Delton looked at the ground.

"Look at me you bastard, or I am going to blow your goddammed brains all over this yard."

"Don't kill him Dad," Tim screamed in horror. "Don't dad, he's not worth it."

Doug moved the weapon a few inches to one side and fired. Delton Davies fell backward and pissed all over himself, holding his hands to his ears. "Get out of here. Now!" Doug commanded.

Delton Davies scrambled into his car on shaky legs, started the engine and drove off. As he left, Doug Grant fired off another round, just over his head.

"If you ever set foot on this place again, I will kill you," Doug shouted.

"Tim, I'm leaving. Go take care of you mother. I think I hurt her pretty bad."

"Where are you going?"

"I'll call in a couple of days. There's money in the safe. It's yours. Take care of your mom and your sister."

"But, dad…"

"I'll call."

"Dad, wait…"

"I can't son. That goddamned preacher will be talking to the law in about fifteen minutes. I need to get on the road."

Doug Grant drove south, headed for Ojinaga, Chihuahua.

CHAPTER XXIII

Doug Grant breathed a sigh of relief when he got on the bridge separating the United States and Mexico. He took another breath to prepare for the next leg of the journey. The bed of his pickup contained boxes. Each box contained AR-15 rifles and ammunition. Doug extinguished his cigarette and pulled up to the Mexican customs official. In his left hand was a hundred dollar bill; resting near his right was the loaded .357.

"What do you have in the back?" the man, asked, in Spanish.

"No *Español*, man." Doug replied.

"What you got?" the man then asked, this time in English.

Doug then came out with the one phrase he knew in Spanish, a phrase he had read in an article about some drug dealer in Mexico and practiced until he got it down.

"*Plomo o plata?*"

Doug held out the bill, and picked up the gun with the other hand, gazing directly into the eyes of the fat Mexican. He then smiled. The Mexican wisely chose the silver, as any fool knows silver is worth more than lead, and then told Doug to enjoy his stay in Mexico.

Doug watched in the rear view mirror. The Mexican resumed working as though nothing had happened. *Smart man.*

A Mexican national who owned a ranch in West Texas and routinely purchased farm equipment from Doug had given him the name of another Mexican in Ojinaga who bought firearms for cash—more than they were worth in the U.S. Doug followed the written directions to the man's house. An elderly woman met him at the door.

"Juan Dominguez?" he asked. The woman took a suspicious look at Doug, and walked back into the house. Doug followed her through the door. A man in his sixties appeared, half clothed, from a back bedroom.

"Who are you?" Mr. Dominguez asked.

"Doug Grant. Carlos gave me your name."

"Carlos?"

"Carlos Herrera. He told me to give this to you. Doug handed a note written in Spanish to the Federale.

"He has mentioned you. What do you have?"

"Convertible AR-15's and the parts to make them fully automatic. A few CAR 15's as well."

"How did you get them here?"

Doug raised his revolver. "I reasoned with the man at the bridge."

"You're lucky. We will have to do better than that next time."

Juan Dominguez went with Doug Grant to another house on the outskirts of town and paid for the weapons. Afterward, he rode with him to the Mexican checkpoint and introduced Doug to the men there. Before they left, he had convinced them that Doug Grant was not to be disturbed. The man who had taken the bribe avoided looking at either Doug or his boss. From there, Doug and Mr. Dominguez proceeded to the bar at the Motel Ojinaga. Doug drank coffee and smoked cigarettes while Juan Dominguez drank Don Pedro brandy and coke with a slice of lime.

"What else can you bring me, Mr. Grant?" the elderly lawman asked.

"Tractors, combines, bulldozers—for that matter, anything on wheels or tracks."

"Good. Do you accept payment in any form other than dollars?"

"What do you have in mind?"

"There are many things. I understand you have a need for land. I have land. I will trade for merchandise. Then there are the drugs your people seem to prize so highly—marijuana, heroin, cocaine, pharmaceuticals—all are available."

"I don't have a market for that stuff," Doug replied.

"You could make much more money if you traded for drugs. They cost me little or nothing. You know how it is. Someone comes through here with a load and gets caught. I end up with the merchandise. I can afford to pay you almost five to one. We have far more drugs than dollars."

"I will see what I can do then, but I will make no promises. In all honesty, I'm afraid of the dope business. Sooner or later, you have to sell it to someone who uses the shit. If he ain't got enough sense not to be doing the stuff, he ain't got enough sense to be doing business with me."

"You—the man who pulled a weapon on a customs official—afraid? I don't believe that."

"Believe it. Most people want to live. Dope heads are different. They're killing themselves already. People like that are not to be trusted." Doug lit a cigarette off of the one he had just finished.

I noticed you don't consume alcohol. I assume you do not use other drugs either."

"Nope," Doug replied, taking a swig of coffee and a long drag on the cigarette. "My only vice is women. Right now, that is a problem. I am doing without."

"How so?"

"Well, the one I had in the United States is no good any more. I don't like prostitutes. I haven't been with a woman for some time. I need to find a good one. The thought occurred to me I might do some looking down here—find me a Mexican woman."

Juan Dominguez paused for a minute before speaking, looking thoughtfully at Doug Grant.

"I have a daughter, Mr. Grant. She has been unlucky at life —married three times; each time something happened. The first two ran away. And the last—a good man, was killed in an accident. The last left a child behind. She is a good woman, and pretty, but many in our town think she is cursed, and are afraid of her. She needs a husband. Would you like to meet her?"

"Yes sir, I would. I don't assign much weight to curses."

"Then tonight, you will meet my Carla."

Doug Grant took Carla out after eating with her at Juan Dominguez's house that night. Unlike her father, Carla spoke almost no English. In spite of their inability to speak, they both sensed an unfulfilled longing that transcended the spoken word. They shared a bed that night. The next morning, Doug went by Mr. Dominguez's house, and bought a house on the edge of the town for ten thousand dollars—the same ten thousand dollars the lawman had given him for the load of guns the day before. Both were satisfied with the arrangement; Doug got a wife and a house; Mr. Dominguez got a husband for his daughter, and a load of valuable guns.

* * * * *

"Did the fucking preacher press charges on me?" Doug asked his son, over the phone.

"I don't think so. No one came by the house."

"How is your mother?"

"She is in her room, mumbling and praying—not makin' any sense. She'll live."

"I won't be coming home Tim. I bought a house. I also found another woman."

"So soon?"

"Don't take long for me to decide whether I like somethin', son. I'll get in touch when I get caught up. May take a while. Been over a year for me."

"You're kidding."

"No sir, I'm not. Is Susan there?"

"Yeah."

"May I speak with her?"

"She doesn't want to talk to you, dad," Tim replied, after a moment's hesitation.

"Can't say as I blame her. Is Ira back?"

"No."

"Go ahead and deliver the bale loader to his place. When he gets back, I'm sure he'll pay for it. You use the money to operate on. I have several other things working."

"How much are you charging him for the bale loader?"

"I told him twenty thousand. I think I'll give him a break. He needs it. Charge him fifteen—cash, of course."

"That's a lot of money. Should I put it in the bank?"

"Hell no, son. Hide it in a couple different places. Don't tell anyone where you got it. Matter of fact, deliver the loader after dark, and tell Ira he's not to say where it came from."

"OK, dad."

"Bye, son."

After the call, Doug returned to his new family. Supper was waiting and the boy child was in bed. Doug ate in silence, sweating through a spicy dish. He was unaccustomed to eating hot peppers, and chased each bite with a drink of coffee, making the burn even worse. Afterward, they went to bed together for the first time in their new home. There, body language sufficed, filling a void no words could fill.

CHAPTER XXIV

Ira woke up dreaming of food, or at least he thought it was a dream, until he fully awoke and realized Angela was cooking bacon and eggs. The smell of the food combined with Ira's very empty stomach caused his salivary glands to flow. Angela walked into the room and thrust a plate under his nose.

"I am not eating anything you earned selling your body to another man."

"Come on, Ira. What does it matter? What's done is done." She offered the plate again.

"You eat it," he told her fighting the impulse to grab the plate.

"I have some. Look, you may not believe this, but what I did was as much for you as it was for me. Do you actually think I enjoy screwing those guys?"

"I would assume so."

"Well, you're wrong. You're the only man that has come close to getting me off. What you did for me last night is the greatest thing I have experienced with a man. I need to be held and caressed. I never had that as a child. You don't understand what it's like to be me. I grew up without love. My step dad fucked me and my mom hated me for it—not him! Sometimes, when I sell myself, I'm getting back at all the men in the world—I use them, take their money, and then throw them away. When they come back for more, I treat them like shit. It makes me laugh when they fall for me—the ignorant bastards."

"You used me too, Angela."

"I know, and I hate myself for it. You don't deserve that. It's not like I wanted to, but I did it anyway, without thinking. I'm cold sometimes—so cold I scare myself. Ira, please eat some food—for me," Angela pleaded. Tears welled in her eyes.

"OK." Ira took the plate from her and ate.

She smiled—a beautiful smile. Her addiction to speed was being broken and she was beginning to normalize.

"Are you going back to Susan?" she asked.

"I don't know what I'm going to do. I *am* going home. I have to do that."

"What about me?"

"You could stop selling yourself and be my wife."

"I can't do that. Not yet. I know you don't understand, but I can't."

"I can't share you either. If you screwed half the world, I would still care, and I would still love you, but I would have to keep my distance. It would kill me."

"I don't know what to do. I can't go back to Lubbock. I don't want to go back to Lubbock. I can't work in Texas. They'll find me."

"Where is you mother?"

"Phoenix."

"Why not go there?"

"And live around my father-in-law? Forget that."

"You're strong enough to deal with that now. Besides, you don't have to live with her. Maybe she can help get you set up with a job and a place to live."

"Ira. I *like* dancing."

"It's your life Angela. Do what you want with it. Nothing I can say is going to change your mind anyway."

Ira finished his meal and watched Angela do the dishes. It angered him that she was so hard headed. Watching her, he realized that underneath it all, Angela had it in her to be a good person. Her bad side was very bad; Ira thought her good side might also be very good. The glimpses of that goodness—the naked honesty with which she sometimes spoke—and the way she made him feel with nothing more than her presence, *made* him want her.

Ira drove to the Western Union office, alone. The first check Ernie sent was there. He cashed it, returned to the villa, paid his bill, and then checked out. The owner was relieved to see him come up with the money; the bill had grown far above what she had anticipated, and she had begun to worry that he might skip out without paying until the check finally did arrive.

Ira took his truck to a mechanic and had a wheel bearing replaced. That evening, he and Angela went out to eat, and later took a cruise on a ferry they had watched go by from the shore many times.

The ferry offered three floors of entertainment. Before the night was over, Angela got drunk, and Ira got into a fight, trying to fend off other drunken Mexican men who wanted to take advantage of the drunken beauty. Once again, he found himself in despair over Angela.

"Where are we going to stay tonight?" she asked, slurring her speech and laughing, after they got off of the ferry.

"You can stay wherever you like. I'm staying on the beach, right over there."

"On the beach? Are you crazy?"

"No. I have just enough money to get home. I can't be sure that second check will arrive, and I'm damned sure not going to spend all my money again, waiting."

"I want a room," Angela demanded.

Ira pointed to a nearby hotel. "See that place? There are all kinds of rich bastards who would be happy to let you share their room. I'm going to be right here." Ira grabbed a blanket and headed for the beach.

"You bastard," Angela yelled. She turned and began walking toward the hotel.

Ira sat on the blanket and watched the waves roll in. The sea sounds comforted him. He heard music and merrymaking in the distance, coming from the open bar near the hotel Angela had gone to. He shut out those noises and concentrated on the natural rhythm of the waves, letting them wash his mind. Finally, he lay down, at peace, and went to sleep. A few hours later, someone's presence woke him. Angela stood there with tears in her eyes.

"You're crazy Ira."

"I know it. Come here, Angela." Ira stretched out his arm and she lay beside him.

"You bastard. How did I ever fall in love with you?" she asked.

"Hell, ain't it?" Ira asked.

They spent the night wrapped in each other's arms, totally immune to the rest of the world.

CHAPTER XXV

When the second check arrived, Ira decided it was time to head for home. Acapulco had proved to be all the fun he could handle for a while. The trip back through the roadblock went smoothly; the sergeant with the Thompson recognized them, and waved them through. Getting through Mexico City proved different. The first time through, while headed south, Ira had sailed through the huge city, but this time, he took a wrong turn, and found himself trapped in a downtown traffic jam unparalleled by anything he had ever witnessed.

The people of Mexico City are notorious for being some of the world's worst drivers. Whoever gets to an intersection first has the right-of-way, and the matter is often decided by a mad dash and a game of chicken, horns blaring and curses flying. Any way you can be cut off, you will be, and any discourtesy is the accepted norm. More than once, Ira found himself ready to drag someone out of the car and fight. Several times, he stopped to ask for directions out of the madness; none of which seemed to help. Five hours of driving in circles, being locked in downtown gridlock—at one point they spent an hour at one light, watching it change from red to yellow to green, without being able to move, because the traffic going in the other direction blocked the intersection each time the light was green, rather than stop and allow traffic going the other way to have a chance—left Ira ready to kill. Rather than do so, he spotted a hotel, stopped, rented a room, and waited for another day.

Angela woke up now in a more agreeable state of mind than she had exhibited the first week of their journey; she had broken her dependency to methamphetamine. They spoke, while still in bed the next day.

"It's going to be hard for me to leave you," Angela said.

"I'm still not sure I *can* leave you," Ira replied.

On the way out of town, Ira had a minor fender-bender. To avoid involving police, Ira gave the guy a hundred dollars, while Angela protested—the wreck had been the other driver's fault, at least by American standards. Ira figured, by Mexican standards, the gringo was always at fault.

Ira drove all the way to Ojinaga, Chihuahua, without stopping for anything other than gas, food, or directions, taking a back route through an uncompleted road from Camargo to Ojinaga, rather than going through Chihuahua City, and thereby avoiding the customs checkpoint. The road turned out to be brutal. They averaged twenty miles an hour over the rock-strewn, pothole filled and winding, dusty path; even at that speed he lost a shock absorber, a tire, and a muffler during the six-hour journey. Angela cursed his judgment for having taken the route, but it did accomplish its intended purpose: getting them to the border without going through a roadblock.

Ira rented a room in Ojinaga. The room was tolerable, but the dirty, trash-filled, bleak looking border town held nothing of interest from Angela's point of view. Ira stopped for one reason. He hadn't yet figured how to get the marijuana stashed in the doors of his pickup back into the United States. The thought of trying the bridge was more than he cared to risk; he needed time to formulate a plan. The only viable option that had come to mind was to remove the product, stuff it into a backpack, and send Angela across with the pickup, where she could retrieve Ira after crossing the river on foot, like so many wetbacks do each and every day of the year. Even this option left much to be desired.

Angela did not want to go out to eat, so Ira walked to a local grocery store to pick up a few things. While there, he ran face to face into Doug Grant and a Mexican woman he did not recognize.

"What are you…" both men started to ask simultaneously.

"You first," Doug said.

"It's a long story—long and painful."

"So's mine. Meet my new wife. Ira, this is Carla."

Ira offered his hand to the woman. She grasped it shyly.

"I bought me a place on the edge of town. From now on, this is home for me."

"I'll be damned. You talked about doing this, but I doubted you really meant it."

"I'm not the type to waste my breath. If I say something, take it to the bank. Why don't you come by the house tonight? You can be our first guest."

"I'm not alone."

"The girl from Lubbock?"

"How did you know?"

"Susan."

"Susan? Oh shit. How did she know?"

"She followed you to Lubbock, and went by that bar, right after you left. From there, she put two and two together. Come on by, and bring the girl."

"But…"

"I understand. Don't forget—I was young once, too."

"But, you couldn't possibly…"

"Let me guess. You were the handsome knight in shining armor, out to save a fair damsel from her evil master. After you got her away, you realized you had stolen his pet dragon instead. Am I close?"

Ira began laughing. "You're close."

"Come over tonight."

"We will."

CHAPTER XXVI

Ira and Angela checked out of the motel at noon and drove to a remote spot near the banks of the *Rio Bravo Del Norte*, or as it is known in the United States, the Rio Grande. Ira stopped under a group of small shade trees, parked, and watched the American side of the river for activity. In spite of the shade, the cab of the truck was soon hot, and Angela once again found something to complain about.

"I hate sweating. What are we doing here?"

"I'm checking out the river, to see if there is any way I can sneak this weed across on foot. I sure as hell don't want to go through customs with it. Do you?"

"This whole damned trip is crazy. Get rid of the damned stuff and let's go home."

"Not yet. We have a couple of hours to kill. Then we are going to see a friend of mine. He invited us over to eat."

"You have a friend—here?"

"I didn't know I did, until I went to the store this morning, and then I ran into the guy."

"Is he a Mexican?"

"No. He's white. He owns a farm near ours. He's Susan's daddy."

"And you are going to take *me* to meet him. Am I going to survive this? From what you've said about that guy, I'm not sure I *want* to go."

"He's crazy, but he's OK. You might even like him."

"This I have to see."

Angela finally tired of the heat and decided to go for a swim in the river. Ira soon joined her. The cool water made the heat bearable, and the day passed.

"Tell me more about this guy," Angela said, before they made the drive to his house.

"Well, first he is a farmer, but he no longer farms. His boy does all the work. He went broke farming, so now he steals for a living, I figure. Second, he probably kills anybody that gets in his way. He's a damn old outlaw."

"So, let's get this straight. You are taking me to see some crazy guy that kills people, and also happens to be the father of the girl you were going to marry."

"Yes, but don't worry. He has probably already killed his quota for the week—just kidding. He isn't really all that bad."

Ira pulled up to Doug Grant's house. A tall fence with jagged metal spikes surrounded the house. Ira hollered from the front gate. Angela stood alongside. They could see Doug Grant sitting at the kitchen table, illuminated by a kerosene lantern, through the front door screen. An automatic rifle was propped against the table, within arm's reach. Doug stood up, rifle in hand, and walked to the door.

"That you, Ira?"

"Yes."

"Come on in."

"You weren't kidding about the killing, were you?" Angela asked, suddenly not sure whether she wanted to go into the house.

"No, I wasn't. He won't hurt you though."

Ira steered Angela to the door.

"Doug, this is Angela. Angela, Doug."

Angela decided that Ira's evaluation of Doug Grant had been understated. One look into the cold fire burning in those ice-blue eyes sent shivers down her spine.

"Glad to meet you, Angela. Come on in. Ira—you met Carla. Carla this is Angela."

The two women acknowledged each other. Carla seemed somewhat intimidated by the larger, blond *gringa*.

"Have a seat. Have you eaten?"

"I'm not hungry," Angela said.

"I guess I'll pass too," Ira said, after noticing what was on Doug's plate. It appeared to be some unrecognizable body part.

"How about some coffee?"

"That would be nice," Angela replied.

"Can you get us some coffee?" Doug asked his new wife. She looked back, confused.

"She doesn't speak English?" Ira asked.

"No, and I can't speak Spanish. We make out all right though. Watch this."

Doug pointed at the jar of instant coffee sitting on the table. She understood.

"Coffee," he said.

"Café," she replied. Both repeated the word several times to themselves, to the best of their ability, in the other's language. Carla then poured hot water for all and sat down at the table with her guests. Coarse sugar with a slight off white color occupied a spot on the table as well. All but Doug partook.

"I like mine like I like my women—dark and bitter," Doug stated. "So, Ira how did you end up in Ojinaga?"

"It's a long story. We decided to take a trip to Acapulco after the incident at the bar in Lubbock. I though it might be fun, and would also give me the opportunity to check out the marijuana situation. I had always heard that Acapulco had the best—this stuff they call Acapulco gold. There is big money to be made smuggling weed."

"I don't know if I would want to take that chance. Ain't it dangerous for a white boy to fuck with that stuff down there? I have always heard Mescans don't like others hoggin' in on their territory. They kill people over that shit."

"Tell me about it. We got busted."

"You got caught, and you're still here to talk about it?"

"It's a long story, like I said. In the end, the same people that busted us ended up selling us a load."

"Do what?"

Ira told the story, from start to finish, leaving the parts out about the constant fighting he and Angela had done and selling pussy in Acapulco in order to eat.

"You're lucky to be alive," Doug told Ira. "And *you* are lucky not to be still fuckin' Mescan soldiers, lookin' like you do," he said, redirecting his gaze at Angela. "There ain't no way in hell I'd bring dope out of the interior. They don't like white men traipsin' around down there. If you want marijuana, buy it at the border. Hell, I already ran into a man that'll sell it to me here, cheap."

"I sure as hell won't try it again," Ira said.

"How did you get past the checkpoint between here and Chihuahua? Normally, I hear they search people coming through."

"I took the back road, from Camargo. They still don't have anybody at the checkpoint there."

"You're lucky. I heard just last week they did have one set up and had a hell of a shoot out between federales and a guy trying to run it with a load of marijuana."

"Like I said, I don't plan on doing it again. I bet I lost a year off of my life from the stress of this trip."

"It wasn't fun for me either," Angela added.

"I bet not," Doug commented.

"So, what brought you down here?" Ira asked Doug.

"You know I've been thinking about this for quite a while now. I have plenty of reasons. First on the list would have to be what I see happening in the United States. They got us by the balls with all those computers and shit. An outlaw don't have a fightin' chance any more. Then, there's that bitch I used to call my wife."

"What happened?"

"Oh, nothin' that hasn't been happenin' for a long time. It just finally reached a head. She wore me out with that religious shit of hers, and then come to find out she has been fuckin' the preacher. Bitch hasn't given me any pussy for over a year and she's fuckin' that goddamned preacher. Can you believe that?"

Ira refrained from comment.

"Truth is, I wouldn't give a plugged nickel for most American women anyway." Doug turned to Angela. "No offense to you, m'am."

"None taken."

"The way I see it, most white women these days are spoiled. Everything has to be their way or no way at all. I wasn't raised that way. When I grew up, the man was the head of the household. Not any more. I ain't putttin' up with some bitch runnin' my life."

Ira prodded Angela under the table. She remained silent.

"You want to see a real woman? Take a look at Carla here. She does what I tell her. She don't argue. She tries her best to please me every way she can. She's great in bed. You may not can tell it looking at her, but she is smart too. I let her do the bargaining when we buy things. She wouldn't spend a dime of my money without asking first, and God help the man or woman that tries to fuck me around if Carla gets a hold of their ass. I have already taught her how to shoot. She is a natural. Show em your gun, Carla."

She looked at him curiously. Doug formed his hand into the shape of a gun. Carla smiled and removed a .380 auto from the pocket on her apron, showing it proudly to Ira and Angela.

"She's deadly with that thing, and I'll tell you something else—she wouldn't hesitate a second to use it, if the need arose. I'll show you. Carla. Boom! Boom!"

Doug pointed at the wall. Carla raised the gun and fired at the wall, knocking a chunk out of the adobe. Both Ira and Angela jumped into their seats. The acrid smell of burnt powder filled the kitchen. Doug laughed heartily. Carla smiled proudly. Angela stared in horror at the smoking gun. Ira noticed there were lots of bullet holes in the wall. He nodded in appreciation at Carla.

"The other day, I told her to shoot a stray dog. She hit him, right in the eye. Wouldn't be any different if it were a man either. I can tell, she's a natural. I got me a hell of a woman." Doug wrapped his arm around Carla's waist and drew her close.

"Me good woman," she stated proudly.

"See there, she's even startin' to learn English, and we ain't been together but a couple of days."

Doug continued his tirade about the advantages of Mexican women over their American counterparts for some time. Periodically, Ira tried to goad Angela into disagreeing, but she remained silent. She couldn't help but notice the .357 in Doug's waistband, and he never let the frightful looking automatic rifle get out of arms reach anywhere he moved in the house. The thought of him yelling *Boom! Boom!* and discovering that his finger was pointed at her also came to mind. There was no doubt in the world what would happen if he did. Under the circumstances, keeping quiet seemed the prudent thing to do. Finally, Doug changed the conversation when he ran out of things to say on the subject.

"How are you going to get the marijuana into the U.S.?" Doug asked his young friend.

"Only way I can see is on foot."

"Can you sell it, once you get it home?"

"Yeah. I know a guy in Plainview that will buy it—a guy by the name of Ernie. You'd like him."

"Can you trust him, though?"

"Yes. He's the one that wired us the money to get home on. He's wild as hell, but he is a good friend."

"Why don't you leave the marijuana here with me? I can get it up there for you."

"You?"

"Yeah. I have developed some connections down here. My man has offered to pay me for my services in dope. I understand he has a way of getting it to the other side of the river. I don't mind takin' it from there. I sure as hell don't want any part of takin' it over the bridge. Problem I have is how to sell the shit. If you can sell the Goddamned stuff, I can probably get you all you want. How much do you reckon Ernie can sell?"

"He can handle at least ten pounds a week. I figure that's about what I have in the doors, maybe a little more."

"Let's get it out of your truck then. There ain't no sense you takin' unnecessary chances."

Doug and Ira moved the pickup into the protective walls surrounding Doug's house and proceeded to tear into the doors.

"That Angela sure is a looker," Doug said, after they were alone.

"She sure is. She's smart too, but she's a whore, and she likes being a whore. She flat wore me out on this trip."

"How did you meet her?"

"I've known her for some time, long before I met Susan. When Susan wouldn't give me any… you know. I got weak and looked her up. Then Susan broke it off with me. Next thing I know, I've got Angela hauled off and don't know what to do with her. I've loved that girl for a long time, but she's a heart breaker."

"What are you going to do with her now?"

"I still don't know. I reckon I'll probably give her some money and send her to her mom's in Phoenix. She'll be on her own from there. Susan must be furious with me."

"S'pect so. Kind of disappoints me that she was so stingy with herself. Hope she don't turn out like her goddamned mom. You don't want no part of that. Never would give you any, huh?"

"No, sir"

"I'd a guessed y'all were getting it on a long time ago. Do what is right for you, Ira. When it comes to figuring out the mind of a woman, I'm at a loss."

The two men put the bundles of marijuana into a large flour sack and carried it into the house. They found Carla showing Angela how to make hot sauce on the wood cook stove.

Doug Grant had never seen marijuana before, so he opened a package. It was gold bud.

"Shit, this stuff is full of sticks and big pieces—and seeds. How the hell do you smoke the stuff?"

"It has to be broken down and cleaned up first."

"Why don't they go ahead and get it ready before they sell it?"

"I think it begins to lose some of its potency once you break it down."

"How much is this worth?" Doug asked, pointing at the sack full.

"Probably seven or eight thousand dollars, wholesale."

"For that little pile. And to think I spent all that time growing alfalfa. That much alfalfa ain't worth a dollar. Hell, there ain't a quarter of a bale here."

"Now you understand why I'm growing some on my dad's place."

"Tim and I talked it over too. I'm a little leery, though. You have to sit on that for a long time and you can't move it if things get hot. What you are after is money. You and Tim can grow that if you want, but I have a better way of makin' money."

"What's that?" Ira asked.

Doug leaned over and whispered, "I am not too comfortable talkin' about this in front of the lady."

"Don't worry about her. She's an outlaw too. She won't talk."

"Well, the way I got it figured, what we all want and need is cash. Instead of goin' through all these gyrations to make money, why not go where they keep the stuff and just take it?"

"I'm not following you."

"Banks. Robbing banks. They have been fucking me over for years. It's payback time. I plan to hit it hard for one year and then retire—down here—away from those damned computers."

"Now that sounds dangerous to me," Ira stated.

"Naw. Nothin' to it. Me and three or four good men can take any bank in the country."

"Well, we better be goin, Doug. I'm going to take a sample of that marijuana with me. Do you have a baggie?"

"I don't believe I would, if I were you."

"I'll just take a little."

"Where are you going to hide it?"

"I'll get it through. Don't worry about that."

"Your ass!"

"I need something to show Ernie. He'll probably come down."

The truth was, Ira needed something to smoke. Doug found a plastic grocery sack and Ira stuffed a generous ounce into it.

"How much is that worth?" Doug asked.

"At least a hundred bucks," Ira replied.

Doug shook his head in disbelief. "No wonder people get into that business."

Ira and Angela said their goodbyes and left. Ira rolled and smoked a joint while they drove. Angela took a few hits also.

"That guy is out of his fucking mind, Ira. You better leave him alone."

"You live your life; I'll live mine."

"You'll end up in jail or shot dead someday. You're crazy. I heard you talking about robbing banks. Now you are going to sneak weed through the checkpoint. And you have the nerve to talk down on me about selling pussy. You're the one playing with fire."

"Who are you to talk? At the rate you're going, you'll be worn out, or dead by thirty."

"Ira, please, don't get involved with that guy. He's ready to go off any minute. When he does, people are going to die. I don't want you to be one of them."

"You live your life; I'll live mine," he repeated.

"What are you going to do with me?"

"I'm sending you to Phoenix."

"Broke?"

"No, I'll give you some money."
"Are you going back to Susan?"
"I doubt she'd take me now."
"Do you still love her?"
"I don't know if I even know what love is any more. Sometimes I think I do, and then something else comes along to prove me wrong."
"Like me?"
"Yeah."

Ira rode for a while before crossing the bridge, allowing the pickup to air out. He stuffed the bag of marijuana into his underwear, right under his balls, almost in the crack of his ass, wedged tightly as possible.

"Here goes nothin'," he stated, turning toward the United States.

CHAPTER XXVII

Robert Salinger had a knack for spotting smugglers. His job as a customs inspector at the Presidio, Texas crossing required making snap decisions. Not every vehicle could be searched thoroughly; there was not enough time or manpower. Robert's job was to select those who looked suspect.

When the black pickup containing Ira Jones and his girl friend pulled into the station, Salinger punched the license plate number into his computer. His experienced eyes searched for signs. He noticed the Mexican visa sticker in the window, indicating they had gone into the interior of the country. The truck was dirty and missing a muffler, causing it to roar loudly. He scanned the bed of the pickup. *Very little luggage. No place to hide a load of marijuana. Maybe hard drugs, though?*

"State your citizenship," he told them.

"American," Ira replied.

"And you?" he asked Angela.

"I'm from Ohio."

"Are you an American citizen?"

"I just told you I'm from Ohio. The last I heard, Ohio was still part of America."

"Where have you been?" he asked.

"Acapulco."

"For how long?"

"Almost two weeks."

Robert Salinger looked closely at the perforations on the sticker applied to the windshield by the Mexican customs officials. The dates checked out.

"Are you bringing anything back from Mexico?"

"A few clothes, a pack of cigarettes. That's about it," Ira replied.

"He's a cheapskate," Angela added.

Salinger checked the computer. *Nothing. The guy's eyes are red and glassy. Looks like he just finished a joint. Not nervous, though. Better check anyway,* he finally decided.

"Pull right over there. We are going to have a look at your vehicle."

"Whatever you say, sir."

"He's going to search us isn't he?" Angela asked.

"Yes."

"I told you not to bring that shit."

"Be cool. He hasn't found anything yet. Let's get out and act like we have nothing to hide."

They stepped out of the truck and sat on a bench near the search bay. A few minutes later, another customs inspector came out and began the search. He opened both doors and looked through the cab. Using a mirror attached to a pole, he checked the underside of the pickup. He opened the hood and removed the breather from the carburetor. He let a little air out of each tire, and smelled it. He removed the spare and did the same, and then rolled it across the ground. Any unevenly distributed weight in the tire would cause it to wobble as it rolled. He then ran a flexible dipstick into the gas tank and probed around. Utilizing a dolly, he crawled under the tank to see if any bolts had recently been removed. While under the truck, he knocked on the tank, and listened to the sound. After he crawled out, he used a flashlight and a small pry bar to look into the doors. Ira and Angela exchanged knowing glances.

"Do either of you use illegal drugs?"

"No," Angela stated.

"I smoke a joint every once in a while," Ira said.

"You do?"

"Yes."
"Do you use anything else?"
"No."
"Let me see your arms."

Ira held out his arms. The man turned them over to look at his veins.

"Do you have any drugs on you person?" he asked.
"No sir."
"How about you?" he asked Angela.
"No."
"Let me see your purse, please."

She sighed and shook her head, and then handed him the purse. "Can't you see we don't have anything?"

"Just doing my job, ma'am."

"Your job is to catch smugglers, not to bother innocent people," she said.

"Sometimes, it is hard to tell the difference," he replied. He handed back the purse. "You may go."

"Thank you," Ira said. Salinger watched him walk around the truck. The small bag of weed felt like it was the size of a football as he walked. The agent noticed nothing out of the ordinary. Ira started the engine, and drove off.

"That was a stupid thing to do," Angela said. "You could have gotten us busted again."

"I know it. I'll never do it again. That scared the living shit out of me. I don't see how people do this."

"I was scared too," Angela confessed.

"You seemed to handle it well."

"So did you. I almost crapped when you told them you smoke marijuana though."

"I figured he could tell. He believed everything I said from that point on—even the lie. If I had denied smoking, I think we might still be there. At least we have something to smoke. I need it after that."

Ira dug the bag out of his pants. "Roll one up."

She did and they smoked.

"Now where?"

"My house. You can spend the night if you want to. Tomorrow morning, I'll go by the bank and get you some money and drop you off at the bus station. I hope you will go to your mom's."

"I hate to, but I guess I will. No one else wants me."

"I do. You are welcome to stay, but only if you quit whoring and dancing. Is that what you want?"

"I'm not ready to quit. Will you come see me?"

"I might. Maybe someday, you will get tired of that life. I hope I'm around when you make that choice."

"I'm going to miss you."

"Me too."

It was late when they arrived at Ira's trailer. They spent the night in each other's arms. The next day, Ira took her to town, withdrew a thousand dollars from his dad's account and dropped her off at the bus station. Saying good-bye proved difficult.

Ira fought off tears all the way home.

CHAPTER XXVIII

At first sight, Ira thought the farm looked pretty good. The barley had headed out nicely. While Jose was obviously behind cutting and baling alfalfa, there was more hay stacked in the barn than when he had left, and the fields were green. The farm had received a rare but timely rain during his absence. Upon closer inspection however, Ira discovered many things in a state of disrepair. Of three tractors on the farm, only one was in operating condition. There were seven irrigation engines on the Jones's farm; only three were running. Two engines had totally shelled out due to a lack of motor oil, and two had cracked heads—the cooling tanks had been allowed to run out of water. Jose had been afraid to operate the new bale loader, so quite a few bales still rested in the field, even though Leonardo and his compatriots had diligently been picking them up, when the tractor was available.

Jose had planted a patch of watermelons and a small plot of chili peppers.

One other thing was doing well. Ira discovered his marijuana plants stood knee high. He immediately set himself to the task of transplanting them into the ditch behind his house.

Ira's heart ached for Angela, but he carried an awesome load of guilt for having left the farm unattended so long and immersed himself into his work, sleeping a total of twelve hours the first three days back; the rest of the time he spent working. When he did lie down, he passed out, exhausted, and slept without dreaming.

Susan showed up one day, catching him at work on an irrigation engine. He looked up at her approach, but kept working.

"Hi, Susan."

"How long have you been back?"

"About a week."

"Why haven't you come to see me?"

"Last I heard, you never wanted to see my face again."

"I didn't mean it."

"You shouldn't say things you don't mean."

"You ran off with that…that stripper, didn't you?"

"You know the answer to that. Why do you ask?"

"Because I want to hear it from you."

"OK. I ran off with her. Satisfied?"

"Why, Ira?"

"That would require some time. I'd rather not get into it."

"Try to explain it to me, Ira. I need to know."

"I guess it started because I wanted some pussy. One thing led to another."

"What did you do with her?"

"I am not going to give you a blow by blow account."

"Is she pretty?"

"Yes."

"What does she look like?"

"Blonde, built like a brick shit house. Kind of muscled up, but in a nice way. Tits ain't big, but stick straight out. Nice ass."

"Was she good in bed?"

"Why do you want to know?"

"I just do."

"The best I ever had. The best I'll ever have."

"Oh Ira."

"Don't ask if you don't want to know."

"You are a bastard, Ira."

"Why, thank you Susan. You can go home now."

"You are not the only one who can sleep around. I slept with Jason Adams."

"Well good for you, Susan. Must be a hell of a dude. I tried for two goddamned years and he got to you in a week. Get the hell out of here."

She went nowhere.

"Leave!"

"Screw you, Ira!"

"You better get off of my property right now," he said, starting toward Susan.

She turned and ran. He picked up a small clod and threw it as she retreated, barely missing her. "I just got rid of one whore. Might as well get rid of another." He threw another clod.

Susan turned to say, "I am not a whore…" when the clod hit her, on the forehead. She fell.

"Oh my God," Ira shrieked, instantly sorry for what he had done. He sprinted toward her.

"Are you all right?" he asked when he arrived; concerned that she might be seriously hurt. He reached down and picked her up. "I didn't mean to hurt you."

"I'm OK. And, I'm sorry, Ira. The thing with that other guy —it was awful. I came to ask you if you would take me back. It just hurts to know you have been with someone else."

"I know, Susan."

"Tell me one thing. Do you love that other girl?"

"I'll tell you like I told her. Sometimes, I'm not sure I even know what true love is. I thought I did."

"What about now?"

"I'm here, and she's in Arizona. That's all I can say."

"Ira, I want you to make love to me."

"Really?"

"Yes."

"Right here? Now?"

"No. Let's go to your house."

"Are you serious?"

"Yes."

"You know you don't have to do this."

"I want to."

"Go on to my trailer, then. I have to pick up my tools. I'll be right behind you."

"Hot damn," Ira said. He threw the tools into the back of his pickup, jumped in, and sped toward his house, before Susan had a chance to change her mind.

Susan was beautiful. But the sex was awkward. Before the night was over, Ira had agreed to marry her.

CHAPTER XXIX

Susan Grant woke up, fighting Ira's advances at her private regions. "What do you think you're doing?" she asked, squirming to get away. "Quit, Ira!" About that time, the sound of an approaching vehicle reached their ears.

"Damn," Ira said, thwarted. "Who could that be at this time of the morning?"

"Go see!" Susan shouted.

While she went on a mad search for her clothes, Ira walked to the window.

"It's your dad."

"Oh my God!" Susan said, in a panic. "Put on your clothes Ira!"

Ira stood at the window with his mouth agape, and an erection jutting straight out into the room. Susan ran for the bathroom and locked herself in. Ira pulled on a pair of jeans, sans underwear, and walked to the door. Doug Grant greeted him when he opened it.

"I see you and Susan got back together," Doug said loudly, for Susan's benefit. "I couldn't help but notice her car."

"Yeah, we did."

"How was it?" Doug asked.

"How was what?"

"Oh come on Ira. You don't buy a pair of shoes without trying them on first to see if they fit, do you?"

"It fit," Ira whispered.

"I figured it would. What did she say about the other girl?"

"We had a fight over it."

"Best pussy you'll ever get comes right after a fight. I'm glad to see y'all tryin' to make a go of it. I was beginnin' to worry Susan would turn out just like her mom. I see you got the bale loader going. I assume you paid Tim?"

"Yeah."

"Good. I'm kind of reluctant to go by there. How is Tim doing?"

"He's OK. Busy."

"You can come out now, Susan," Doug Grant yelled through the door.

Susan walked into the room, blushing.

"Come here," he said, inviting her into his arms.

Tentatively, she approached. He gave her a hug.

"You're not mad, daddy?"

"Mad? Hell no. Overjoyed would be more like it."

Ira hoped Doug would not notice the small knot on her forehead, from the clod.

"Your mom ain't goin' to like it. If I were you, I wouldn't spend too much time worryin' about that though. Susan, I'm not coming home. I got me a place in Mexico, and another woman. I'm not looking for approval. I just wanted to be the one to tell you."

"OK."

"Who is she?"

"Her name is Carla."

"She's a Mexican?"

"Yes. And a good woman. Don't look down on her. She put a smile back on my face."

Susan had to admit, something did seem different about her daddy. Prone to being less than concerned with cleanliness, Doug stood with clean pressed clothes, a clean shaven face, and reeking of after shave. His hair was freshly greased and combed into place, at least what she could see of it from under the cap, cocked back in its customary position.

"What about your mom?"

"She's OK. She's seeing Reverend Davies."

"Good. Goes to show, there is probably someone for everybody. They are two of a kind. She still at home?"

"No. She moved to town. Tim and I are alone at the farm."

"Good deal. Guess I'll go by and see Tim then. See you later, Susan. Ira, pull on your boots and come out here for a minute. I have some business to discuss with you."

Ira pulled on his boots and a t-shirt, gave Susan a quick kiss, and walked out the door. Doug waited by his pickup.

"So, the bale loader worked out for you?"

"Yeah, it did. Way I got it figured, it may cut my losses in half."

Doug laughed. "How many bales do you reckon you'll end up with this year?"

"Around fifty thousand."

"Let's see. Normally, you'd lose about a dollar a bale. If that machine cuts your losses by half, that means I just saved you twenty five thousand dollars. Not bad, for a fifteen thousand dollar investment. Course, anywhere else, it would have cost you fifty thousand. You work what? Five thousand hours a year? That means you're only paying the bank five dollars an hour for the privilege of bein' a farmer. Not bad! Wait a minute though. I forgot to figure in the barley and the cattle. That might push it up to seven or eight dollars an hour, but you can get that back down some if you don't sleep. This farm is probably worth half a million or so—maybe you'll get to keep it another four or five years at the rate you're goin, before they foreclose on you."

"At least I got rid of my cotton habit," Ira replied, grinning.

"I've been trying to get Tim off of that stuff, but cotton is a tough one. I've seen people work theirselves into a grave over that stuff. It can really get a hold on you. They ought to make it illegal. It sure has Tim by the balls. We ought to start a new group. We can call it—Farmers Anonymous."

"Seriously, Doug, has it always been this bad? I just don't see how we can make any money."

"Well, you have a lot of people to thank for that. Start with the banks. Where else in the world can you get off so light—just paying for your property four times over before you own it? Then there is the government. Property taxes don't amount to much. Shit, when you die, your kids may even get to keep as much as thirty per cent of what you earned in your life. Ain't that wonderful of them? No wonder the Russians are switchin' over to the free enterprise system."

"I think Communist countries have it a lot worse than we do," Ira replied.

"You're right Ira. Know why? Communism don't work. They go out and tell the people right up front—you don't own nothin', you have no personal rights, and you all work for us. People earn the same, so long as they show up, so no one works hard. Productivity is low. They go fuckin' broke. Over here, we have developed a much more effective system for controlling the masses. It works similar to casino gambling. The whole thing is based on deception. They say you own your property, yet you have to pay taxes for owning it. What are taxes? Rent. Don't pay them and see what happens. You can't fart in this country without payin' taxes. Since we think we own our own property, we work harder. It is human nature. They let about one man in a thousand hit it big, and break out of the social barriers that keep the rich, rich and the poor, poor. They control the news media. They hold this guy up for the world to see and say, *if he can do it, anybody can,* kind of like they do the big winners at Vegas. Everybody sees this shit and runs out, borrows more money and works their ass plumb off. Productivity is high. The banker sits back and laughs behind your back, getting rich off of you. They manipulate prices and the market. Ever now and then, they let things go to hell, and repossess the whole country, and then they sell it back to us again. Shit, I'm getting mad just talking about it."

"So, what do we do?" Ira asked.

"I've lived long enough to know you can't change it. People are brainwashed or just don't give a damn cause they are one of the lucky ones. They've got kids praying the pledge of allegiance way before they have any idea what those words mean. Before long, they can be persuaded to do just about anything in the name of the almighty United States of America, and feel good about it. Stand up against anything this government wants to do and they will slap your ass down quick, even if you have the best interest of the people in mind. I gave up on the best interest of the dumb ass motherfuckers sittin' back and takin' this shit. The only one I am concerned with now is me and mine."

"I can't go that far, Doug. There are a lot of good people in this country."

"Lots of dumb asses. Tell me that ten years from now, after they have taken everything you own. See how many people stand up to help you when you are down. A man only has so much power. You best use yours takin care of your own, cause no one else will."

"I'm still holdin' on to a little hope. Just in case though, I've got something else workin'. Come over here and let me show you something."

Ira directed Doug to the ditch full of weeds behind his house. Amongst the kochia weeds, marijuana plants stretched their leaves toward the morning sun—a glorious sight, in Ira's eyes.

"You know what that is?" he asked the older man.

"Sure. I've seen enough of those leaves on hippie's ass pockets to know what they look like."

"Well, what do you think?"

"I still have mixed emotions about that stuff. It takes a long time to grow. You can't sell it without involving others who use it, which means you're doin' business with a bunch of dope heads—instead of reliable people. One thing about it though—it seems to be worth a lot of money. How much do you figure you can make off of a patch like that?"

"I'm hoping for a hundred grand—bare minimum, maybe more."

"Not bad. Personally, I prefer my way of doin' things."

"What do you mean by that?"

"Repossessin' farm equipment. They steal it from us; I steal it back from them. Good money in it, but it too has one big flaw."

"What is that?"

"Just like marijuana, you have to sell it to someone. Repossessin' it is the easy part. Sell enough equipment, sooner or later, the word gets out, and they catch up to you. I have something else in mind."

"Banks?"

"You got it. The object of what we both are doin' is to get cash money in our hands. So, why beat around the bush, when all the money is piled up in one place, ready for the taking? The way I see it, banks are our biggest enemy anyway, so I get the additional satisfaction of fucking them too. The government insures the bastards, so it doesn't come out of any individual's account anymore, and I can get my licks in on them too, while I'm at it. Only problem about it—to do it right, you need help—about four good men, way I got it figured. Hard to find four good men of a like mind. I have two, which makes three counting myself—one more and I am in business."

"Who?"

"You and Tim."

"Whoa there partner. I don't know about that. The thing that scares me is the possibility of having to hurt someone."

"Done right, you won't have to. I can guarantee it."

"I don't know. I need some time to think about it."

"Time is something I'm runnin' short on, Ira. It gets away from you. None of us may have as much as we think."

"What do you mean by that?"

"You know I am not a churchgoer. Don't mean I don't have beliefs. I just see things a little different than most. You ever hear about the end times, and the mark of the beast?"

"You mean 666 and all of that shit?"

"You got it, only I think it is a lot closer than people realize. I may not be a good man, but I see things goin on that worry me. We are gettin' sucked in, piece by piece, losin' more and more of our freedom, and they got us likin' it. Here is how I think it is all goin' to come down."

"First, a ruler will appear with many solutions to problems in this world. His plan will earn him the support of almost everybody, and he will be widely recognized as the savior of the world. Part of this guy's plan involves abolishing crime and controlling unauthorized, tax-free business. In order to do that, he has to get rid of cash money. Without cash money, you can't sell pussy, stolen products, dope, and, what's more, there will be a record of every transaction you make. Even income tax fraud will be eliminated. It will happen in stages though. They'll try computerized cards. Your wages will be credited directly into your account. Anything you sell will also be credited to your account, by presenting this card to be run through a scanner, deductin' money from one and adding it to another, minus the taxes and user fees, of course. When you get ready to buy something at a store, let's say, you will just swipe this card through the scanner. Then criminals will figure out how to steal or copy the cards, forcing them to come up with a better idea. *Why not install a computer chip directly into a person's body, perhaps in the forehead, or the hand?*"

"The mark of the beast?"

"You got it pal. It's 1983 right now—I can see something like this happenin' before my kids are dead. This system will give the government absolute control, which is what they want. Just think of all the other problems this will solve. They could track everybody all the time. Think about that. How can you commit a crime when they can track you anywhere you go? You can't go to a whore house they don't know about, rob a bank, a store, another person—cops will be on your ass and there ain't no way you're getting away unless you cut off you hand or your head. Child molesters, kidnappers, drug dealers, murderers—all will be out of business. No need for so many jails—cause the whole world will be one big electronic jail. Bodies can be recovered from accidents, runaway kids located. This will be the answer to all the world's problems. But, that assumes that the people runnin' the show are good and have our best interests in mind. They ain't, and they don't. Once they take cash money away, they got us."

"Even if you're right, what can you do about it?"

"I don't know, but you can rest assured of one thing. I am not going down without a fight. In the meantime, I plan to live as well as I can and I need cash to do it. I have bought some land, and I hope to fix it up. By the time I'm done, it will look like a castle."

"And when they come to take it away from you?"

"Then it's my time to die, and I ain't afraid of that. I am goin' to take as many as I can with me on that day. Anybody comes around my place is goin' to be dodging lead."

Doug and Ira walked back to Doug's pickup. Doug removed a large suitcase from the back of the truck and handed it to Ira.

"Here's your marijuana," he said.

"How did you get it up here?" Ira asked.

"Come to find out, my father in law knows a few American customs agents dissatisfied with how much money they make."

"I'll be damned."

"Look, Ira, like I said, I ain't too crazy about this dope thing, but if you can show me there's quick cash in it, and you have someone reliable to sell it to, I can get you all you want."

"It'll sell, Doug. Take my word for it. Matter of fact, I'll call Ernie and have him come down today. Why don't you stop back by tonight?"

"OK, I will. Remember, banks are where *all* the money is."

"Maybe so, Doug."

Doug left to go see Tim. Ira returned to his trailer, called Ernie, and got him started south, and then tried to con Susan back into bed.

A man spends nine months of his life tryin to get out of there and the rest tryin to get back in.

CHAPTER XXX

Ernie Coontz blew into Southwest Texas like a desert thunderstorm, hard rock music blaring from oversized speakers and dust billowing from speeding tires. He brought the party with him, in the form of a carload of girls and drugs.

Ira cringed when he saw Denise. Luckily Susan had already gone home and was not due back for several hours.

Denise walked up and kissed him, whispering, "Are you well yet?"

"Yeah," Ira said.

"Good." Denise then kissed Ira again, tongue probing deep into his mouth and hands traveling all over his body. As soon as Ernie could manage, he got her off and pulled Ira to one side to conduct a little business.

"Damn it Ernie. Why'd you bring her? I told you I got back with Susan."

"Hooked on another one, are you? I'm just trying to save your life. Looks like I arrived just in time again."

"This one is special."

"The one in Lubbock was special too, wasn't she?"

"Yeah."

"They all are special, Ira. That don't mean you have to marry them. Why buy the cow, when you can get the milk for free? You mix up sex and love."

"Maybe so, Ernie. Still, I would just as soon Susan didn't know about Denise. Please take the girls to town and rent a motel room. I'll see you there. I have a friend who wants to meet you."

"I am kinda running low on smoke, Ira. You got any handy?"

"Sure. Matter of fact, let me get a little out of the load, and you can take the rest now, while you're here. That way, you won't have to come back by the farm."

Ira was thinking ahead, trying to keep Susan from running into Ernie's wild entourage.

Doug and Tim Grant showed up that afternoon. Ira led them to the motel in McCamey for the meeting with Ernie. Ira found the room by consulting with the receptionist, an eastern Indian woman. He could have just as easily located the room by listening for the music and by trailing the cloud of marijuana smoke issuing from under the door. A naked girl answered the door. Ira barely avoided getting drawn into the fray, and somehow extracted Ernie at the same time. He led him to Doug Grant's pickup and introduced him, leaving the party behind.

Doug Grant looked at Ernie.

"Follow me to the restaurant," he told Ira.

After a few minutes of talk over coffee, Doug Grant decided he liked Ernie, and they got down to the business at hand. Ernie spent a good while trying to convince Doug to keep him supplied with marijuana, while Doug tried to sell his idea of robbing banks to the group. Before all was said and done, both parties had made concessions. If Doug and Tim would keep Ira and Ernie supplied with marijuana to sell, they in turn would help the Grants rob banks. Both parties left somewhat apprehensive about the new fields they were soon to enter, but determined to give it a shot.

Ira walked back to Ernie's room. The orgy was still in progress; this time Ira did not emerge unscathed. By the time he was able to extricate himself, Denise had thoroughly worked him over and the dawn of a new day was at hand. Meanwhile, Susan Grant lay sleeping, alone, in Ira's bed.

Ira arrived to find the bed still warm and Susan gone—a nasty note left in her place.

That evening, when Susan did return, Ira took the most logical approach he could think of—he lied. For some reason, Susan chose to believe him.

CHAPTER XXXI

The expectations Ira had for what a relationship involving sex with Susan would be like far exceeded the reality. Susan was seldom interested and acted as though the whole process was something nasty. When they did get around to it, she lay there, passively. She seemed consumed with thoughts and preparations for marriage, as though she were more interested in the concept of being married than whom she was marrying.

Ira immersed himself in his work. Favorable weather gave him an excellent looking barley crop. A neighboring farmer contracted custom combiners to harvest his grain; as soon as they were finished, they moved to Ira's field. Ira followed the first load of harvested grain to the elevator and watched it weighed. Using this as an average, he determined the field would make almost a hundred bushels to the acre. Prices were bad, but the huge yield would help make up for that. Ira returned to the farm, and watched the rest of the loads leave, headed for the grain elevator, while he did other jobs on the farm.

He kept tally of how many loads the field produced. The combines worked fast, and the field was harvested in one day. Ira was ecstatic over his success, after calculating how much the field had produced and decided this was cause for celebration. He and Susan drove to Odessa, ate out at a nice restaurant, and spent the night in an expensive hotel, watching movie channels not available in the rural area where they lived. The next day, they went by the grain elevator to pick up the check. The man at the elevator avoided making eye contact. Ira walked into the office, and a secretary handed him a sealed envelope. He opened it.

"This can't be right," he said.

"Is there a mistake?"

"The weights on these loads. The first load weighed almost twice what the rest did. How is that? I watched them leave the farm. Each time, the trailer was full, just like the first load." Ira felt the blood rushing into his ears and his scalp began to tingle.

"I work with the figures they give me sir. You will need to talk to the boss about that."

"Where is he?"

"He's not in today. Try back next week."

Ira walked to his pickup in a state of shock.

"What's wrong?" Susan asked."

"They fucked me out of half the grain."

"What do you mean?"

"I don't know exactly how they did it, but they fucked me. Look here. The first load—the one I watched them weigh, weighed twice what the rest did. I saw those loads leave. They were all the same. I should have watched them weigh every last load. You just can't trust anybody nowadays."

"What can you do about it? They shouldn't be able to get away with that."

"Not a damn thing. There is no way I can prove what they did. I must be the dumbest bastard walking the face of the earth."

"No, you're not."

"Who's dumber?"

Susan thought for a minute. "That West Texas oil man running for governor."

"OK, so there's one, but who else?"

No one else came to mind right away.

Half the money earned in six months of hard work was gone. Had he received all of it, it wouldn't have been enough to turn a profit.

CHAPTER XXXII

Ira dropped Susan off at her house and drove to the farm, finding the men hoeing in the watermelon patch.

Farming irrigated land in desert climates requires constant cultivation of the soil. Each time the ground is irrigated, the sun begins extracting the moisture out of the ground. A few days after the watering, a crust forms, and then that crust begins to contract and crack. The cracks go deep, exposing the soil underneath and allowing moisture to escape. In addition to removing weeds, which compete for the moisture, cultivation loosens the top layer of soil, which stops up the cracks.

Watermelon plants spread on the ground in vines. They are planted in rows far apart. The first cultivation can be accomplished mechanically, but once the vines begin to run, the only way to do the job is by hand, with a hoe.

Ira left three of the wetbacks hoeing, and sent the fourth, and the only one capable of driving a tractor, to cut alfalfa. While at the field, showing the men how he wanted the work done, a local boy by the name of Mike Perez drove up. "Hey Ira. What's happening?"

"I'm OK. How about you?"

"I need a job."

"I can't use you right now, Mike."

"But, I really need the work."

"Why'd you leave me hanging last month? I needed you then. I can't afford to hire people who work one day, get a check, and then don't come back, leaving me with hay laying in the field."

"Sorry I didn't call. Something came up."

"Yeah, I know how it is. Remember. This isn't the first time we have had this discussion. You work long enough to get yourself drunk or high, and then I don't see you again for two weeks. When you are here, you hardly work. I don't need people like that."

"Look at those guys," Ira said, pointing in the direction of the Mexicans, madly hoeing away at the cracked earth. "They work their asses off for twenty dollars a day and never complain. I get about ten to twelve hours a day of hard labor for my money, and they are here every day. Are you willing to do that?"

"No, but then, I ain't no wetback."

"Then you best take you ass on down the road. Sorry Mike, but that's the way it is."

"Can you at least give me a joint or two?" Mike asked.

Ira looked at the young man disgustedly. "Yeah, I guess so. You got a pack of cigarettes?"

"Yeah."

"Give me the cellophane wrapper off of it."

Ira took the wrapper and dropped a small amount of marijuana into it and handed it to Mike. Mike took the offering without saying thanks and drove off, spinning the tires on the gravel road as he left.

* * * * *

Later that evening, Ira was moving the water on a patch of alfalfa, when Leonardo came running, on foot. He was breathless and looked terrified.

"Señor, la migra está aqui!"

"Slow down Leonardo. Now, what is happening?"

Leonardo continued on, in Spanish. "The border patrol is here, and they caught my friends."

"Oh shit! Where are they?"

"At the melon patch."

"I will go see what I can do."

"What about me?"

"Hide, unless you want to get caught too."

"No, Señor."

"When every thing is cool, I will come back by this well. Stay close enough so you can see my return."

"Si, Señor."

Ira drove toward the watermelon patch, thinking to himself. *First the bastard at the grain elevator, and now, this.* He pulled up to a lime green Suburban. The three Mexicans sat in the back, peering out through an expanded metal cage—looks of fear etched into their faces.

The border patrolman stepped out of the vehicle. He was a large man—a big gut hung out over his beltline. He wore mirror-like sunglasses, which kept Ira from being able to see his eyes. The man extended his hand, as if to shake. Ira ignored the gesture.

"Don't I know you from somewhere?" The border patrolman asked.

"I don't think so," Ira replied.

"I assume you are Ira Jones?"

"Yeah."

"Well, Ira. I am going to have to haul these guys off. They have no documentation proving they are here legally. Would you like to tell me where the other one is?"

"What other one?"

"Would you like to pay these guys before I go?"

"Can I?"

"I wouldn't ask if I didn't have to. Makes me no difference one way or the other."

Ira wrote a check for each of the Mexicans and handed them to the border patrolman.

Ira then said, "I guess you're really proud of what you do for the country."

"Matter of fact, I am."

"What gives you the right to say who can be here and who can't?"

"The law."

"Well, sometimes the law sucks."

"We have to have laws to keep these folks out. We would be overrun if we didn't. There aren't enough jobs for the people already here as it is. Each one of these guys takes a job away from a law abiding American citizen."

"Where did your ancestors come from?"

"What does that have to do with anything?"

"Everything."

"My folks are from Kansas."

Ira looked at the man's name tag. "Schmidt, huh? Good Kansas name. Sounds German to me."

"My great grandparents were German."

"The blood in these folks you have in your wagon here is at least ninety percent Native American. While your ancestors were running around Europe, theirs occupied this very ground where we now stand. Now you come along and tell them they have no right to be here."

"That's the law." Officer Schmidt replied.

"Law my ass. We came over here—raped, robbed, and pillaged to get this ground, then made laws—no more raping, robbing, or pillaging. Talk all you want about the law being fair, but I ain't buying it."

Officer Schmidt was getting mad now. "The lifestyle you enjoy would not be available if it weren't for us. We have a higher standard of living because of our government and its laws. I won't stand here and listen to you bad mouth my country."

"Anything we have was earned by the sweat of our parents," Ira said, "and their parents before them, not the people running this government. Anything this government has was taken from citizens, and is used up by a bunch of leeches like you."

"I won't stand for any more of this."

"You will as long as you are standing on my property. I hire Mexicans for one reason and one reason only. They work harder and do jobs no American wants to do. Sure, I can find someone to come out here and take a check from me, after fucking off half the day, but I cannot find people willing to work like these guys. A law that punishes them for that is not just. Big corporations hire them down south of the border for a lot less than I pay them and bring the stuff back without paying taxes on it. But you fuck with little guys like me."

"I have heard enough. It is my duty to tell you one more thing, before I go. The law is changing. Soon, you will face fines and possible imprisonment for hiring illegal aliens. If you do not comply with this new law, I will personally see to it that you are one of the first in line to suffer the consequences."

"Get off of my land."

"I will be back."

By now, the Mexicans in the back of the suburban were wishing Ira would shut up. They were the ones who had to ride off with the guy.

When officer Schmidt got back to his office, he filed a report on Ira Jones, branding him as a possible revolutionary terrorist. From that day forward, his name would occupy a prominent place in government files.

CHAPTER XXXIII

Ira walked into the farm co-op. Walter Dean and Bubba Cooper occupied their normal positions in the store, making sure their two favorite chairs didn't run off.

"Howdy Mr. Dean. Mr. Cooper."

"Hello son, what can we do for you?" Cooper asked.

"I need another piece of that orange tarp we use for irrigating."

Both Dean and Cooper looked at the roll suspended from the roof near a back wall in the store, but neither made a move toward it. "Go ahead, and cut off what you want. The yard stick is over there, right by the roll."

Ira rolled off and measured what he needed, cutting it with his pocketknife. When done, he went over to talk to the old timers.

"How are things going on the old place?" Cooper asked.

"Not good. Just about the time I was starting to get caught up, the border patrol showed up and hauled off my help."

"We heard."

"I don't know why they hit me. People all around here got wets working, and they get me."

"There's a reason for that," Dean responded.

"Really. What is it? I'd like to know, so I could keep those bastards off of my ass."

"It is too late for that now. You got them pissed off at you son. You wouldn't want to do what's necessary anyhow."

"Try me."

"Well, I've heard tell that certain farmers around here have an agreement with the border patrol. They notify them, every time they see a wet. Then, when they need hands, the agents let them be for a while. The farmer gets done with them, he gives the border patrol a call, and they come pick them up. The farmer gets by without paying their wages, and the border patrol gets his quota filled."

"You're shitting me?"

"Afraid not, son."

"Who does that kind of shit?"

"I am not inclined to name names. Look around you. You'll figure it out. A man has to learn how to live with the law in this life to get by, not spend all his days buttin' heads with it.

"Fuck the law."

"I told you you weren't prepared to do what you needed to do. Don't get mad at me over it son."

"I hope I don't ever get so sorry I'll stoop to that to survive. How much do I owe you for the tarp?"

Cooper made out a receipt for the tarp, charging it to the Jones's account. After Ira left, he turned to Dean and said, "That boy is trouble. These young ones think they can come in here and change the way we've done things for years."

Dean added, "And they either learn to adapt to the way things are, or they go broke. He won't last another year."

CHAPTER XXXIV

Ira found Leonardo up early in the morning, hoeing furiously at the earth around a pepper plant. Jose stood by, watching him work.

"What are you going to do, now that your friends are gone?" Ira asked the wiry young Mexican. "I am afraid the border patrol will return for you."

"I will stay. As long as you let me, I will stay, and I will work."

"You don't fear getting caught?"

"Sure, but that is a chance I must take."

Leonardo loosened the soil several inches under the surface and then pulled the softened earth up to the base of the plants.

"These pepper plants are doing very well," Ira said.

"It is because of the hoeing," Jose added. "It fills the cracks—the ground breathes, and the roots do better, because the soil is not so heavy on them."

"Have you considered growing a large field of them?" Leonardo asked. "I think you have a good climate for raising peppers."

"I am sure we can grow good peppers here, but who would pick them? People here don't want that kind of work. If they do take the job, they won't work hard, and they charge too much for their labor. It'd end up costing me more to raise peppers than they're worth."

"I know how to make money off of this land," Jose offered.

"Oh yeah?" Ira asked. Normally, Jose refrained from giving advice on the running of the farm, preferring to take his orders, do his job, and draw his wage.

"Yes sir, I do. You try to make money growing food. People in this country have too much food. They are fat with food. They don't care about people who grow food. But, their spirits are poor. They want drink. Plant grapes; make wine. Plant barley; make beer and whiskey. The poorer they get, the more they want drink."

"You might have something there. Those grapes growing by your house do very well. With drip irrigation systems, we could water much more land and use less water. They like heat and sunshine; we get plenty of that, and they are tough as hell. They stand up well to the wind."

"I'm right Ira. I have thought long about this. I spend my money on drink. All my friends do the same. Everybody wants to forget his pain. There is much pain in this world, so there is much need for drink. The rich want it for they are poor in spirit, and the poor want it to forget their pain."

"But, don't you think we would only add to their problems by selling them booze?"

"You did not ask me how to help people. You asked how to make money with this land. Helping people is another matter. There is no money in that."

"Very true, my friend. Thanks for the advice, Jose."

"I did it for me. I like working here. You will go broke growing food for people. People are too fat in this country. Food is everywhere, but drink—the people never get enough to drink."

Ira heard truth in the old man's words. He also saw a measure of sadness in his eyes. Sometimes the truth bears a measure of pain.

CHAPTER XXXV

Ira woke on a Sunday, bathed in sweat, after a restless night, plagued with nightmares, in which he was involved in a deadly shootout while robbing a bank. He rolled over and reached for Susan, but she repelled his advances.

He persisted.

"I'll trade you," she finally suggested. "You want me? I want a favor."

"What is the favor?"

"Susan straddled Ira and kissed him seductively, teasing him, without giving up the prize.

"Oh come on Susan, don't do this to me."

"Will you do me the favor?"

"Yes."

Susan rolled over and let Ira have his way with her. Afterwards, she jumped up and stated, "Get up Ira. We have somewhere to go."

"Oh yeah. Where is that?"

"We need to pick up Tim on our way to church."

"Who said anything about going to church?"

"The favor…"

"Oh no. Please, no…"

"You promised."

"But church. Not church."

"You promised!"

"OK, but I'm not wearing a suit, and I'm sitting in the back row, and I ain't standing up when they announce visitors, and I ain't singing, and…damn it Susan, why are you making me do this?"

"You promised."

"Please Susan. Think of the rest of the church members. What if it causes an earthquake or something? The holy water might start boiling and burn someone."

"We don't have holy water! Shut up and get dressed. You promised, and that is that."

"Tim is going too?"

"Yes, Tim and Lisa are going."

Ira put on his best pair of jeans and a white western shirt. The two drove by the Grant place to discover that Lisa had also corralled Tim. Tim came out clutching at the knot of a tie, as though it was choking him. Martha Grant was waiting when they arrived at the church, staring in approval as the two pairs walked up to the building.

"Hi, Ira," Martha Grant said.

"Hi, Mrs. Grant," he replied.

"That is no longer my name. I am Mrs. Davies now."

"Oh, OK. I'm sorry, I guess. I mean..."

"When are you and Susan planning to get married?"

"Uh... I don't know for sure..." Ira looked at Susan, hoping for some support.

"Mom wants us to have our wedding two weeks from now."

"Here? A church wedding? I just kind of figured we'd go to the justice of the peace, or something."

"You should be married in the church, to make it stick."

Ira looked around for support and got none. Tim jabbed him in the ribs.

"Aren't you ready to get married?" Susan asked. The remaining three all had looks on their faces like, *yeah, don't you want to marry her?*

"Of course I am," he said. *I think,* he thought.

"Why not in two weeks, then?"

"Well, but, shit...excuse me Mrs. Grant...I mean Mrs. Davies. Sorry... Why not?"

Susan shrieked and grabbed Ira around the neck.

"What about you and Lisa?" Mrs. Davies asked Tim. "You have been procrastinating long enough also. We could have a double wedding and save some money."

Tim went from laughing to standing with the blood draining from his face. *They had been set up.*

"What about it Tim? Do you really love me, or have you just been leading me on?" Lisa asked.

"But...I don't have anything to offer you right now. How can we go on a honeymoon, when the crops aren't in?"

"I don't care about any of that. I just want you. We can't go on living in sin. What if I get pregnant?"

A sinking feeling hit Tim in the pit of the stomach. He didn't think his mother knew he had been carrying on with Lisa. He could barely meet her now steely gaze.

"Well Tim?" his mother asked.

Tim tried to say *yes* but the word kind of hung in his throat.

"What was that?" Ira asked.

"Yeah, I will."

Lisa now shrieked with joy. Soon, they were surrounded by other members of the church, congratulating them.

The call to the service was sounded, and the group of soon-to-be-weds wandered into the building. Ira turned into the last pew, but Mrs. Davies rerouted him with one wave of a crooked finger and a sharp look. They ended up on the front row. Ira had never before been to a Pentecostal service, having been raised a non-practicing catholic, and soon found himself surrounded by dancing, hand-waving, song-singing church members, but that was nothing compared to what followed. People began breaking out into strange *tongues*. Ira turned around and realized that only he and Tim and a handful of bored looking children were not caught up in some sort of trance. One of the little kids smiled at him as if to say, *can you believe this?*

Ira maintained his composure until one young man standing beside him dropped to the ground in what appeared to be an epileptic seizure. The young man's body writhed and convulsed, spit flew from his mouth. Ira stared in horror.

"Praise God!" the boy's father shouted. "My prayer has been answered. My boy is slain in the spirit! hallelujah!" The boy's dad danced with joy around his writhing son. A few members of the congregation clapped the father on the back and joined in on the hallelujahs. Ira wondered if he should try to keep the boy from swallowing his tongue. The spasms subsided just about the time he was about to make his move.

* * * * *

After the service, Martha Davies asked, "Wasn't it wonderful when Ed Connelly's boy accepted the Holy Spirit?"

"Yeah, I guess. I can't say I ever saw someone accept the spirit quite like that. I was raised a Catholic, you know."

"If you come around a few more times, you'll accept him too, just like that boy did," Mrs. Davies stated confidently.

I goddamned sure hope not, Ira thought to himself. *Nothing looked very holy about that spirit.*

CHAPTER XXXVI

Angela lasted only three days in her mother's house before a heated argument broke out. Angela's new stepfather couldn't take his eyes off of her, and her mom wanted to stop things before they got started. Once again, she accused Angela of tempting her man. The resulting fight drove Angela to the one thing she knew well—stripping at a seminude bar and selling herself on the side. She got a job in the first place she tried. Another dancer offered her a place to stay on the second night. A motel room at a client's expense took care of the first.

The roommate turned out to be a lesbian, and Angela found herself repelling advances almost immediately after moving in. The men came in all shapes and sizes, all wanting the same thing in a slightly different flavor. She catered to their fantasies, playing whatever part they desired, but her heart was no longer in the work.

New girls showed up at the club—younger than Angela—also possessing near perfect bodies, and a lust for the trade. Before long, they were the main attractions. Angela was getting old, at the ripe old age of twenty-three, and she knew it.

CHAPTER XXXVII

Officer Kelly Brown was Upton County's finest, or so he liked to think. Brown was a big man, especially around the waist.

Brown arrived in Upton County after being dismissed from a similar job in Georgia when he was accused of having sex with a thirteen-year-old girl. The charges were dismissed and dropped with prejudice when he agreed to leave and never return. Kelly swore his innocence to the end.

Kelly Brown's wife and four daughters lived in a remote ranch house and were seldom seen in town. His wife taught the children in home school. Once a week they visited the local Pentecostal church. Kelly liked the idea of keeping his women in church.

Deep-seated insecurities seemed to vanish when Kelly Brown strapped on his uniform: shiny badge and boots in place, the thick black belt, complete with handcuffs and holster containing his revolver riding low on broad hips, mirrored sunglasses shining brightly from his plump face. When on duty, his chest stuck out another inch or two and his gaze seldom wavered. He loved it when criminals cringed at his arrival, and delighted in stories circulating, describing how he had roughed up a local scumbag drug dealer in a fight.

Kelly also took pride from an event where he single handedly arrested two smugglers whose plane crash landed near McCamey; but this had been two years ago and the thought didn't carry the weight it once had. Kelly Brown wanted something new to feel good about. That morning he got a lead—from the preacher no less—a lead bearing the name of Doug Grant.

Rumors had circulated for some time about Grant's comings and goings. Kelly did a background check and discovered that Doug was suspected of stealing farm equipment in his home state of Kansas, but had never actually been charged nor convicted. Kelly Brown operated under the premise that where there's smoke, there's fire.

* * * * *

Doug Grant had heard of Kelly Brown though he had never spoken to the man. When he saw the unusually colored police car pull up, a color Doug described as a cross between piss yellow and puke green, his face hardened. Doug was sitting in a small café drinking coffee. In his pickup, waiting outside, was a load of marijuana, destined for Plainview, Texas, and the house of Ernie Coontz.

Doug puffed on his cigarette and took a large gulp of hot coffee, scarcely noticing that it scalded his tongue.

Kelly Brown lumbered out of the piss yellow, puke green car, and surveyed his domain, stretching out like a sleepy old lion. One look at a young Mexican kid sent him scurrying. Kelly strode into the café and sat down. His eyes immediately found Gloria, the main reason he frequented the place, and he bellowed a loud greeting to her.

Gloria was seventeen. At one time she had made the mistake of offering sexual favors to Kelly Brown in order to keep her older brother from going back to prison. She now despised the man, but could not afford to let her true feelings be known. She had seen a dangerous, sadistic side of him and it left her scared.

Kelly watched the pretty young Mexican girl's every move. Only after having received his coffee did his gaze wander elsewhere; when it did, it ran squarely into the ice blue eyes of Doug Grant. Kelly looked away. He felt his pulse quicken. His breathing became laborious. After a moment, he looked back. Doug Grant stared at him. Once again, Kelly looked away.

The feeling of power and authority he had worn when entering the café was nowhere to be found. He could feel the crushing weight of Doug Grants stare, pressing into his back. Subconsciously, his hand slid down to make sure his revolver was still in place. It was, but brought little relief.

Doug Grant stood up and walked by officer Brown's table; as he did, Kelly Brown cringed. Doug paid for his coffee, turned one final time to glance at officer Brown and walked out. Kelly noticed his hand shook when he tried to take a drink of coffee.

A minute or so after Doug left, Kelly regained his composure, jumped up and headed for the door without paying his bill, or saying goodbye to Gloria—something she found quite unusual.

Outside, Kelly looked both ways, trying to discern which way Doug Grant had gone. He got into his car and started the engine. His heart was racing and sweat beaded on his forehead.

"Son-of-a-bitch!" he hollered. "I am going to get you, you son-of-a-bitch!"

Kelly sped off in pursuit of Doug Grant; fortunately in the wrong direction.

CHAPTER XXXVIII

Doug Grant showed up at Ira's with Tim riding alongside. "Ernie hasn't made it down with your money yet, but he did say he got the marijuana sold," Ira explained.

Why don't we run up there and pick it up then," Doug suggested. "I have more for him."

"I have mechanic work I really need to get done. The border patrol took all my wets but one and work's stacking up all around me."

"I'll make a deal with you then. Come with us tonight. The four of us will sit down and discuss a little business. I need twenty-four hours of your time. When we get back, I'll help you with your mechanic work."

"The robbery?" Ira asked.

"Not yet. I have something else in mind."

"What's that?"

"I'll tell you on the way. Get you men lined out and let's go."

"We'll be back by tomorrow night?"

"Yes sir."

Ira gave Jose and Leonardo instructions and left without talking to Susan, opting to leave a note behind instead.

"Tim told me you are going to have a double wedding next week," Doug stated, soon after Ira hit the seat.

"Yeah."

"I figured you were smarter than that."

"I did too," Ira said. "I've been cussing myself ever since those awful words slipped out of my mouth, but it's too late now. Mom and dad and the whole crew are coming down."

"It won't kill you—right away, anyhow. Who knows, you might even learn to like it."

"Are you coming to the wedding?" Ira asked.

"Hell no. I would sooner brave the fires of hell. They got nothin' I want or need in that church"

"You ever see anyone get slain in the spirit?" Ira asked.

"You mean when they get down and roll around on the floor?"

"Yeah, that's it."

"There's more than one spirit on this planet, and they ain't all holy."

"That's kind of the way I got it figured too."

"I heard you got screwed on your barley crop."

"Yeah. Sorry bastards cheated me on the weight."

"I've seen it done. They rig the scale by wedging a board into the springs underneath the platform. That's what I wanted to talk to you about. It's time you learned how to get even. We are going to pay a couple of visits to the grain elevator."

"We're going to rob them?" Ira asked.

"No, nothing like that. We are going to get your grain back and sell it to them again. In order to do that, we'll need a few trucks and trailers. I have two. Tonight, I'm getting a third. I'll need help. You and Ernie are going to give it to me."

"Is this going to be dangerous?"

"Of course. Driving down the highway is dangerous. What does that have to do with anything?"

"Well, I'm not particularly interested in the prospect of getting killed at this point in my life, and I don't particularly want to kill anyone else if I can avoid it either."

"Don't worry about that. Anyone needs killin'; I'll take care of it. All you got to do is help me load them trucks and get paid. Can Ernie drive a truck?"

"Of course. He's a farm boy, same as me."

"Is that right?"

"Yeah. His dad still has a farm, but I don't think they farm it any more. They have it leased out."

"We're in business then. How's he doing with the marijuana?"

"It's a little slow. The stuff you have been bringing isn't very good. People are crying for better weed."

"My man in Mexico tells me this is all they have until the new crop comes in. I'm makin' a couple of grand a week off of the shit, but I take a lot of chances."

"Wait until you get some good pot. I guarantee you'll make money then."

"Maybe so. In the meantime, I'm going to show *you* how to make money, and get back at the sorry bastards that fucked you over—all at the same time."

Ira looked at Tim. Tim smiled. Ira was about to be introduced to the noble art of repossessin'.

CHAPTER XXXIX

"Susan is pissed at you," Ira told Doug Grant. "Why?"

"I'm not sure if it is because you didn't go to the wedding or if it is because you dragged her husband off two days after the wedding. One or the other did the trick."

"What does she expect? You need to make some money, son."

"Yeah, it's her fault anyway. I don't know why in the hell she had to get in such a rush to get married."

"Show up with a pocket full of cash and a nice gift and you'll be OK."

"So, how are we going to do this, Doug?"

"Just like we discussed. It'll be a piece of cake. Here we are."

Doug dropped Ira off at a semi-truck with a grain trailer behind. Ira started the engine, and let it warm up. Ernie came over, after starting his, and offered Ira a snort of crank. Ira took him up on it.

"What do you think about this, Ernie?"

"I've been looking all over for some reason it ain't gonna work, and I just can't find one. Damn it. We got no choice but to go on and do it, I guess."

"I guess you're right. Won't hurt my feelings to get back at that bastard."

"Let's go for it, then."

Doug led the way. Behind followed three grain trucks. Doug pulled up to the gate of the mill, opened the lock and led the trucks to the loading area. The night watchman approached and unlocked the elevator and helped fill the trucks with grain. When all three trucks were loaded, they cleaned up any evidence of their having been there. Bright and early the next morning, Ira arrived at the mill with his compatriots and sold the grain back to the same mill, telling the owner it was some he had cut and stored in his own silo. They rested throughout the day at their homes, and then returned to the grain elevator again that night. The group repeated this process for an entire week.

At one point, Ira had to stifle a laugh when the man docked him for too much moisture in the grain, telling him it would have to be dried before he could put it in the storage silo to keep it from spoiling—the same silo he had removed it from about four hours earlier.

Ira decided it was tough to make money selling grain, even when you stole the stuff. His share of ill-gotten gains for a week's work barely covered what he had been shorted by the mill.

CHAPTER XL

Tim and Lisa pulled up to the trailer house where Susan and Ira lived after Susan invited them over for supper. After the meal, Ira and Tim left the women at the trailer, and then went out, supposedly to check on an irrigation well. No sooner had they cleared the door, than the serious talk began.

"Man, I didn't know being married was going to be like this," Ira stated. "Susan wants to run my life now she has that ring on her finger."

"Tell me about it. Lisa hardly resembles the girl I dated for the past two years."

"Has she said anything about our escapades?"

"That's *all* she talks about."

"Susan too. I think they are ganging up against us."

"Think hell, I know they are. And mom is in on it too. She's teaching them. I don't know how it happened, but Lisa is pregnant. We've been having sex for two years, and nothing. One month of marriage, and she's pregnant. How the hell did that happen?"

"I better be careful too."

"You're too late."

"Think so? What are we going to do Tim? Your dad is hell-bent on robbing banks. That ain't exactly my idea of a steady job to raise a family on."

"I don't know either. My cotton crop is looking pretty good. I'm hoping…"

"What about the prices?"

"Not too good, but better than expected. I may have a hell of a yield though."

"Are you scared Tim…I mean, about robbing banks?"

"Yes…shitless."

"I am too. I don't think your dad is."

"He ain't. That's what worries me. Dad just doesn't give a damn."

"I know what you mean."

Ira rolled a joint and the two young farmers headed to Ira's weed patch.

"Damn, Ira. That stuff must be over six feet tall."

"Sure is. My bank robbing days are going to be over before they begin if this stuff makes it. I don't need a whole lot of money."

"Me, neither. Has Susan said anything to you about smoking weed?"

"Yeah. She quit. Now she's trying to get me to quit. What's worse, she keeps trying to make me cut this patch down."

"Lisa quit too. Funny thing about it though. She don't mind spending the money we make off of the stuff."

"I haven't ever seen Susan turn down any money either."

"How's Ernie doing, but the way?"

"He's still selling a few pounds, but in all honesty, he ain't gonna be able to sell much until we get some better pot. Nowadays, if the weed is no good, people'd just as soon get their high out of a bottle. Ernie's friends like that pharmacy shit."

"I noticed he seemed pretty fucked up a time or two."

"He tends to stay that way. We better get on back to the house. The girls will be mad. Somehow or other we need to come up with an excuse to go to Plainview."

"It will be hard for me to get away. I've got ass loads of work to do."

"Me too, but Ernie has some money for us. I'm about half a mind to go, even though we *don't* have any more marijuana to take him."

"Why is that?"

"You know me. There are good women, and there are bad women. I can't seem to wean myself off of that second type. I know the stuff is bad for me, but I just keep going back for more. You ever sleep with anyone other than Lisa?"

"Nope. Doesn't mean I don't think about it, though." Tim looked at the small roach in his hand and smoked the last little bit. "I just don't see how we can get away. I have too much to do."

"I guess you're right. Hell bein' a grown up, isn't it?"

CHAPTER XLI

Shorter days brought changes to the Trans-Pecos region of Texas and the lives of Ira Jones and Tim Grant. Both stayed home more, as crops neared maturity—hoping for a miracle—hoping to survive without resorting to robbing banks.

Doug Grant and Ernie Koontz did not allow themselves to get caught up in the harvest madness, choosing rather to continue working in their respective fields of expertise, selling dope and stealing.

Both Susan Jones and Lisa Grant became pregnant, and managed to reel their somewhat wild husbands in a notch or two, but it took plenty of conniving and conspiring to get the job done. Many a day and night were spent working on strategies.

The sheer load of work associated with the end of summer was, of itself, enough to keep the two newly wed men in line. There just wasn't enough time for anything but work. For once, it appeared, hard, dedicated labor on a farm might pay off.

Ira had a decent year raising alfalfa, considering the slow start. The new machinery enabled him to get his crops baled and removed from the field effectively. Ira's hopes did not however, rest entirely on alfalfa. In an inconspicuous looking ditch full of Kochia weeds, stood several hundred monstrous cannabis plants, and in them rested Ira's hope for a successful year.

Tim had no marijuana, but even Doug Grant had to concede he had the best field of stripper cotton ever grown in the region; row after row of huge plants, loaded from top to bottom with hundreds of bulging bowls covered his field, and prices held at steady levels.

One day, the two young farmers converged at Tim's field.

Ira said, "I got to hand it to you, Tim. That is the most beautiful crop I have ever seen. You got a stripper lined up yet?"

"Yeah. I'm not waiting for a freeze, not with this kind of crop at stake. I hired an aerial sprayer to put out arsenic acid so I can get this out of here before bad weather comes along."

"I'd say that is a good idea. Can't ever tell what the weather might do. Who you got to spray the field?"

"Mr. Dean hooked me up with some guy from Pecos. He is supposed to be here tomorrow."

"Tomorrow? You know that shit works fast. You will need to be ready to harvest in a week. Are you sure you have your stripper ready?"

"He says he is ready when we are. Dad is supposed to go by and make sure for me this afternoon."

"He's around?"

"Yeah, he blew through last night on his way to Lubbock. He'll be back tonight."

"Where are the strippers working?"

"Some farm near Coyonosa. Not much cotton ready yet. Later, It may be hard to get someone out here."

"Your dad say anything about robbing banks?"

"Don't he always? At least he's giving me a chance to see what I can do with this cotton crop. I'm hoping I'll make enough to carry me through the winter. You know him. He's impatient. Even the dope business doesn't make money fast enough to suit him."

"I think we got a shot at pacifying him. Between your cotton crop, my marijuana patch, and what Ernie generates selling dope, we're going to make a pile of money."

"I sure hope so."

CHAPTER XLII

Doug Grant pulled his pickup up to a cotton field where three four-row strippers worked; two more sat near the edge of the field. Grease and dust covered men worked on the disabled machines, occasionally letting a cuss word fly when things didn't go their way.

Doug walked up to a large man, watching the others work.

"Mr. Nuehoff?" he asked.

"Yes sir," he answered, with the hint of a German accent in his reply. "What can I do for you?" he asked, offering a huge, meaty hand to Doug in greeting. Doug accepted the handshake, noting strength in the man's grip.

"I'm Doug Grant—Tim's dad. I understand Tim contacted you about stripping his cotton."

"Yes sir, he did."

"How are things coming along here? It looks like you still have quite a bit to do."

"It has been slow so far. You know how it is, getting your machines going at the beginning of harvest season. Belts are worn, bearings rusted. Everything that can happen will happen."

"I know. Tim is ready to spray tomorrow. I don't think he should if you're not going to be on time."

"Tell him to go ahead and spray."

"Are you sure?"

"Yes sir. I will be there."

"I just want to make sure. Once that stuff is put on, the plant dies and becomes fragile. It also costs quite a bit to get it sprayed. Damn near every year, we get some bad weather around here. We don't have insurance. I'd hate to see him lose his crop."

"I'll be there."

"I'm taking your word on that. Don't let me down."

"I won't."

"You'd best not. It ain't healthy."

Doug Grant turned and walked off.

"I wonder what he meant by that?" Nuehoff asked one of the mechanics, who had listened in on the conversation.

"I don't know boss, but something tells me we better be there the day his cotton gets ready."

"He can wait his turn, same as anybody else," Nuehoff replied.

I don't know about that, the mechanic thought, watching the retreating figure of Doug Grant.

CHAPTER XLIII

Tim watched the yellow bi-winged plane swoop down for the last time across the field, spraying its lethal cargo of arsenic acid in misty clouds which settled slowly to the plants below. By the next day, all the leaves were wilted and the sun's rays started drying the plants. Many bowls were already open; any near maturity popped after the application of the poison. What earlier that year had been eighty acres of barren dirt now was covered with beautiful white rows of cotton stretching from one end of the field to the other.

Tim called Nuehoff's secretary. Everything was on schedule.

Harvest day arrived, but not Mr. Nuehoff. Tim called again. There had been a small delay. Tomorrow was now the word.

Tim drove by the cotton field. A feeling of pride swelled in his chest, checked only by fear of losing the crop.

That evening, a few clouds developed, but no rain fell. Tim spent most of the night watching thunderstorms on the horizon. The next day came and went. Still no strippers. Then another. And another. The secretary gave Tim the runaround.

Finally, late one afternoon, Nuehoff and his crew showed up. He had run another farmer in ahead of Tim. Of course, he didn't bother telling Tim that.

"You scared the shit out of me," Tim told the man. "At least you're here now."

"Had some trouble getting parts for some of my strippers. Sure is a pretty field of cotton you have there son. Best I have seen by far. Must be three bales to the acre."

"You think so?"

"I know so."

"Are you ready to get started?"

"Yeah, we'll make a few passes this afternoon. Should be able to knock it out tomorrow with no problem."

That afternoon Nuehoffs's men stripped about fifteen acres before shutting down for the day. The piece they stripped averaged over three bales to the acre by Tim's calculations.

That night, Tim sat at the dinner table with his young wife.

"How's the cotton looking?" she asked.

"Beautiful. I swear, that is the best field of cotton I have ever seen."

"Good, honey. You deserve it."

"I don't know about that, but it is good."

Just as Tim was dozing off for the night, he heard a sound, a sound he did not want to acknowledge.

"Is that thunder? he asked.

"Yeah, but way off in the distance," Lisa answered. "It has being doing that every night. Don't worry Tim."

A few minutes later, a bolt of lightning flashed near Tim's home. Tim walked to the front porch and looked out. The sky was pitch black; the smell of rain was in the air. The wind swirled, stirring dust from the powder dry desert floor. More lightning flashed, nearer this time, followed by a clap of thunder. Tim watched quietly. A drop hit the roof. Then another. Lisa came out and stood by Tim. She held his arm and peered out into the inky blackness. More drops fell—big drops.

"Will that hurt?" Lisa asked.

"It's not good, but it hasn't hurt us yet," he answered.

The tempo of the rain increased gradually. Tim commented as it did. "We won't be stripping tomorrow—it'll take a day or two to dry out now."

The wind began to blow. Flashes of lightning revealed ominous, dark, swirling clouds, billowing high into the night sky. Seconds later, sheets of wind-driven rain began to fall.

"Is that bad?" Lisa asked, fearing the reply. Tim did not answer. Stonily, he stared out at the sky.

"Please, Lord," he whispered.

As if to answer Tim's plea, another noise joined that of the rain. *Tick,* then *Tick-tick,* then *TICK!* On the roof.

"Oh my God," Tim pleaded.

"What is it, Tim?" Lisa asked in alarm.

The ticks turned into a roar, steadily pounding the Grant home.

"It is goddamned hail! Haven't you ever seen hail before?" Tim exploded.

In minutes, the ground was covered with golf balls sized hailstones, and then, almost as quickly as it had come, the storm was gone. The rain stopped, leaving eerie silence in its place. Tim broke from Lisa's grasp.

"Where are you going?" she yelled after him. He did not reply.

Tim ran to his pickup and drove to the cotton field. Using a powerful spotlight connected to the cigarette lighter, he surveyed the field. He could scarcely tell any difference between the rows that had been stripped and those that hadn't. All were bare, except for a few tattered shreds of dirty, mud splashed cotton, which still hung on to the spindly stems.

Tim drove to town and bought a bottle of whiskey. He drank most of it on the way home, and laid down in a drunken stupor. His pregnant wife lay next to him, crying.

CHAPTER XLIV

The storm totally devastated some areas; others only miles away remained unaffected. Ira walked out to his marijuana patch, fearing the worst, to discover that the wind had caused a few plants to lean over some, but nothing more. What he saw on the way to Tim's house sickened him.

Mr. Nuehoff and his crew were loading their equipment and leaving. Where beautiful rows of cotton had been the day before, stood row after row of bare, stick-like stalks, with occasional shreds of tattered bits of useless muddy cotton dangling from the branches. Between the rows were thick piles of crud—a mixture of cotton, leaves and mud, laced with arsenic; had it not been poisoned, it could have served for cattle feed—as it was, it was useless.

Ira continued on to Tim's house without bothering to stop and talk with Nuehoff. There was nothing to be said. Lisa met him at the door.

"Where's Tim?" he asked.

"He's still in bed," she replied.

"In bed?"

"Yeah. He's drunk, Ira."

"Tim…drunk? Damn. He must have taken it hard."

"Is it? Is it all gone, Ira?"

"Yes. I'm afraid so."

"Tim worked so hard. It just isn't fair. What are we going to do?" Lisa looked grief-stricken.

Ira hugged her. "Don't worry. We'll think of something."

The words were little consolation. Ira started toward Tim's bedroom.

"He won't get up. I already tried."

Ira continued walking into the bedroom. The smell of alcohol laced vomit struck him in the face.

"Start a bath," he told Lisa.

Ira began to tug at his friend. "Get up Tim."

"Leave me alone. Can't you see I'm sleeping?"

"You have puke all over you. Get up!"

"It was a bad storm, Ira. Wiped me out."

"I saw. What good is this going to do?"

"You see Nuehoff?"

"Yeah. He was just leaving when I went by."

"Son of a bitch. If he'd been here on time, none of this would have happened."

"You didn't insure the crop, did you?"

"No. Of course not. You know how it is. If you have insurance and make a crop, all your profit goes to the insurance company. Besides, you know dad. If I were to take out an insurance policy, he would disown me."

Ira guided Tim to the bathroom. "Get cleaned up and get your clothes on. I'll be back for you."

"Why? The crop is gone."

"Yours ain't the only crop in the country. I need help. I can't possibly get all that shit harvested by myself. The hail missed me."

"Is it ready?"

"It is ready to start on. I am not going to harvest the whole plant. I'm just going to cut individual buds."

"That is yours, Ira."

"I'm cutting you in. There's more than enough for the both of us and I can't do it all myself. Get your crying ass up and come help me."

Tim looked at Lisa. She didn't want him involved with marijuana. However, she much preferred seeing him do that than what they did with Doug Grant. Whatever that was, it had to be worse. Tim refused to talk about it, even in his weakest moments.

"You might as well. You're going to anyway," she said.

Tim clothed himself and the two headed for Ira's marijuana patch.

CHAPTER XLV

Clipping buds off of the marijuana plants turned out to be more difficult than Ira anticipated. The branches of the marijuana plants were abrasive, and the resin coating them irritated the skin. Ira was also allergic to Kochia weed and Johnson grass, both of which were in full bloom around the plants. A few minutes in the patch had his eyes itching and watering, his nose gushing snot, and sneezing violently. Smoking joints brought relief, but only temporarily: the result being Ira smoked non-stop. By the end of an abbreviated day, they had cut enough buds to yield a hundred pounds of dry marijuana and had more to go.

Ira put the buds into burlap tow sacks, filled only half full and then laid out the sacks on rocks, loosely spreading the contents along the entire length of the bag. Ira hoped the marijuana would dry more slowly this way, preventing it from breaking down into shake.

Ira and Tim got back to the trailer about the time Mike Perez drove up. Ira looked suspiciously at Mike, believing he had been the one that called the border patrol.

"Hi, Ira," Mike said.

"What do you want?"

"I'm still looking for work."

"I can't use you."

"Come on Ira. I really need the money."

"Sorry Mike. I need a hand, but not you."

"Do you have any marijuana I can borrow? At least give me something to smoke."

Ira shook his head, reached into his pocket, and removed a baggie he had been smoking out of. The weed was some of his own, harvested only days before, and still not totally dry.

"Thanks, Ira."

"Don't come back, Mike. I'm tired of seeing your face."

Mike took the bag and left. One look at the semi-dry weed set his mind to working. He'd seen homegrown before. Mike drove about a mile down the road, parked his pickup and snuck back into Ira's place on foot. He picked up the men's tracks and followed them to the ditch containing the marijuana.

That night, Mike and a friend returned and helped themselves to all of the sacked buds. It almost filled the bed of his truck in its green state.

* * * * *

Ira woke early and walked back to the marijuana patch. One look told the whole story. Mike's tracks were everywhere. He had taken only the harvested weed, but that represented the best of the crop. Most of the remaining buds were smaller or not totally mature. Ira went berserk.

His first impulse was to find Mike Perez before he had time to dispose of all of the marijuana. Ira drove straight to his house without considering what he would do once her arrived. An older woman, Mike's mother, answered the door.

"Is Mike here?" Ira asked, trying to conceal his anger.

"No, I haven't seen him since yesterday afternoon."

The phone rang.

"Excuse me, I'll be right back," she said. Ira watched the old woman shuffle back into the house. As she talked, the blood seemed to drain from her face. Ira watched as the woman grabbed a chair and dropped into it. He saw her write something on a scrap of paper. After she hung up the phone, she sat staring blankly at the wall for a moment, then got up and walked back to the door, starting to cry.

"That was the police. Mike was shot last night. They said he's dead."

"What? I'm sorry. Did they say why?"

"They said it involved marijuana. Who are you?" the woman asked.

"Ira Jones. He came by looking for a job yesterday. I decided I might need him after all. I'm really sorry ma'am."

Ira rushed back to his house, speeding all the way, stopping only to pick up Tim. The pair pulled the remaining plants. When done, Ira drenched the entire ditch with diesel, threw tires in for added fuel and set it on fire.

They loaded the remaining marijuana into the back of Tim's pickup and covered it with irrigation tarps. Ira instructed Tim to drive to Plainview and to leave the marijuana with Ernie. Less than five minutes later, Ira's favorite deputy and Upton County's finest, Officer Kelly Brown showed up. The ditch was still burning.

"What you burning there?" he asked.

"A ditch full of Kochia weed. Getting ready to irrigate."

"Mind if I have a look around?"

"Of course not."

The law officer heaved himself out of the puke green, piss yellow car and walked alongside the ditch. "Why didn't you let the weeds dry before you burned them? They burn better that way."

"I got hit with a horrible case of hay fever this morning, and couldn't stand them Kochia weeds one more minute. Stuff makes me sneeze my head off."

"You mind if I take a stroll down to your barns?"

"What're you looking for? I might be able to help you."

"Can't say. I'll let you know if I find it."

Kelly Brown drove to Ira's equipment shed, stopped the car, got out and went in. A few minutes later he drove back to the ditch. Susan stared at him as he drove by the house going and coming. He stopped to speak with Ira again.

"You know a fellow by the name of Mike Perez?"

"Yes sir, I know the piece of shit. I fired him not too long ago. Why do you ask?"

"Old Mike managed to get himself killed in Odessa last night. The word is, he had a huge load of freshly grown marijuana. Rumors say it was grown right here on your place."

"Marijuana, here? Bull shit!"

"I'm just telling you what's being said. The police think someone killed him and stole the load. Normally, I wouldn't be inclined to believe that, but there was something that made me wonder."

"What was that?"

"They found a bag of fresh cut buds in his coat pocket. A friend of his tells me he stole it from you, along with a whole lot more."

"Mike was a lyin' son of a bitch. I doubt there was any marijuana. If the guy is a friend of his, he's probably a liar too."

"You might be right," Officer Brown stated, "but this time, I believe the prick. He has nothing to gain, coming up with a story like that. Let me tell you something, Mr. Jones. You so much as fart in Upton county and I'm going to bust you for it. This is not over."

"Thanks for the warning."

"I'll be back. You can count on that," he added, punctuating the remark with a finger jab to Ira's chest.

"Keep your hands to yourself," Ira warned.

Kelly Brown stared. Ira met his gaze.

Kelly got into his piss yellow, puke green car, and drove off.

CHAPTER XLVI

Ira met Doug Grant at the front door of his trailer.
"Hi, Ira. Where is Tim? I went by his place and Lisa said he was gone."

"He went to Plainview."

"What?"

"It's a long story."

"What happened to the cotton?"

"The guy with the strippers showed up a week late. He got fifteen acres stripped, and then that night, a hail storm came along…"

"Son of a goddamned bitch. I told that bastard not to be late. How did Tim end up in Plainview?"

"That's another story." Ira went on to explain what had happened to the marijuana and Mike Perez.

"You're lucky. You could be sitting in jail right now."

"Don't think I ain't aware of that. It was a close call. Too close."

"Get a set of clothes Ira. I'm goin' to need some help."

Just then, Susan stepped into the room from the kitchen, where she had been eavesdropping on their conversation.

"Ira, don't you dare go with him."

"This doesn't concern you, Susan."

"Doesn't concern me? I have watched daddy screw up for years. I'm grown now. Daddy, if you want to ruin your own life, go right ahead. I'm not going to stand by and watch you ruin mine too. Leave my husband alone."

Doug turned toward his daughter.

"What are you going to do? Spank me? If you lay a hand on me, I'll call the police."

"You call the police on me, that will be the last call you ever make."

Susan did not reply, but stood her ground, staring defiantly.

"I'm going," Doug finally said. "Are you coming, or is this bitch going to run your life?" he asked Ira.

Ira picked up his hat and followed Doug Grant out the door.

"You bastard!" Susan screamed. "I won't be here when you get back."

* * * * *

Victor Nuehoff and his crew stared in shock at the field where they had been working the day before. All of the cotton strippers were gone. Only the module maker was still in place.

"Who would do this to me?" he asked, to no one in particular.

One of the mechanics looked at a driver and smiled. "I told you we should have done that man's field first. There are some people in this world you had best not lie to. It ain't healthy."

The next day, Victor Nuehoff's secretary received an envelope containing cash and an invoice for fifteen acres of stripping. The invoice was marked:

PAID IN FULL,
Signed, Doug Grant.

CHAPTER XLVII

Ira approached his trailer. In the front yard he noticed a pile of partially burnt belongings, including all of his clothes. Inside, he found windows broken, pictures mutilated, and vulgarities written on the walls. Any and everything belonging to Susan had been removed. Ira drove to Tim's house, to see what had happened.

"Looks like Susan left me," he commented.

"That ain't half of it."

"What do you mean?"

"According to Lisa, she's getting the marriage annulled. If she can't, she is going to divorce you. She moved in with Jason Adams."

"Do what?"

"Yeah. She called the cops on you and daddy too. Lord only knows what she told them. I heard she was going to file an injunction on both of you."

"You're shitting me."

"No, I'm not. I can hardly believe it myself. What are you going to do?"

"Hell if I know."

"I'm going to pick up the check for the little bit of cotton I sold. You want to come?"

"Sure. I don't have much else to do."

Tim and Ira spent the next few days collecting money from all their various endeavors. Harvest season was almost over. Between all the crops, all the dope, and all the stealing, the two young farmers had managed to break even for the year. After retiring their debts, they had no money left.

Doug and Ernie, on the other hand, had done quite well for themselves; both of them had enough sense to quit the nasty habit of farming.

CHAPTER XLVIII

The phone rang. Ira picked it up. It was his dad. "Ira, I want you to bring all your records to Lubbock tomorrow," the elder Jones ordered.

"I'm pretty busy. Can't it wait?"

"No, it can't. Mr. Jenkins needs to see them."

"All right, dad. I'll see you tomorrow."

Ira hung up the phone and sighed. There weren't any books to bring. Ira had been doing predominately cash business, taking what he needed out of the pile, more than often, an excessive amount, and putting back into the same pile whatever income came his way, from whatever source, legal, or otherwise.

Ira spent the entire day and most of the night trying to fabricate a semblance of records, scrapping together what receipts he could find, and falsifying others. He drank cup after cup of coffee and smoked plenty of marijuana during the endeavor, further complicating the procedure by clouding his already scrambled mind. At times, he found himself dreaming about something miles away, while the hours passed and the work got nowhere nearer completion. No matter how he juggled the figures, on thing remained evident—he had spent all the money he made. Where it had all gone, he had no idea.

Ira left the next day, without having slept, and drove to Lubbock.

James Jones glanced briefly through the books and shook his head. "Don't guess it makes a damn, anyway."

"What was that, dad?"

"It doesn't matter. Mr. Jenkins is going to shut us down. I wanted to tell you personally. I'm sorry son."

"But..."

"It's not entirely your fault. These are tough times. I'm on the verge of bankruptcy. Even if you had made money this year, I believe they would have shut us down."

"But, that isn't fair, Dad. It takes time to make a place productive."

"Not much is fair in this world, Ira."

"So, what am I supposed to do?" Ira asked.

"Well, first of all, you need to let the hands go. Shut down all the wells. Mr. Jenkins wants you to stay on the place for a while to make sure things don't get stolen. Eventually, someone will be by for the equipment and the irrigation engines. Tomorrow, a man will be coming by for the rest of the cattle."

"They're taking everything?"

"That's about the size of it."

"But, you bought a lot of that stuff with your own money—money from other places. They can't take all of that."

"Yes, they can. Everything on that place is collateralized against our loan, even the land itself. It too, will be sold."

"So, Mr. Jenkins wants me to sit out there and do nothing, while they disassemble our place?"

"Yeah."

"What am I supposed to live on in the meantime?"

"I guess you will just have to find a job. You can stay in the trailer for free."

"I'm sorry dad, but I can't do this."

"There is a place for you here, Ira. I can get you a job..."

"I need some time to think, dad."

"Do you have any cash?"

"A little over a thousand bucks."

"Keep it. Your account has been frozen. Don't sell any more hay. It will all have to be accounted for."

"What?"

"Yeah. We are through, just like that," James Jones told his son, snapping his fingers.

"Sorry, dad," Ira replied, getting up to leave. His father followed him to the door.

"Are you going back to the farm? If not, I need to let Mr. Jenkins know."

"Yeah, I'm going back. I owe it to Jose and Leonardo. By the way, Susan left me."

"What?"

"It is a long story and I would rather not talk about it right now. Dad, will you do me one favor?"

"What?"

"When you see Mr. Jenkins, tell him to kiss my ass."

"Ira, you know I can't do that."

"Why not? We don't have to please that bastard any longer."

"I am going to get screwed here. Mr. Jenkins has control over how deep."

Ira turned and left. He couldn't stand to see his dad, such a proud and honest man, subject to a man of Jenkins's caliber. Ira drove to the bank where Floyd Jenkins worked and parked by his car, right before lunchtime. A few minutes later the banker came out of the bank in the company of a pretty secretary.

"Hello, Ira," Mr. Jenkins said, as he approached the car.

"Fuck you too, Cocksucker," Ira replied. After a moment, he started the engine, and drove off.

"Who was that?" the secretary asked.

"Ira Jones. We foreclosed on them."

"You better watch him."

"He's just a kid. He'll get over it."

The secretary watched the retreating pickup. *I don't know about that,* she thought to herself.

CHAPTER XLIX

Rather than drive straight home, Ira went by way of Plainview, first to replenish his marijuana supply, and also, to pick up a couple of thousand dollars Ernie still owed him for the last of the marijuana he had grown. Ira left Ernie's house with $3,500 in his pocket. That money, the pickup he drove, one horse and several sets of clothing comprised everything he owned. Ira drove in a daze.

Usually when such calamities came along, the first thing that came to Ira's mind was a wild woman. Ira couldn't go to the tit bars in Lubbock because of what he had done there, so he drove on to Odessa. He stopped at a bar and drank until drunk. He left the bar alone, almost running off of the road a few times on the way home. At McCamey, he drove by Jason Adams' house, and saw Susan's car parked there. He imagined the two of them huddled together in the same bed, his baby growing between them in Susan's womb. The thought made him want to stop but better sense prevailed. He went home instead.

The next day, Ira delivered the bad news to Jose and Leonardo. Afterwards he could not tolerate sitting at the farm; too many memories haunted the place.

That night, Ira started driving, first north, then east, but finally west, headed toward Phoenix, where hopefully, he would find the one person on the planet he wanted to see—Angela Romano.

* * * * *

Ira was shocked to discover how large Phoenix had become. Only when he had driven for several hours around the city did he realize how monumental the task of finding Angela might turn out to be, assuming first, of course, that she was in fact still there. Ira had failed to get Angela's address or even her mother's last name, which was different than Angela's.

Ira checked into a motel and took a look at the massive Phoenix phone book. Ira concentrated on a mental image of her. Where would she be? He spoke to her in his mind, hoping spirits would convey the message. He got no answer. Then logic took over. *Where did I find her the first time? In a tit bar.* For the first time ever, Ira hoped Angela had not changed her ways—not yet anyway.

* * * * *

Angela peered out through the dark, smoke filled room as she danced, going through the moves almost automatically, covering the stage from one end to the other. Her body was still hard and beautifully proportioned, the kind that fantasies are made of. Angela knew which of the men had money and which would give her some, perhaps before they did. She played the game: a smile here, a kiss there, a crotch in the face, a flip of the hair, a twist of the hips, sultry looks; by now, she knew all the tricks of the trade and which would work on what man.

Angela spotted a man in a suit. *Hello, Mr. Moneybags,* she thought to herself. She gave the man a little sign to show him he was special. She knew who he was and didn't like him, but by now she realized she could make more money by being one rich man's plaything than by playing the crowd.

Mr. Moneybags was a married forty-year-old lawyer with baby soft, manicured hands and a potbelly. He was a wimp and a doughboy but he had piles and piles of money taken from people headed to prison. He drove a Rolls, when he wasn't in the Ferrari. Angela played him for all he was worth.

When her routine was over, Angela put on her sexiest outfit and strolled to his table.

"Hello, my queen. How are you today?"

"Great, honey," she replied, with a cheerful smile. Inside, she felt anything other than cheerful. "Would you like a drink?"

"Yes, but sit down. Let the waitress bring it."

"I have to go to the bar anyway. Give me the money and I'll get it for you."

Mr. Moneybags handed Angela a hundred. "You keep the change."

"Why, thank you baby," Angela said, cupping his face in her hands and kissing him. Angela knew there were many more bills where that came from, and she felt no guilt about taking her share. Mr. Moneybags was a money whore on a scale that made anything she did pale by comparison—a real piece of shit.

Angela sauntered toward the bar, shrugging off a few handsome young studs with hard muscular bodies on the way. The move was not missed by the lawyer and left him smiling profusely. He looked at the young men victoriously. Angela knew the boys would have no money, thinking their good looks alone would stop her in her tracks. Men like that came a dime a dozen to a woman like Angela.

Angela stopped to talk to the bartender, a woman, and her current roommate.

"Guess who is here again," she told the woman.

"You lucky bitch. Why can't I find something like that?"

"I'm tired of him."

"Well, then, let me have a shot."

"No way. I said I am tired of him. I am *not* tired of his money."

"What is he like?"

"You don't want to know."

"Yes, I do."

"He is a freak."

"Oh yeah? Just my type then."

"Well, it's not mine. He actually pays me to piss on his face."

"You're kidding."

"No, unfortunately, I am not."

"I love it."

"He makes me spank him and he calls me *mother*. I'm telling you, this guy is a real worm. I thought about getting some pictures of the guy and blackmailing him."

"Is he married?"

"Aren't they all?'

"I guess so."

"Give me a light." Angela put a cigarette in her mouth and waited for her friend to light it. After doing so, the bartender placed two drinks on the bar. Angela got a weird feeling, like someone was staring at her. She looked at the men sitting at the horseshoe shaped bar. Her eyes moved quickly from one to the other, until she saw a face that looked familiar. *Must be someone I fucked,* she thought to herself. She picked up the drinks and took one step toward Mr. Moneybags, and then stopped in her tracks. She turned around again, and looked closer at a cowboy staring at her from across the room, dressed in a faded Levi jacket and silver belly cowboy hat. The drinks dropped to the floor.

Angela stood paralyzed, staring into the eyes of Ira Jones underneath the brim of the hat. She saw pain in those eyes.

Angela started toward Ira, almost against her will. When Ira saw her, it was like looking at a reflection of himself. All pretenses were stripped and beneath all the layers was pain.

"Why?" she asked.

Ira stared, but said nothing. Finally, he stood up and kissed her, a short kiss, but one packed with emotion.

"Angela." The bartender's voice brought Angela back to the bar.

"Wait a minute, Ira. I will be right back. Don't you go anywhere," she ordered.

Angela walked back to the bar.

"Who is that?" the bartender asked.

"Do you remember me telling you about that crazy trip to Mexico?" she asked.

"Of course. That was the only thing you talked about for the first month you were here."

"That's the guy."

"What about him?" the girl whispered, nodding toward the lawyer. He smiled in her direction.

"Give this to Ira for me," Angela said, scribbling a note rapidly on a napkin, "and keep your hands off of him."

"My, he must be something."

Angela walked over to the lawyer's table. "I feel really bad tonight. I think I'm going to go home early."

"That's all right. I'll take you home."

"I don't feel like company."

"We don't have to do anything, Angela."

"Look, Steve, I really feel bad. I just started my period. I am going home. Come back tomorrow night. Please."

"OK, Angela." Mr. Moneybags got up to leave. About that time, Ira walked by, also headed for the door. The lawyer asked, "Is there anything wrong, between you and me?"

"No, not at all, honey. I just don't feel good. I'll make it up to you tomorrow."

"Good. You know I love it when you're bleeding."

"Sure honey, whatever turns you on," Angela said, smiling. Inside, she cringed.

Ira drove back to his motel. An hour later, he called the number on the napkin.

Angela answered. "Where are you?"

Ira gave her the name of the motel and the room number.

"I will be right over."

CHAPTER L

Ira opened the door. Angela stood there, looking like an apparition from his dreams. He couldn't help but stare. Finally, he stepped aside.

Angela was dressed in jeans and a black leather jacket. She walked into the room and set her purse on a nightstand. She then turned and asked the same question she had asked at the bar.

"Why?"

"To see you, of course."

"What about Susan? Did you marry her?"

"Yes. She is divorcing me."

"What did you expect, Ira. You're crazy."

"I want you, Angela."

"No, you don't, Ira. You want what you think I *could* be, not what I am. I'm no good. You said so yourself once. I hurt anyone that gets too close to me. I hurt you once; I'll do it again."

While Angela's mouth said one thing, her look said something else. Ira found her irresistible.

"Angela, I want you. I love you, and I need you." Ira took her hand in his own. "I want you to be my wife."

"No you don't, Ira. You want my pussy, like everyone else. That's what everybody wants from me."

Ira kissed her, not sensuously, but gently, on the forehead. He wrapped his arms around her and hugged. He felt her body shake. After a moment, she returned the hug. They stood several minutes without moving or saying a word, powerful emotions coursing between them—emotions long since pent up and repressed.

"I missed you," Ira exclaimed

Angela pulled her head back so she could see Ira's face. "Now I remember why I fell for you. You *are* crazy, Ira. You should never have allowed yourself to get mixed up with me."

"I couldn't help myself."

The young pair sat on the edge of the bed. Angela removed her jacket.

"So, Ira, tell me what happened after I left."

"Well, Susan came back to me. Her mother conned me into getting married right away. I thought I wanted to, so I can't put all the blame on her. I didn't really know Susan. Either that, or she changed an awful lot after we got married. She wanted me to go straight—you know, eight to five at some job, little house in a suburb, church every Sunday in a fancy suit, and kissing the ass of all the right people to get ahead. She wanted to run my life for me."

"You ever consider she might be right?"

"Hell no. I'm not going to be anyone's slave. Anyhow, one day I came home and she was gone. She moved in with another guy in town and got an injunction against me. He is just the kind she wants; sits on the front row at church, kisses all the right asses, young, handsome, the whole works. His father has big bucks."

"What about your farm?"

"We're going to lose it."

"What are you going to do then?"

"I don't know. Thieves got most of my pot patch and what money I did make got fucked off somewhere."

"I can still get you some girls. There is good money in it, Ira. You could make sure nobody bothers us. It would be easy, and you'd get rich."

"I'm not a pimp. I never will be. There are other ways to make money."

"Like what? Robbing banks with that crazy dude?"

"If it comes down to it, I'll do that before I become a pimp."

"You'll end up in jail or dead. What good will that do? You can stay here and live the life of a king. Please Ira, listen to me."

"I didn't drive all the way from Texas to argue with you Angela." Ira kissed her again. Passionately this time. When he proceeded to remove her clothes, she stopped him.

"I'm on my period," she said.

"Shit," he exclaimed. "That's all right." Ira wrapped his arms around her and pulled her close.

After a time, she whispered. "I love you." Those words had not crossed her lips since the two had parted ways.

"I know," Ira replied.

Ira and Angela spent the night in each other's arms. They didn't make love, but they loved. The next morning Angela got into the shower with him. Being near her naked body aroused Ira. They made love standing in the shower allowing the water to wash away the blood. Afterward they stood holding each other, luxuriating in the closeness.

During breakfast, Ira caught her staring pensively at him. "What are you going to do?" she finally asked.

"I still don't know."

"I don't want to be poor, Ira."

"There's more to life than money."

"I know, but I have needs. I refuse to be poor, not when I can do something about it."

"All I know is that I want you," Ira replied.

"Ira, I'm cold. Ice cold. Like a diamond—pretty to look at —but I give no warmth to those who try to hold me."

"Bull shit."

"I'm telling you the truth. Go back to Texas and forget me."

Ira saw the pain saying these words caused Angela, even as she said them. When they finished the meal, Ira walked her out to her car.

"Go home, Ira. I won't marry you. I'm sorry, but I can't. I do love you, but there's more to marriage than that. Good bye."

Angela shut the door and started the car.

"Wait. Where do you live? Wait a minute!"

Angela backed up and drove off. Streams of tears clouded her vision. She looked at Ira in her rear view mirror, standing in the parking lot, wounded, as though she had ripped his heart from his body.

"You're too good for me," she whispered.

* * * * *

Ira rented the room for another night, determined not to give up so easily. That night he returned to the bar where Angela worked. She didn't show up. No one would tell him where she lived. Ira called the phone number she had given him. No answer. Ira went back to the motel and spent a long, lonely night, thinking of her. The next day, he stayed in the room, smoking joints and waiting. Once again, he returned to the bar, just in time to see Angela walking toward the Rolls Royce with her lawyer friend. He pulled up beside them as they were getting into the car.

"Please go home. I will hurt you," she said.

"You are doing that now."

"I know. I told you I would. I always do. That's the kind of woman I am."

"You don't have to be."

"But I am. Angela leaned into the cab of the truck and kissed him, and then turned toward the lawyer's car. After a step or two, she stopped, turned, and whispered, "I love you," and then continued on, getting into the Rolls.

"Who was that?" the young lawyer asked.

"An old friend from Texas. Let's go."

"He drove all the way from Texas to see you?"

"Yes. Come on, let's go."

"He must really care about you."

"Leave!" she shouted.

Later that night, while the lawyer was pumping in and out of Angela's body, tears ran from her eyes. Her mind was elsewhere.

* * * * *

Ira drove back to his motel room. He tried to sleep, but could not. Finally, he went for a late night walk that turned into a run through the streets of Phoenix. Ira ran, and ran, and ran, faster and faster, forcing his body to the point of breaking. The more tired he became, the faster he ran, until it felt like his heart would explode. Nearing a doughnut shop, his legs failed to keep up with the pace he demanded and he collapsed into a heap on the sidewalk, moaning—deep painful moans.

A policeman pulled up, got out of his car, and walked up to Ira.

"Are you all right son?" he asked.

Ira struggled to get up. "Yeah, I was just running and fell down. I'll be OK."

The policeman looked at Ira's clothes. They were not the typed typically used for jogging. "Kind of late for jogging, isn't it?" the cop asked.

"Yeah... It 's about a girl..."

"You'll be OK, then?" the cop asked, understanding written in kind compassionate eyes.

"Yeah. I'll make it. Ira turned and walked slowly back to the motel, saying a prayer for Angela as he moved through the artificially illuminated streets of Phoenix. When he got back to the motel, he gathered his things and headed back to Texas.

* * * * *

For a few nights, Angela watched the door of the club. A part of her hoped Ira wouldn't show—another hoped he would. He was gone. The third night after Ira's departure, Mr.

Moneybags showed up again. He walked up to her and wrapped his arms around her from behind.

Angela broke from his grasp, turned around and beat him to the floor. "Keep your fucking hands off of me," she shouted.

Two bouncers immediately showed up and hustled the confused lawyer to the door, where they proceeded to bruise his soft body. A totally bewildered young lawyer got into his Rolls Royce and drove home to his wife.

Inside the club, Angela's bartending friend asked, "What has gotten into you, Angela? You just ran off one of the richest Johns in Phoenix."

"Money isn't everything," Angela said, with tears in her eyes.

Now the bartender too was bewildered. Money had been everything for Angela, that is, until that West Texas cowboy had come along.

CHAPTER LI

Bubba Cooper, the former owner of the Jones's farm called Floyd Jenkins and informed him that Ira had abandoned the farm. Jenkins immediately notified local law officials that nothing was to be removed without his permission. Jenkins then hired Bubba Cooper to oversee the place. Cooper gladly took the job. All the farm equipment was parked in a neat row, close to the barn, the cattle shipped to market, and new locks installed on the gates.

* * * * *

Tim Grant walked into the farm co-op to pick up a few parts needed for an irrigation engine. Mr. Cooper and Mr. Dean avoided his eyes. Tim helped himself to the parts he needed and walked to the office, which consisted of nothing more than one desk, two chairs and a filing cabinet. Cooper sat behind the desk, working on an antiquated adding machine. Tim placed the parts on the desk and waited for Cooper to make out the receipt.

Normally, Tim did all his business at the co-op on credit. They allowed him to run a bill until harvest time, charging a monthly interest rate that was as high as the law allowed. Tim had recently paid all but four hundred dollars of his bill.

"Tim." Mr. Cooper began. "Walter and I have been talking things over. Please don't take this personally, but we have decided we can no longer afford to extend you credit. This is purely a business decision. Neither of us sees how you can possibly make it through another year. We're not prepared to jeopardize our own business on the hope that you somehow will."

"Haven't I always paid my bills?"

"Yes, you have. That doesn't mean you will be able to in the future. Please understand. We don't want to lose your business. You have been one of our best customers. Matter of fact, we are willing to give you a five hundred dollar credit line, but no more than that."

"I can't believe this. First you move on Ira and now me, when we did more business here than anyone else in the country."

"Business decisions are not always easy to make or enjoyable. We are simply protecting ourselves."

Bubba Cooper adjusted his bifocals and looked at the parts Tim had placed on the desk. They totaled up to one hundred and fifty dollars—fifty dollars more than they would cost anywhere else in the country. Tim looked angrily at Mr. Dean. Dean nodded his head slightly, indicating that he too supported Cooper's position on the matter.

"Keep your parts," Tim told the men. "I can get them cheaper somewhere else." Tim turned and walked out the door.

"Are you going to pay the balance of your bill?" Cooper asked.

"It will be paid," Tim replied, over his shoulder.

"Sure hated to do that to him," Cooper told Dean.

"You did the right thing," Dean replied.

Tim noticed a small bulldozer doing some dirt work on co-op land as he walked to his pickup.

Yeah, don't worry about a thing. I'll repay you bastards, he thought.

* * * * *

Tim ran into Ira on the way back to his house. Ira had just returned from Phoenix. Tim pulled to a stop; Ira did likewise, pointed in the opposite direction.

"Howdy Tim. Why so glum?"

"A lot of shit has been going on around here the last few days."

"Like what?"

"Have you been by your place?"

"No, I just got back."

"You'd better follow me back to the house. We need to talk."

Tim drove on. Ira did a U-turn and followed. At the house, Lisa prepared a cup of coffee for each of the young farmers. They sat at the kitchen table while she went back to house cleaning. Ira noticed the bulge of her newborn baby for the first time. Lisa had the glow often associated with a mother to be.

"Ira, we've got big problems. Are you aware the bank has closed you down?"

"Yes, that's why I left for a few days. I've gotten over it now. My dad told me Mr. Jenkins needed me to stay on for a while."

"Things have changed. Jenkins hired Bubba Cooper to watch the place. Cooper has already hauled off half of your things."

"Why, that dirty bastard." Ira jumped up from the table.

"Wait, Ira. Sit down a minute."

Tim pointed at the chair. Ira sat back down, with a flushed face and a temper ready to boil over.

"They've chained up the gates with new locks and posted no trespassing signs all over the place."

"I can't believe Cooper would do this, not after all the money I spent in his store."

"Well, he did, and that's not all he did. He cut me off today." Tim glanced over at Lisa, who immediately stopped working.

"Why?" she asked.

"He says he don't see how we can make it. Worst thing about it, he's probably right. Sure does hurt though. I don't know what to do"

"I don't know about you, but I am fixing to go get some of my things and sell them."

"You better not, Ira. Dad and I already talked it over. Anything comes up missing from that place and they will start looking for you."

"They can't stop me from picking up my own personal things. I don't care if they have the *fucking US army* guarding the place."

Ira jumped from his seat and headed for the door.

"Where are you going?" Tim asked.

"To get my things."

"The gate is locked."

"How long do you think that will slow me down?" He did not wait for a reply.

Lisa came up from behind and hugged Tim. Together, they watched Ira speed out of their driveway, tires spinning, and dirt flying.

CHAPTER LII

Ira firmly grasped the steering wheel and aimed toward a spot in the barbed wire fence. The pickup hit the fence doing about fifty. Wires screeched, staples popped, and then gave way, and the pickup careened into the alfalfa field. Ira continued to floor board the pickup through the field, turning one way and then the other, eating ruts in the otherwise level ground. Eventually, he ended up at the barn. All his hand tools were gone—tools that had taken years to accumulate. He drove to his trailer. What few personal things he had were still there. He loaded them into the bed of the truck. Afterwards he hooked up his two-horse trailer and loaded his horse and a saddle. About a hundred yards after he exited the ready-made gate, Officer Kelly Brown rounded the corner, lights flashing. Ira pulled over.

"Where are you going?" Brown asked him.

"That is none of your business, best I can tell."

Kelly Brown surveyed the things in the back of the pickup. "Where did that stuff come from?"

"Those are my personal belongings."

"That is not what I asked. Where did you get them?"

"I got them out of my own trailer."

"You mean that trailer over there?" Officer Brown asked, pointing towards Ira's home.

"Yes sir."

"That trailer is now property of the bank. If you were on that land, you were trespassing. Did you not see the sign?"

"No. I guess I must have been going too fast to notice."

"What about the horse trailer?"

"It belongs to me. Call in the license number if you don't believe me."

"There might be a dispute over that," Kelly Brown suggested. "I think you better follow me to town."

"Are you arresting me?"

"No, not unless you refuse to come."

"For what?"

"I hardly know where to begin. Trespassing, theft, destruction of private property, maybe possession of marijuana…"

Ira shook his head. He couldn't stand a search. "OK, let's go."

A half-mile or so further down the road, Ira saw Bubba Cooper, who obviously had been sitting in his pickup with binoculars watching the confrontation from a distance. Cooper waved at Deputy Brown, who returned the salutation. When Cooper waved at Ira, he got nothing but a cold stare in return.

At the sheriff's office, Kelly Brown called Floyd Jenkins and talked briefly while Ira listened. After a moment, he hung up the phone.

"Well?" Ira asked.

"Jenkins says you can have the trailer and the horse. However, you are not to set foot on that land again without his permission, and you will also need to notify Mr. Cooper before you do. You are not to remove any more property. Should you disobey those orders, I will be more than happy to see you prosecuted to the full extent of the law."

"Is that all?"

"Yes."

"Then I can go?"

"For now. Just remember one thing. If anything comes up missing from that farm, I know where to look. In all honesty, I hope you do try to take something. I would thoroughly enjoy putting your ass in jail, and I am sure it wouldn't hurt Sheriff Garcia's feelings either, after what you did to his son."

"I hate to disappoint you deputy, but that place has brought me nothing but pain and misery. I won't go back."

On the way to his truck, Ira fought off an insane desire to throw a large rock through the windshield of the only piss yellow, puke green car in the parking lot.

CHAPTER LIII

Ira took his horse to Tim's house and in the process got invited to stay for supper. Tim built a fire using mesquite hearts, and allowed them to burn until nothing but coals remained. Meanwhile, Lisa marinated boneless chicken breasts in a secret sauce. Tim broiled the breasts over the coals while Lisa prepared a guacamole salad. To top things off, she fried some potatoes and heated a pot of red beans. After all the restaurant food Ira had been eating, real food was a welcome change.

Following the meal, Tim broke out a few Lone Star longnecks, a local favorite. No sooner than they had popped the tops, Doug Grant pulled up. Tim handed his beer to Lisa, who secreted it in the refrigerator. Lisa reheated some of the food for Doug. Doug watched disapprovingly as Ira finished off his beer and got another out of the icebox, but said nothing. As soon as Lisa got out of earshot, Doug began a conversation with the two young men.

"I have more marijuana for Ernie. They tell me this is supposed to be better than what I have been getting. Damned sure better be, because I had to pay more for it. I hope I didn't get fucked. It is all big pieces, and smells like a pine tree."

"Sounds like buds to me," Ira stated. "If that's the case, we're about to make some money. How much do you have?"

"I got one small bale. I think it weighs twenty five pounds."

"All right!"

Tim and Ira brought Doug up to date on the latest events around the Bakersfield valley and the surrounding area. Before they were finished, he was furious.

"I wanted to take that equipment so bad I could hardly stand it," Ira stated. "I still do."

"You have to use your head, Ira. That's exactly what they'd like you to do. It's time for a change in strategy. We're ready to make a withdrawal from the bank. Take the marijuana to Plainview and sell it. Once you have the money together, call Tim. We'll come up there and meet with you and Ernie in Lubbock. How's that sound?"

"Fine. I got nowhere to stay around here anyhow. It'd do me some good to see Ernie.

"Good. Tim and I have preparations to make. I've already selected a site for us to hit."

"How's Mexico?"

"Great. I bought a ranch. Land is cheap. Carla's dad sold me the place for a quarter of what it would cost here. He's trying to keep me in the family, which don't bother me a bit. Carla is one hell of a woman. Don't think I could find one like her up here."

Ira noticed Doug looked tanned and that his hands were calloused. "Looks like you have been working," Ira commented.

"I have been. That woman has given me reason to make something out of myself again. I've got hands building another house on the ranch at this very moment. I've been helping them a little."

"Where is this ranch?" Ira asked.

"South east of Ojinaga, about twenty five miles, near a little town called San Carlos. It's rugged country. The people have taken me in for the biggest part. Half of them are outlaws, and the other half wish they could be. Hell of a place."

"Sounds like it."

"Maybe I'll take you down and show it to you in a couple of weeks. You may want to buy a place yourself when you see it. They have pretty good cattle down there, stolen from America's finest herds."

"Leonardo told me he has relatives in that area," Ira commented.

"What happened to him?" Doug asked.

"I gave him that old red dodge pickup. Last I saw, he was headed north, looking for work. Sure hated to see him go. He's a good hand. Never heard him complain about anything, the whole time he was here. I guess if I'm headed for Plainview, I better be getting on the road."

Doug walked out and transferred the marijuana from his pickup to Ira's. One look at the weed told Ira it was top grade *sin semilla*.

"Buy yourself a gun or two with some of that money while you are up there. Get Ernie to do the same. Practice up a little on your shooting."

"I have a gun, Doug."

"I'm not talking about a deer rifle or a shot-gun. Get yourself something like this." Doug Grant pulled a semi-automatic, nine-millimeter Browning from his waistband. He worked the action, ejecting a shell.

"You ever see anything like this?" he asked, holding up the bullet.

"I don't believe so," Ira replied.

"Teflon coated. It'll go right through a bulletproof vest. You'll need a back-up also—something like this," he said, pulling up his pant leg to reveal a snub nose .38 strapped to his leg. "Personally, I believe in being prepared for the worst," he added. Seconds later a tiny Italian-made .25 auto appeared in his hand, from who knows where. "You get the picture?" he asked.

"Yes, sir."

"What about rifles?"

"I have plenty of those. Most of our work will be close order stuff. A rifle is too bulky."

"Well, I better be hitting the road," Ira stated.

"Be careful. Can't have you getting busted with that damned stuff when things are looking so good on our other proposition."

"Don't worry. This is money in the bag. You be careful too, Doug."

"The rest of the world best be careful when I am around," Doug replied with a malicious grin, "cause I'm ready to fuckin' go off."

Ira departed for Lubbock.

Tim and Doug Grant paid a visit to the Co-op. Doug started and drove the same small bull dozer Tim had seen working that morning through a wall of the store. Tim pulled his pickup near the hole left by the dozer and filled it with merchandise while Doug loaded the dozer on his trailer. The two then headed for Mexico. By nine am the next morning, Tim was back in bed with Lisa, and his pockets were full of cash.

* * * * *

Two days later Bubba Cooper watched the workers repairing the gaping hole left in the wall of the building. The mailman came by and handed him his mail for the day. He opened a letter from Tim Grant. Inside was four hundred and thirty dollars in cash and a short note.

It said:

Paid in full,
Signed, Tim Grant.

CHAPTER LIV

Ira stopped the van in the parking lot of the apartment complex. Doug Grant exited from the passenger side door; no sooner than he did, a car appeared from behind the van. Ira's breath seemed to freeze in his lungs when Doug placed his hand on the butt of the gun. The car drove by. Ira exhaled. Doug walked over to a Chevy Blazer and broke the driver's side window, and then unlocked and opened the door. Seconds later, Ira heard a loud noise as Doug broke a chunk out of the steering column.

Doug then broke the linkage that ran from the ignition switch through the steering column with a large screw driver, hooked the tip of the screwdriver into a small *tit* left on the linkage, and started the engine.

"Damn. That only took thirty seconds," Ira exclaimed. Ernie shook his head in disbelief. Tim just smiled.

Doug waved at Ira and he pulled out of the parking lot; Doug followed close behind. The two vehicles drove east from Abilene, down a rural road, rather than the interstate. After going through the small town of Clyde, they continued to another smaller road, turned off, cut a hole in a rancher's fence and concealed the van. The time was 5 am.

"Listen," Doug ordered. The three men did, attentively. "I have been watching this place. The president of the bank has a bad habit of coming in to play with his money several hours before the bank opens. We probably have an hour to get this job done, but I want to get in and out as fast as possible. Do any of you have any questions about your assignments?"

Doug turned to each man, one at a time. As indicated, they understood.

Ira felt his pulse rate quicken and got an uneasy felling in the pit of his stomach, similar to what he had once felt before high school football games. He looked at his peers; they too were obviously nervous. Tim patted his feet. Ernie unconsciously picked his nose and ate the buggers, and Doug Grant smoked, one cigarette after another; at one point he had two going at the same time—one in his hand, and another in the ashtray. The wait seemed to last forever.

Finally Doug gave the order to start the Blazer. Ernie was selected to serve as the driver. While they drove toward the town of Baird, the town selected for the morning's activities, each of the three young men went over his assignment again, opening chambers to make sure they were loaded, checking pockets for stocking masks, and back up weapons. The first sign of light was beginning to show on the eastern horizon when they entered Baird. Ernie slowed as they passed a small, local restaurant.

"There he is," Doug commented, pointing at a brown Lincoln Continental. "Little sawed off son of a bitch will be coming out of there soon." A smile broke out on Doug's face. Ira looked nervously at Tim and Ernie, fighting back a sudden sense of panic. Neither of them was smiling. Ernie drove through the town and pulled over momentarily.

"Ernie, Ira tells me you are a driving son of a bitch," Doug commented. "I sure hope so."

"You just get a grip on that seat with the cheeks of your ass and don't let go. Nobody will follow me. If they do, it will be a first."

Ernie turned around and drove through town again, in the opposite direction this time. As they passed the restaurant, a small man in a western suit walked out of the front door.

"Drive one mile, and turn around," Doug ordered. Ernie followed his instructions. Tension built in the cab. Ira found himself grinding his teeth. He tried to stop his knees from shaking. As they neared the bank, they saw the banker getting out of the Lincoln.

"As soon as he walks around the corner, pull in right beside his car. Ira, Tim, give me sixty seconds, and then walk to the front. Walk, don't run. Don't pull on your stockings until you are at the front door. I will make sure the bastard doesn't get a look at you. Try to look natural while you are on the street. If anyone sees you, keep walking."

The banker walked around the corner. Ernie pulled alongside the Lincoln and parked. Doug got out and started after the banker, looking around to see if anyone was out to notice. There were two or three cars on the main street, but no people. Just as the banker unlocked the door, Doug stuck a 9 millimeter handgun into his lower back.

"Guess what, mother fucker?"

"Oh my God," the man exclaimed.

"No, it ain't God, but you'll be meeting him real soon if you don't do exactly as I say. Now, walk into the bank."

A few seconds after they entered the door, Tim and Ira followed, guns drawn and ready for action.

"Give me the key to the door," Doug ordered. The man fumbled through his pockets and relocated the key. When he offered it to Doug his hand shook.

"Please don't hurt me," the banker squeaked. "I've...I've got a family."

Doug laughed. "All the more reason to kill you. If there is one thing this world don't need, it's more goddamned bankers. Now you listen to me and you listen well. We're going to open that vault. If you set off an alarm, I'll kill you. If cops show up, I'll kill you, whether you called them or not. If anyone shows up, I'll kill you."

"But, I have no control over that. What if another employee comes in for work early?"

"Then I'll kill you."

"But...that isn't fair!"

"A banker—worried about playing fair? Why, that must be a first. Is there any money in the drawers?"

The banker did not answer immediately. Doug kicked him viciously.

"NO! There isn't. It is all in the vault. Please don't hurt me." The man dropped to his knees.

"Open the goddamn vault!"

The banker stood up and walked to the vault; Doug followed closely behind. Ira came along behind, carrying two sacks. Tim remained near the front door, looking out toward the street.

"Open it!" Doug ordered.

The banker didn't move fast enough for Doug's liking. He raised the 9 mm to the man's head, instantly putting him into a higher gear. When the door was open, Doug guided the banker to the bathroom. Ira entered the vault and began sacking money, looking carefully to make sure he picked up no dye packs.

Doug produced a roll of duct tape and began taping up the banker, leaving him unable to move, see anything, and barely able to breath.

Ira dragged the sacks out of the vault, stopping to look into the bathroom on the way to the door. "We're done. Let's go."

"This will serve as a little reminder of this meeting, both for you and me." Doug produced a razor sharp folding hunting knife, grabbed the man's ear and cut it off, smooth with his head. A muffled scream escaped from the thick wad of tape, but the man was powerless to resist. Blood spewed from the wound. Doug turned and followed Ira to the door, pocketing the ear on the way. At the door, each of the men removed his mask and pocketed his weapon. The two younger men carried the money while Doug relocked the bank door and then calmly walked to the Blazer and got in.

"Drive slow and easy," Doug told Ernie. "I don't think anyone has seen us." Ernie drove through town one last time, continuing on to where the van had been stashed. There, the group exchanged vehicles, leaving the stolen Blazer behind.

Doug looked through the money. "Not bad for a one horse town. But, this is the real prize," he added, holding up the banker's bloody ear. Ira tried to smile, but couldn't.

CHAPTER LV

The farmers hit three more small town banks in a two-week period, most of which catered primarily to other farmers and ranchers. Bank robberies are common; cutting the ears off bank officials is not, and this activity soon drew national attention, attention neither Ernie nor Ira cared for. Doug, on the other hand seemed to derive satisfaction from the sudden wave of fear generated by this activity. There was one thing Ira and Ernie did like; each earned in excess of a hundred thousand dollars for their efforts.

Doug was not satisfied, and seemed obsessed with a desire for more and more money. After an argument, Both Ira and Ernie convinced him to let them take a break from the action. The young duo went to Plainview, leaving the father-son team to continue alone. Ernie and Ira took advantage of this time and the huge amount of cash at their disposal. One night, after drinking plenty of booze, they ended up in a Lubbock tit bar, freely showering money on the dancers. During a temporary moment of lucidity, Ira stated, "You know, Ernie, we probably shouldn't be here. Angela told me those bikers own all these places."

"Bull shit. They don't own this town, and they had no right to think they owned that girl. You can't own slaves in this country. Have a good time." Ernie grabbed a passing dancer and stuffed a twenty into her thong. She kissed him aggressively. Another approached and he did the same for her.

"Ain't you something? I need to take you home," she said. Soon, they were surrounded. The girls weren't the only ones to recognize the young men. In the crowd sat a meth dealer employed by the Desperados. He recognized both young men; he sold speed to Ernie, and he had witnessed the fight the night Ira took Angela from the bar.

Ira and Ernie went separate ways from the bar, each with a whore in tow. Ira's girl produced cocaine and the two locked themselves into a room and partied throughout the night. The girl left at daybreak and Ira fell asleep. He awoke to the sound of the maid knocking on the door.

"I'm going to stay another night," he told her. I won't be needing maid service." The maid was Hispanic, and nodded that she understood.

A few hours later, Ira awoke, and realized it was his birthday. He got into his truck and drove toward Plainview, hoping to catch Ernie in the lull between parties that occurred during morning hours. When he turned into Ernie's street, the house was surrounded with police cars. Ira kept driving. *Is it a dope bust? Have they found out about the banks?* Ira's mind raced through all the possibilities he could think of. There were many. Ira knew Ernie would keep his mouth shut, but what about all his friends? Which of them might know? Ira drove to a local restaurant, stopped and dialed Ernie's number from a pay phone.

"Hello," an unfamiliar woman's voice answered.

"Hello, is Ernie there?" Ira asked.

"You haven't heard?" the woman asked.

"Heard what?"

"Who is this?"

"Ira. I am a friend of Ernie's"

"Ira, this is Ernie's mother. I think we met one time."

"Yes ma'am."

"Ira, something happened. Ernie is dead."

"What?"

"Ernie died about 2 am this morning. I just got here."

"I'm...I'm...so sorry. How? I just saw him yesterday. He was healthy."

"We don't know for sure, but it appears to be a drug overdose. There was a needle mark in his arm."

"That can't be. Ernie would never shoot dope. He hated needles. He wouldn't even let a doctor give him a shot."

"I'm just repeating what I have been told. I don't want to believe it myself…" Mrs. Koch fought back tears.

"I'm so sorry, Mrs. Koch. Look, let me tell you something. I know Ernie well. He is a good guy. He did smoke marijuana. Sometimes he took pills, but he would never put a needle in his arm. Something is wrong here."

"I'm not ready to talk about it, Ira. It won't bring him back."

"I understand. I'm very sorry, Mrs. Koch. Good-bye."

Ira hung up the phone and walked into the restaurant, stunned and dazed, stopping to buy a local paper on the way in. Inside, he trudged to a booth and opened the paper. There was nothing in it about the incident. Ira noticed the date at the top of the page. *Happy fucking birthday!* He thought to himself.

A waitress approached Ira's table, merrily humming a tune. "Coffee?" she asked.

"Yes, please," he answered.

"Would you like some breakfast?"

"No, thank you."

About that time, Denise walked into the restaurant. Her eyes were red and puffy. When she saw Ira, she burst into tears. Ira invited her to sit beside him and wrapped an arm around her as she sobbed. For some reason, he could not share in her tears.

"How did it happen?" he asked, once she got control of herself.

"We were having a party, you know, like always. Drinking, snorting crank, nothing out of the ordinary. Ernie came in with a girl and two guys that looked like bikers, from Lubbock I think. Ernie took them to his bedroom. I figured he was going to do a deal, because that's where he goes when he wants some privacy. About twenty minutes later, the girl and the bikers came running out of Ernie's room. One of them said, "Hey something is wrong with that dude. He passed out on us."

Denise broke into tears again, remembering the incident anew. "I went into the room and Ernie was on the floor. He had pissed his pants, and he wasn't breathing. I tried, Ira. I was scared, but I tried. He just wouldn't breathe. I tried…"

"I am sure you did all you could."

The bikers left before the cops got there. The ambulance got there about the same time as the cops. I kept trying to make Ernie breathe, but he wouldn't. How could someone so healthy die like that?"

"His mother said they found a needle mark in his arm."

"Needle mark? Ernie didn't shoot dope. That can't be."

"That's what I thought. Who were those guys in the room with him?"

"I don't know them. You know Ernie. He was a friend to everybody. One of them used initials."

Ira began to panic. "Was it RJ?"

"Maybe so. Do you know the guy?"

"Not really. I know of him. What did they look like?"

"One was kind of big, six foot or more, with long dark hair and a full beard. He had brown eyes and tattoos all over his arms. The other guy was scraggly looking, with long blond, greasy hair. I think I remember him selling Ernie crank before."

Ira's face went white.

"What's wrong, Ira?"

"I think those men killed Ernie."

"What? Why would anyone want to kill Ernie?"

"They didn't want Ernie. They wanted me."

Denise stared silently at Ira for a moment. "Why?"

"It is a long story."

"Ira, there's something you should know. Ernie gave me some money to hold…lots of money. I don't know what to do with it."

"How much?"

"Nearly a hundred thousand dollars. He didn't want to keep it at his house. Ernie told me what you do. He always talked to me. You know, a lot of people used Ernie, to get dope, or for a place to party, but to me, he was a real friend. He was wild, and I guess I am too, but I really loved him. I would have died for him."

"Do you know Ernie's brother, the one who lives in Lubbock?"

"Yeah."

"Take about twenty thousand dollars of the money to him. Tell him it belongs to Ernie, and give it to him. He'll make sure his parents get it to cover the cost of his burial, and he'll be smart enough to keep the cops from getting involved."

"What about the rest of it?"

Ira thought for a moment. "You keep it, Denise. I think that's what Ernie would want, but be careful, and don't tell anyone. Don't go out and buy a bunch of new stuff. Do you know anyone with a business you can trust?"

"I think so."

"Maybe you can approach them to help you launder it, or you can just spend it a little at a time."

"Are you going to the funeral, Ira?"

"No. He's gone. I can't bring him back. I have business to take care of."

Denise looked suspiciously at Ira. "What are you going to do?" she asked.

"You don't want to know," he replied with a faraway look.

"Don't go and get yourself killed too."

Ira did not respond, but got up and left. The look on his face scared Denise. Something bad was about to happen and there was nothing she could do about it. As Ira walked out of the door, Denise whispered a prayer on his behalf.

CHAPTER LVI

Ira looked nervously at his watch. It read 2 am. *Closing time,* he thought. Ira drove by the bar where Angela had once worked. He saw the black Cadillac. Ten minutes later, he returned, warily. Cops patrolled the streets, looking for drunk drivers. This time, rather than drive by the club, he pulled into the shadows of a nearby parking lot and waited, and watched.

A group of bikers exited the club, with their old ladies. Most climbed aboard motorcycles; Ira watched for the one who would go toward the Cadillac. There was no mistaking the man. He dressed in black leather; long, dark hair hung to his waist; gold jewelry adorned his hands and neck, and a beautiful girl walked under each arm.

Ira started the truck's engine, pulled out his weapon, and drove slowly toward the group. No one seemed to notice his approach.

When Ira neared, RJ's back was to him. He rolled down the window and slowed to a crawl. RJ turned, just as Ira was about to shoot. Ira hesitated. RJ immediately shoved one of the girls between himself and Ira. Ira momentarily lost sight of his target, seeing nothing but the terror stricken look in the girl's eyes. Ira punched the accelerator to get her out of the line of sight. RJ moved, but too late this time. Ira fired one shot. All the bikers hit the ground. Ira punched the accelerator and sped off.

* * * * *

Ira wandered through the rows of graves, looking for Ernie's final resting place. Finally, he found a fresh grave, marked with nothing more than a small plaque bearing Ernie's name, date of birth, and date of death. The date of death was Ira's birthday. Ira fell to his knees beside the mound of fresh earth surrounded by flowers.

I got him for you Ernie. I'm so sorry. Ira looked skyward. *Why? Why him? I'm the one that deserved to die. Not him!*

He received no answer. After a time, Ira stood up and wandered through the gravestones, pausing occasionally to read one. Many people had died before their time in the small town of Plainview. Finally, Ira decided to leave. One of Ernie's brothers waited at his pickup. Ira tried to speak, but the words hung in his throat. Tears rolled freely down his face. Ira removed a newspaper clipping from his pocket and handed it to the man. He shook the man's hand, got into his pickup, and drove off.

Ernie's brother read the clipping. It described a drive-by shooting in Lubbock. The victim of the shooting, according to the article, was in the U.S. Marshal's witness protection program. He had survived a wound to the body, but doctors predicted he would be paralyzed for life; the bullet had severed his spinal column. The article went on to say that the attack might have been an act of retribution. The victim of the attack reportedly had cooperated with the government in a number of cases, and the list of those who wished to see him dead was long.

Jimmy Koch looked at Ira's retreating figure. "Thanks," he whispered, sadly. He put the clipping in his pocket. Ira's secret would remain a secret.

CHAPTER LVII

Ira walked into the door of Tim's house. When he spotted Susan sitting in the living room, he turned around and walked back out. Susan followed.

"Wait, Ira. I need to talk to you."

Ira stopped.

"I still love you," she said.

"Well, that's great. I wonder what your husband thinks about that?"

"We are not getting along very well."

"Why not?"

"I can't seem to get over you."

Ira noticed Susan wasn't any larger in the waist. "Why aren't you showing? Lisa is already starting to get pretty big."

"That was one of the things I need to tell you. I had an abortion. Jason couldn't handle me having your baby. I'm sorry."

Ira stared at Susan for a moment and then said: "You talk to me about love and then in the next breath tell me you murdered our unborn child. I'd hate to see what you do to someone you dislike."

"I've been so mixed up." Tears formed in her eyes, and she started toward Ira.

"Get back," he commanded, holding a hand up to stop her progress. "I am not your fucking husband any more. Go cry on Jason's shoulder."

"But Ira, I still want you."

"Susan, you may not believe this, but I'm glad Jason came along. He saved my life. You're worse than your mother."

"I am not."

"I'm not going to argue with you. I don't even owe you that privilege. Go argue with you husband." Ira continued to walk toward his pickup.

"Ira, come back here. You can't do this to me!" Susan screamed.

Ira backed up and drove off, his mind in a daze. First his best friend had been killed, then his unborn child. Life had not been kind to Ira Jones.

CHAPTER LVIII

Doug, Ira, and Tim sat at the kitchen table of Doug's Mexican ranch house. The house was built of concrete reinforced adobe and stucco outside, with a spacious circular-shaped central room with walls three feet thick. The front door was made of solid iron. Ira realized he was in a fortress, built to withstand a siege.

"We can't afford to mess around much longer," Doug told his two younger counterparts. "I can feel it in my bones."

"What's the rush?" Ira asked. "We've made enough money to live well for several years."

"Ira, I'm telling you—now is the time to get your money together and buy land. You won't be able to much longer."

"I have a hard time believing that. I know things are bad out there, but things have been bad for a long time. People have been saying Jesus is coming back for two thousand years now. I can't believe it is going to happen right away."

"Look at it this way, Ira. According to the Bible, four thousand years passed from the time of Adam to the time of Jesus. During those four thousand years, man went from walking to riding animals, and pulling wagons. Eighteen hundred more years went by and man was still riding horses and pulling wagons. Look what has happened in the last two hundred years. They're riding rocket ships to the moon, for Christ sake. Things are changing fast. We've got men fucking other men and women marrying women. Kids hate their parents, and parents hate their own kids. You can't fart without the government knowing about it. Local law has succumbed to state law; state law has lost its power to the feds; now international corporations are taking over countries. Fucking churches are there to justify whatever the government wants to do. Science comes up with one miracle after another; before you know it, they'll have us believing we created ourselves."

"I understand all of that, Doug, but what can we do about it?"

"Some are willing to lay down and take a fucking. Not me. Right or wrong, I ain't going down without a fight."

"The Bible says if you live by the sword, you will die by the sword," Ira stated.

"Sure does. Doesn't say there is anything wrong in dyin' by the sword though, does it? I would much rather be dead than keep swallowing this shit. God ain't going to do nothing for us if we don't get off our asses and start doing for ourselves."

"But killing...I don't know, Doug. We might end up killing an innocent person. I won't do that for money."

"Innocent you say? You don't think they'd kill you? Even those too weak to pull the trigger on you will pick up the phone and send someone else in their place to do it for them. Most cops aren't anything other than hired killers and bullies. They sit around dreaming of getting to kill folks like us. The man that picks up the phone is just as guilty as the man pulling the trigger. For that matter, when you pay taxes to support those bastards, you are guilty in my eyes."

"I can't give up my hope for something better Doug. I have dreams—dreams of a good woman, kids, good food, and good times. I can't drop all that."

"The day will come when they take it all from you, unless you join them. If you think you can go to church once a week, pay your taxes, and make no waves, while these evils go unchecked all around you without lifting so much as one finger to stop them and then call yourself a man, you're dead wrong. I will concede one thing, Ira. I may be jumping the gun, but—the time will come when every God fearing man on the face of the earth will have to make a choice—a choice of going with the flow and giving up his soul, or resisting and suffering, maybe even to the point of death. Ira, you balk at the thought of killing a few folks. What about all the folks the government kills? Hell, Charles Manson didn't kill but a half dozen or so, and most people think he's the devil himself. Why don't they apply the same standard to the fuckin' President of the United States, who sends hundreds of thousands to a grave in the name of democracy? Why is one so terribly evil and the other not?"

Ira did not reply. Doug continued the tirade.

"The president is a murderer. The churches condone what he does. They have blood on their hands too. You say I'm a killer, but I haven't killed anybody—yet. Who are the real murderers?"

"I'm not ready to take that chance Doug. I'm sorry, but I am through with this. I'll rob no more banks."

"You're young, Ira. You still have the hope and optimism of youth, Someday you'll remember what I've told you today, and you'll understand. Boys—I do have one confession to make."

Both Tim and Ira looked at Doug.

"I've done a little better at my trade than I let on. While you were wasting your time digging in the dirt, I was out making a pile of money. Follow me."

Doug led the two young men to a horse barn. Unlike barns in the United States, this too was constructed of adobe. Doug removed a padlock from a door of the barn and revealed a room partially full of alfalfa hay.

"Help me move these," he instructed, grabbing a bale and passing it to Ira. In quick order, part of the stack was moved. Doug then bent over and began to pry boards from the floor. When several had been removed, he disappeared into a hole in the ground.

"Come on down," he hollered.

Tim and Ira crawled down a makeshift ladder into the dark hole. Doug turned on a battery-powered lamp, revealing a small room. Four crates lined one wall.

"Now, you know why I have calluses on my hands. You didn't honestly believe I would build my own house did you? I dug this myself. No one besides you knows it's here. Doug opened one of the crates. It was full of weapons. Another contained ammunition. A third contained sealed packages of freeze-dried food. The last was full of money—stack after stack of American dollars.

"That's over two million in cash you are looking at. It all belongs to the two of you, should something happen to me. We have plenty of money. The reason I'm still repossessin' is personal. I'm out for revenge." A wild look came into Doug's eyes, accentuated by the shadows the lantern cast upon his face. I want only one thing from each of you in return."

"What's that, dad?" Tim asked.

"If any of us is arrested, the survivor will do what he can to continue to support the families left behind. I need your word on it. Also, no one else is to know about this. What will it be?"

"You have my word," Tim replied immediately.

Doug turned to Ira.

Ira surveyed the huge pile of money. "Me too," he finally replied.

Doug shook the hand of each, looking them squarely in the eye. Neither wavered.

"Carla has instructions to turn over all I have in the event of my death. She doesn't know about this though. Once again, no one besides us is to know about this. Do you understand?"

"Yes," both replied.

"Good."

All three returned to the surface and re-covered the entrance to the room with the boards and the hay.

"If either of you needs a place to stay, this place'll be here for you. Very few know about it, and the ones that do are outlaws. I should probably retire and spend the rest of my days here, but something just won't let me. They pissed me off real bad, and I am not even yet."

CHAPTER LIX

Kelly Brown heard the dispatcher announce that the Blue Sky hardware store's burglar had gone off again. The owner of the store was a personal friend of his.

Officer Brown arrived at the store just seconds before two local policemen. "It's probably just that new burglar alarm. It goes off nearly every night. It's sound sensitive and I guess it just works too well. Any noise will set it off."

"We've already answered a few false alarms ourselves," the local policemen said.

"I'll go in and check it," Kelly offered.

"Do you want back up?"

"No, just wait out here."

"Fine with me," the policeman answered.

Kelly Brown hoisted his body out of the piss yellow, puke green car, hitched up his belt, and started toward the door. He slid a key into the lock and started in.

* * * * *

Ira stood near the hole in the roof of the hardware store, looking around. *What is taking him so long,* he wondered? He looked up at the night sky. A few drops of rain started to fall. The sound of an engine reached Ira's ears. Simultaneously, Tim's head popped out of the hole, with an armload of rifles.

"Did you hear something?" Ira asked.

"No."

"I think I did."

Both men listened for a moment.

"Your ears are playing tricks on you," Tim said, ducking back into the hole, and climbing back down the ladder for another armload of guns. Ira remained unsatisfied. As quietly as possible, he walked over the tar and gravel roof toward the front of the store. Near the edge, he dropped to his hands and knees and crawled. Every move made a horrendous sound. The gravel dug into his knees. Ira peered over the edge of the building and saw three police cars in the parking lot.

Oh shit, he thought. He looked over the edge once more, to make sure his eyes had not deceived him. One of the cars belonged to Kelly Brown; the other two were city cops. Ira saw the cherry red glow of a cigarette in one of the cars. Ira backed from the edge of the building, trying not to make noise as he walked. He fought the impulse to panic and run.

Tim arrived to the top of the ladder. "Where the fuck are you, Ira?" Tim asked, standing with arms loaded. About that time, Ira arrived; before he could say anything, a loud popping noise came from within the store.

"What the hell," Tim exclaimed.

"Cops!" Ira told him. "Come on, let's get the hell out of here."

"Wait. Dad is still down there."

Tim ducked back into the building. Another shot rang out, and then, another. Ira jumped involuntarily. Tim's pickup was parked behind the building. Ira ran in that direction. When he looked over the edge, a flashlight beam hit him squarely in the face. Milliseconds later, a shot flew over his head, missing by inches, followed by another. Ira dropped to the roof and grabbed his gun, but quickly reconsidered. He didn't want to shoot or be shot. Ira sprinted for the side of the building, seeing Tim emerging from the hole out of the corner of his eye.

Ira reached the edge. Now, both Tim and Doug were also on the roof, headed toward the back of the building. "There's a cop back there!" he warned.

"So's our truck," Doug yelled in reply.

Ira looked down. The roof was fifteen feet above the ground. Doug and Tim arrived at the ladder. Gunfire erupted. Ira jumped. He hit hard, knees driving into the asphalt surface, sending a wave of pain through his body. Ira jumped up, ran toward a wooden fence, cleared it, and fell on the other side. Seconds later, a policeman stuck his head around the corner. Seeing nothing, he ran toward the firefight still going on behind the building.

Ira ran. He covered the first quarter of a mile in a minute flat, in heavy hiking boots. His chest burned and his vision clouded, but still he ran. More shots rang out, just as he started to slow down. Ira stepped into a hole and fell. The roar of an engine and the sound of sirens got him on his feet and running again. Ira dove into a hedge near someone's yard.

Seconds later, Tim Grant's pickup roared by, followed by two cop cars. As they passed, a rifle sticking out of the back of Doug's pickup spit flames into the dark; the sound pierced the night air. The first police car swerved and hit a trash dumpster, showering the road with glass and pieces of metal. Steam erupted from the radiator. No one moved in the car.

Overhead, a light came on in the house where Ira was hidden, and a neighbor's dog began to bark. Ira jumped up and started running again, around the house, over the back fence, down the alley, over another fence, through a yard, across a street, and over yet another fence. Soon, he found himself on the outskirts of town. Sirens wailed in the distance; the strobe of red, white, and blue lights illuminated the night sky.

Ira walked until McCamey was nothing more than a bright spot on the Northern horizon. Still, he walked.

* * * * *

Dawn's first light found Ira stumbling along: tired, hungry and thirsty. The familiar sound of an irrigation engine came, borne on the morning breeze. Ira realized he was less than two miles from his father's farm. The engine he heard came from Mr. Dean's place. Ira walked toward the sound. When he arrived, he found a cement ditch of cool clear water running by, headed for a field of grass. He lay on the bank and drank deeply. Afterward, he dunked his head into the water and allowed it to carry away the accumulated sweat and dirt.

Now what? Rest seemed to be the answer. The shade of a dense pile of brush provided the place. Ira lay down, exhausted, and allowed the drone of a Minneapolis-Moline engine to lull him to sleep.

CHAPTER LX

Bubba Cooper stared down the wrong end of Doug Grant's pistol. Tim lay on the floor of the barn, his face chalky white. One leg of Tim's jeans dripped blood from a wound in the thigh.

"Help me get him into the house, Bubba," Doug ordered the elderly man.

Bubba Cooper calmly walked over and helped Tim to his feet. "How do you feel, son?" he asked the young man.

"Weak. Dizzy. I think I may throw up." Tim gagged for a second or two, but nothing came out. Once he got control of himself, Mr. Cooper helped him hobble to his house. Doug followed behind.

Bubba Cooper's wife answered the front door. The sight she beheld shocked and scared her. Tim's leg was drenched in blood. In the background the television continued to describe the shooting of the night before. According to the report, one deputy sheriff and one policeman had died; several more had been wounded and were in critical condition, and their assailants had escaped the scene. A manhunt was on, and people were being warned not to stop for anyone on foot.

"I'll call an ambulance," she said.

"No, you won't," Doug said. It was then she noticed the handgun.

"It was *you*, wasn't it?" she asked

Doug Grant did not reply

Bubba Cooper looked squarely at Doug Grant. "Doug, I'm an old man. I've lived a good life, and I'll be dead soon enough, one way or the other. You don't scare me with that gun, so you might as well put it away."

"I need to lay down," Tim said, starting to fall. Bubba and Mary Cooper came to his aid and led him to a couch.

Mr. Cooper then turned to face Doug Grant. "You need to turn yourself in. The whole county is crawling with policemen."

"Can't do that, Bubba. I've gone too far. I ain't going to jail."

"Tim has lost a lot of blood, Doug. He needs to go to the hospital. He may very well die if he doesn't. Think of him, for God's sake."

Doug looked at his son. Tim looked weak, barely conscious. Doug was prepared to die. He was not prepared to watch his son's death.

"You'll never get out of here," Mr. Cooper stated again. At that minute, the beating of a helicopter reached their ears.

Doug went over and kissed his son's pale face. "Good-bye Tim," he said. "I'm going to leave you here with Mr. And Mrs. Cooper."

"Where are you going?" Tim asked his father.

"Back to Mexico. You stay here." Doug Grant turned back to Mrs. Cooper. "Call the ambulance," he ordered her. "You come with me," he told her husband.

"Don't you hurt my husband, Doug Grant. He's a good man!" she shouted as they walked out the door.

"Bubba, I'm going to tell you what happened. You listen. Understand?" Doug said.

"Yes."

"The whole thing was my idea. We cut a hole in the roof. Tim waited on top. He never went into the building. I disarmed the burglar alarm and went after the guns. Somehow the cops knew I was in there. One came in on me I got the drop on him. I told him to lie down, that I wasn't going to jail, but he decided to be a hero. He said, *you're under arrest,* and tried to draw his weapon. I shot him in the stomach with a twelve-gauge shotgun. I told him to lie still, but the crazy bastard kept grabbing for his gun, so I shot him twice more. I ran for the hole in the roof and Tim and I ran for the back of the building. Another cop was waiting for us. He shot Tim and I shot him, three or four times. Another cop came running around the building about the time we got to the truck and shot at us. I shot at him. We got into the truck. Two cars followed us. Tim drove while I shot out the back sliding glass window. I think I hit one of the cars and he crashed. The other car followed, but at a distance. When we got to the cutoff to your old place, we turned off. At the cattle guard, I made Tim stop. I got out with a shotgun; Tim continued on. The cop kept coming; I jumped up and shot him through the windshield. I ran out of shells, dropped the gun and ran. Tim picked me up and we went cross-country until two tires blew and we were forced to stop. We tried to walk, but Tim was hurt too bad. We made it here on foot. *Tim never fired a round.* You got that?"

"Yes sir."

"Get in your pickup, Bubba. You're taking me out of here."

"Doug, there is no way out. The police have roadblocks set up and the whole country is looking for you."

"I'm not going to jail. Get in your truck."

Bubba Cooper got into the driver's side seat of his pickup and started the engine. About the time they started out of the drive, the distant sound of sirens reached their ears.

"It's too late, Doug. They're here."

"Stop your truck by that tree."

"Doug, don't be a fool."

Doug Grant slumped down in the pickup. Two police cars and an ambulance approached.

When the first policeman's car started through the cattle guard, Doug Grant jumped out and opened fire, blasting the windshield full of holes. The second car swerved off the road and stopped, broadside to the action. The policeman jumped out and knelt on the ground, hiding behind the front tire. Doug turned his fire on this vehicle, moving toward it as he shot. As he rounded the car, weapon blazing, the report of another weapon sounded. Doug Grant staggered and then fell to the ground.

"Forgive me, Lord," Bubba Cooper prayed as he lowered the lever action deer rifle he had removed from the gun rack of his pickup. The crouching policeman never fired a round.

Bubba Cooper walked to where Doug Grant had fallen. He was still alive, shot through the torso.

"I'm sorry, Doug. I couldn't stand by and watch you kill another innocent man," the old man said.

Doug Grant whispered. "Remember, Tim never fired a shot."

"I remember."

Doug Grant passed out.

* * * * *

Ira watched Tim's house. He saw Lisa get into her car, and leave, speeding toward town. No one else appeared to be around. He dug a hole and buried the handgun he carried. He felt in his pocket and removed the keys to his pickup. Ira snuck up to the house, unlocked the door to his pickup, started the engine, and drove south. After being waved through a roadblock, he turned east on interstate 10 and drove all the way to San Antonio. There, he checked into a motel room and sat, quivering and shaking, while the TV described events that had shattered a tiny little West Texas town. The television reported that two suspects had committed the crime; an elderly rancher killed one in a shoot-out, and the other was in police custody, fighting for his life in a hospital in Odessa. Not once did they mention a third suspect.

CHAPTER LXI

"Do you have anything to say for yourself before I sentence you?" the judge asked.

Tim rolled his wheelchair as close as he could to the microphone and spoke. "Maybe I would have killed to protect my dad, but the fact remains I did not. I'm guilty of burglary. I'm guilty of helping my dad flee the scene. I lost my dad. I lost a leg. My wife is soon to have a baby and will be left alone in this world. I regret what my dad did. I regret what I did. If I could undo all of it, I would. I feel terrible for the families left behind, but *I did not kill anybody.* Sentence me for the crimes I committed, but not for crimes I did not do. I've done a lot of thinking since that day. I am a changed man. I will never do such a thing again."

"Is that all?" the judged asked.

"Yes, sir," Tim replied.

"I understand from reading these letters sent in on your behalf you now have found religion. Where was your religion the night you and your dad sent three officers of the law to their graves? You speak of your pregnant wife. What about their families? Why didn't you think of her before you chose to steal, armed with lethal weapons? You are of age—a legal adult. You must pay for your actions. I have taken into consideration the fact that you lost a leg. I do believe your role was secondary to that of you father. Were he here today, I would have given him the death penalty."

The judge then ran down a list of crimes for which Tim had been convicted, listing the years he would receive for each. Tim added them up in his head. The last crimes listed were for his participation in the murder of three police officers. He received thirty years apiece for these. *I'm dead,* he thought.

"Due to the fact that you are young, and may someday deserve another chance at life, I hereby order that all of these sentences are to run concurrently." The judge slammed down his hammer.

"What does that mean?" Tim asked his lawyer.

"It means all your sentences will run at the same time. You have a thirty year sentence, and will someday be eligible for parole."

* * * * *

Ira watched the sentencing on the evening newscast. The prosecutor was mad, feeling Tim should have received a life sentence.

What could I have done? Ira asked himself.

Ira lay down, but sleep would not come. A promise he had made to Doug Grant played over and over in his head.

CHAPTER LXII

Tim approached the desk. A guard checked his name off of a list and told him he could proceed. He propelled himself into the visiting room on crutches, wondering who had come to see him. He was shocked to see Ira, sitting at a table near the back of the room.

"Howdy Tim," Ira said.

"Hi, Ira. This is quite a surprise. I didn't figure you'd come."

"It wasn't easy, but I had to."

"I bet not. I never told them, Ira. No one knows."

"I figured that much. They would have come and got me long ago. I made a promise to your dad and I intend to keep it. You know what I am talking about."

"Yeah."

"What can I do?"

"Not much, Ira. I can't beat the case. They don't let a cop's death go unpunished."

"I feel guilty."

"Don't. It could have been the other way around. I am glad you didn't get caught. Was it still there?"

"Yeah, just like he left it."

"Take care of Lisa. Take care of Carla. Dad would want that. Visit my son, Ira. Raise him as if he were your own. And, don't let him grow up to be an outlaw. Dad was full of shit, Ira. I know things are bad out there, and a lot of unfair things happen in this world, but the day you kill innocent people, you've gone too far. I understand that now. It is too late for me, but not for you, and not for my boy."

"It must have been awful to watch your dad go out that way."

"Bubba Cooper told me the truth, Ira. Dad left him no choice. He died like he wanted to. After killing those cops, they would have hunted him to the end of the earth. Ira, this may sound strange coming from me, but I've changed. In here, I have a lot of time to think. Dad was very convincing, and he used the scriptures to justify what he did. He missed the most important part of Jesus' teaching—the lesson of love. There may be a time to fight, but it's not now. My dad saw injustices —real injustices, but the day he picked up a gun, he crossed the line. Innocent people suffered and died because of him— because of us. I knew it was wrong and didn't stand up to him. Did you know one of the men he killed had four children?"

"I heard that."

"Well, I saw them, face to face. They are innocent. They lost their daddy. Cops are people, just like you and me. Some are good; some are bad. It is the same in here. I have met guards who are decent people, and others who are assholes. I understand each of those cops has a fund set up for surviving family members. I want you to anonymously donate half of my share of the money to them."

"Are you sure? That's a lot of money."

"It has blood on it, Ira. I don't deserve it. If it weren't for the fact that I have a family in need, I'd give it all to them."

"What do you think your chances of getting out look like?" Ira asked.

"I'm told I will do between ten and fifteen years, if I'm lucky and get paroled. That's a long time, Ira. I can't think about that. I have to serve one day at a time. I'm studying to be a minister."

"No fucking way."

"Don't get me wrong. I'm not claiming to be some saint, but this thing changed me—for the better, I hope."

"I can't see you being a preacher, Tim."

"I sure as hell won't be like any of them I know. That doesn't mean God don't have room for an ex-con in His plan."

Tim and Ira visited until Ira was forced to leave.

CHAPTER LXIII

The Jones's farm was sold by auction. Floyd Jenkins was shocked to see Ira Jones at the proceeding, accompanied by an elderly Mexican man and his daughter. He was even more shocked when the old man out bid the representative he had in place, hoping to buy the farm for pennies on the dollar.

* * * * *

Ira walked into the co-op. "Give me the keys to the gate of our place," he told Bubba Cooper.

"What are you talking about?" Cooper asked. "I heard some Mexican bought it."

"They did. I'm his new foreman."

Bubba Cooper's jaw dropped. He pulled the key out of his pocket and handed it to Ira. "What can we do for you, Ira?" he asked.

"Nothing, Mr. Cooper, nothing at all."

Outside, Jose and Leonardo waited. They smiled as Ira waved the keys at them.

* * * * *

Ira drove through the streets of McCamey. It felt good to be home, although the Blue Sky hardware store still brought back bad memories. Ira was glad to be farming again. New opportunities had come along. The government was now paying farmers *not to farm*. Ira set aside over half the land and was set to receive a yearly check for doing so. Soon after Ira acquired nearby pastureland containing flattop mesas, a power company wanted the right to set up wind generators; each month landowners qualified for royalty checks from the power they produced. One thing the Bakersfield valley had an ample supply of was wind. Oil was discovered under his farm; Ira got an owner's royalty on that. A European company set up a winery on a neighboring place and agreed to buy all the grapes Ira produced. Utilizing submersible electric pumps and elaborate drip irrigation systems, he started a small vineyard. It would be a number of years before they produced, but as Jose said, *the people want drink.* Potential yields looked promising. Jose and Leonardo both went back to work for him; this time Leonardo had a visa. Ira's biggest problem was one that had plagued him since puberty. He needed a woman.

Ira drove by the church and noticed Susan's car in the parking lot. Without thinking, he pulled in and parked. Ira walked to a window and peered in. Everybody in the small country church had his or her hands in the air, waving from side to side. Ira searched the room and found Susan on the front row. To her right side was Martha, Doug's ex wife: to her left, Jason Adams, all decked out in suit and tie. Reverend Davies noticed Ira through the window. About that time, Jason Adams fell to the ground and began writhing on the floor. Both Martha and Susan began shouting hallelujahs, which caused a whole series of hallelujahs and Praise Gods to erupt from the crowd. Jason's body jerked and spasmed like a man in the final throes of death. Ira turned and walked away.

Thank God it's him instead of me. Ira started the engine and drove away.

CHAPTER LXIV

Angela sat in the back corner of the club, alone. Her heart was no longer into the work. She had seen too many smiling faces, too many naked bodies, heard too many lies, fucked too many men. She had tired of lying in order to get at the money in someone's pocket. Her house was full of material possessions; none brought what she wanted or needed. Angela put out a cigarette and looked at it disgustedly. Even that no longer brought enjoyment. It was just a nasty habit.

Angela sensed someone's approach. She looked up and into the eyes of Ira Jones. This time there was no big scene, no expression of jubilation—just a sigh of relief.

"Are you ready to get out of here?" Ira asked.

Angela took one final look at the scene around her. "Yes, I am, and yes, I do—that is—if you'll still have me."

Angela stood up, joined hands with Ira, and they walked out of a tit bar for the last time.

EPILOGUE
Ten Years Later

"How did things go at School today?" Ira asked Angela as she entered through the front door of the adobe farmhouse.

"You know first graders. I'll be glad to see next week over with. I'm as ready as they are for summer vacation."

"I got some good news today."

"Oh yeah?"

"Tim is going to be paroled."

"Great! Lisa will be so happy."

"Yeah, she has waited a long time."

Ira showed Angela a ledger he had been working on. "You are not going to believe this. We almost broke even on the farm this year."

Ira and Angela cracked open a beer and walked out to the back porch to watch the sun set. Squaw tit peak loomed in the background. Evening rays filtered through rows of lime green grape leaves; in the distance two foals played with each other while their mothers grazed green pastures. Carla milked a cow in the corral while her calf waited patiently for his turn. The evening breeze turned wind-powered generators on nearby mesas: each turn of a blade put money in Ira's account at the bank. Pump jacks lifted oil; each stroke helped pay another bill. Tim Grant's son tossed a football with Carla's boy; both dreamed of how they were going to be the next local star as they ran and lept gracefully. Jose and his wife watched glimmering rivulets of water course through rows of tomatoes, chilies, and melons; the clean smell of water and fresh tilled earth permeated the air.

Leonardo checked the supplies in the wetback shack. Beneath the shack, through a concealed trap door in the closet, a ladder led to secret underground room, which hid three tired wetbacks on a journey to parts farther north, and work. Turns out, it wasn't against the law to feed and provide water for illegals, as long as you didn't hire them. The border patrol still came by looking, but had apprehended no one in years.

Maybe there is a little hope in this world, Ira thought to himself, wrapping his arm around his wife and drawing her near. *At least for some of us.*

Both smiled.

The end

Don Henry Ford, Jr. describes himself as a cowboy, writer, horseman, seeker of things spiritual, social activist, former dope smuggler, convict, bronc rider, dope-addict and general no-good. Still not so good but aspiring to be.
He lives with his wife, Leah, in Seguin, Texas.

Also by Don Henry Ford, Jr.:

Contrabando: Confessions of a Drug-Smuggling Texas Cowboy
A Cowboy's Observations: On Drugs?
Ruminations From the Garden
The Devil's Swing

www.unrepentantcowboy.com

www.ingramcontent.com/pod-product-compliance
Ingram Content Group UK Ltd.
Pitfield, Milton Keynes, MK11 3LW, UK
UKHW041431180426
11947UKWH00007B/385